Whitby Toll
A DCI Finnegan Yorkshire Crime Thriller
Ely North

Red Handed Print

Website: https://elynorthcrimefiction.com

To contact ely@elynorthcrimefiction.com

https://www.facebook.com/elynorthcrimefictionUK

Cover design by Cherie Chapman/Chapman & Wilder

Cover images © Gail Johnson / death_rip / Adobe Stock Stock Photo
Disclaimer: This is a work of fiction. Names, characters, businesses, places, events, locales, and incidents are either the products of the author's imagination or used in a fictitious manner. Any resemblance to actual persons, living or dead, or actual events is purely coincidental.

Published by Red Handed Print

First Edition

Kindle e-book ISBN-13: 978-0-6455982-6-1

Paperback ISBN-13: 978-0-6455982-8-5

Also By Ely North – DCI Finnegan Series

Book 1: **Black Nab**

Book 2: **Jawbone Walk**

Book 3: **Vertigo Alley**

Book 4: **Whitby Toll**

Book 5: **House Arrest**

Book 6: **Gothic Fog**

Book 7: **Happy Camp**

Book 8: **Harbour Secrets**

Book 9: **Murder Mystery** – Pre-order (Dec 2024)

DCI Finnegan Series Boxset #1: **Books 1 – 3**

DCI Finnegan Series Boxset #2: **Books 4 – 6**

Prequel: **Aquaphobia** (Free ebook for newsletter subscribers)

*Note: All books are available from Amazon in ebook, paperback, and in **Kindle Unlimited** (excluding Aquaphobia). Paperbacks can be ordered from all good bookshops. **Boxset print editions are one book compiled from three books. They do not come in a box. *** Pre-orders only apply to ebooks.

1

Thursday 26th November

The car swings onto the forecourt and screeches to a halt next to a petrol pump.

Heart pounding, mind racing. The chemical mixture he snorted, and injected after the robbery has a created a cauldron of dangerous highs, blocking logic. He turns to the old woman in the passenger seat.

'Nearly out of gas, grandma. Shall I fill her up or will you do the honours?' He laughs manically as he glances casually in the wing mirror. A car pulls up behind and an overweight man exits and ambles forward. 'Hello, what's this fat prick want?' He slides his hand under grandma's leg and retrieves the pistol.

The unwanted visitor nears the Subaru and pulls something from his pocket.

'Fuck! That's a Barney if ever I saw one. There's no way I'm going back to the castle, grandma.'

DS Jason Cartwright taps on the window and bends to peer inside. The glass rolls down. He flashes his warrant card, but before he can speak, he spots the barrel. It's followed by a burning sensation in his chest. His legs collapse. Staring at the blue sky, he wonders why. A roar of an engine and a voice screaming his name.

Her shocked face hovers over him.

His eyelids flutter, then close.

The surrounding sounds become muffled, then stop.

2

Sunday 29th November

Zac marches into Frank's office, face as hard as granite, leather bomber jacket tightly zipped up.

'You ready, boss?' he asks.

'Nearly.' Finnegan slips into his 1920s style, long, black overcoat and pulls on a pair of leather gloves. 'Just one more thing—I need Long Tall Sally.'

'Who?' Zac screws his face up as he watches Frank rifle through his desk drawers.

'Here she is.' Frank smiles with satisfaction as he locates his police issue telescopic baton. He jerks his arm downward, and the baton extends to its full reach with a satisfying click. 'As good as new,' he says, collapsing the weapon and dropping it into his coat pocket.

'You have a name for your baton?' Zac quizzes.

'Aye. Sally and I go way back. She's helped me out of many a tricky situation over the years. Although, she's been redundant for a while now. But tonight, she's going dancing.' He grins, buttoning his coat up as he studies Zac.

His amiable demeanour changes. 'You don't have to do this, you know.'

'I'm not letting you go alone.'

Frank contemplates. 'It was different in the old days. Surveillance cameras were rare. These days they're everywhere. If we're reported, we'll be for the high jump—you do know that?'

'Aye.'

Frank smiles at him. 'Mobile off?'

'Yes.'

'Okay, sergeant, let's go find our snouts and ruffle some feathers.'

'What's your informant look like?' Zac asks, as Frank parks the car on a dimly lit street in the middle of Scarborough.

'Like an emaciated rat. Hence the nickname, Rizzo.'

'Rizzo?'

Frank eyes him wearily. 'Rizzo the Rat from The Muppets?'

Zac shakes his head. 'I've heard of Kermit and Miss Piggy, but not Rizzo.'

'His real name is Martin Henshaw. My informant... not the Muppet,' he adds as an afterthought. 'Probably in his early forties, but looks about sixty. Missing teeth, sunken cheeks, dead eyes. Weed, booze, and the horses have been his downfall. He's been on my payroll for twenty years or more.'

'Good intel?'

'Patchy. Depends if he's on a bender or not. Rizzo likes his snooker, hence why we're here on a Sunday night. Cheap beer and it's open twenty-four-seven.'

Zac steps from the car and stares across the street at the snooker club. 'What's the plan?'

'We see how many customers are inside. If there's only a handful, we get rid of them and take Rizzo into the toilets for a little chat. If there's too many, we'll wait outside in the car for him. First, we need to disable the CCTV.'

'Leave that to me. I'll rewind the footage to before we make our first appearance.'

Sauntering across the road, they both stuff their hands deep into their pockets and shiver.

'Christ, there's a bloody cold snap on the way. Wouldn't be surprised if it snowed.'

Skipping up the worn stone steps, they enter the brick-built Victorian building and emerge into the murky clubrooms. There are nine full sized tables in all, and only one of them is lit up at the far end of the room. A pall of blue smoke hangs lazily over the table, the downlights obscuring the faces of four men. The occasional clunk of a snooker ball melds with good-humoured banter. Behind the bar is a solitary male, early twenties. Busy scrolling his phone, he fails to notice the new arrivals.

Frank and Zac approach, their sudden appearance like ghouls in the night, making the man jump.

'Evening, gents. You members?'

Frank shakes his head and emits a low grunt. 'No.'

'Then you'll either have to sign a membership form and pay your annual fees or get an existing member to sign you in.'

Zac flashes his warrant card. 'Police. CID,' he says quietly, slipping the ID away before the barman can read his title. 'Name?'

'Harry.'

'Harry what?'

'Harry Thwaites.'

Zac pauses, as if contemplating the information, making the barman edgy. 'Is Rizzo in tonight?'

'Yes, he's...'

'Never mind. We need to look at your CCTV footage from last night. There was a serious assault outside the club. We want to see if we can identify the attacker and if he exited from these premises.'

'Oh, okay,' the barman says hesitantly. 'It's in the back room,' he adds, pointing at a closed door behind him. Zac lifts the hatch of the bar and moves behind the counter.

'Were you working last night, Harry?' Frank asks, following Zac.

'No. Sunday to Wednesday nights are my shifts. The boss never mentioned anything about an assault, though.'

Zac pushes open the door and studies the disorganised box room, his eyes resting on an antiquated computer sitting on a desk in the corner. 'The footage... does it store to the Cloud or the hard drive?'

The barman half-laughs, nervous. 'My boss thinks the cloud are those fluffy white things in the sky.'

His lame joke falls flat. 'Can you log-on, please?'

'No need. It's not password protected.'

'You run a tight ship around here,' Zac says, taking a seat. He taps at the keyboard, and the computer monitor begrudgingly yawns into life. 'I haven't seen a computer with a cathode-ray tube for about a decade or more.'

'Yeah, the boss is a bit tight when it comes to upgrading things. The icon for the cameras is that blue one on the top right of the screen.'

'Got it,' Zac says as the CCTV programme fills the monitor.

'While we're here,' Frank begins, 'we may as well make sure everything's tickety boo with the club. Have you a current liquor licence?'

'Yes. It's framed and hung up behind the bar,' the barman replies, becoming increasingly concerned with the cold disposition of the officers.

'Lead the way,' Frank says, voice low, serious.

As Frank and the barman head out of the room, Zac studies the icons for the six CCTV cameras on the screen. Cam 1 Outside Entrance. Cam 2 Inside Entrance. Cam 3 Front of Bar.

'That should do,' he murmurs. Clicking on Cam 1, he quickly scrolls through the video until he spots himself and Frank walking up the steps of the club a few moments ago. He pauses the recording, selects the frames, and hits the delete button. Repeating the process for Cam 2 and Cam 3, he closes the program and shuts down the computer, pulling the power cord from the back and sticking it in the desk drawer.

Frank hands the photo frame containing the liquor licence back to the barman. 'Hmm... seems to be in order.' He spins around and stares into the far corner, where the blue haze hovers like an ethereal ghoul in the air. Frank points at a "No Smoking" sign on the wall.

'You do realise it's been illegal to smoke in enclosed spaces of a workplace, including pubs and clubs, since 2007?'

'Erm... ye... yes,' the barman stammers.

'It's two and a half grand fine for the employer, and a two-hundred quid fine for the employee.'

'I didn't think it would... I mean, if someone complained then I... but most of the punters smoke...' he says, losing the grasp of coherent English.

Zac joins them. 'There's nothing on CCTV, boss. It's all clear.'

'I see.' He eyeballs the barman. 'Have you a police record, Harry? And I want the truth because it's easy for me to check.'

Harry shakes his head vigorously. 'No. I've never been in trouble with the police.'

'Well, you're in trouble now. Allowing patrons to smoke inside the club.'

'But I can't... I mean, I need this job to pay my rent. If my boss is fined, I'll get the sack.'

The two officers exchange meaningful glances. Frank drapes a friendly arm around Harry's shoulders and manoeuvres him towards the back office. 'I tell you what I'm going to do, Harry,' he says in a fatherly tone. 'You look like a good kid, and it's easy to make one mistake. You shouldn't lose your job over it. Especially these days. Work is hard to come by. So, I'm going to turn a blind eye to the smoking offence—on this occasion.'

'Thanks, I really appreciate it.'

'I'm sure you do,' Frank replies with a smile as he leads Harry into the back office. 'Now, one good turn deserves another, yeah?'

'Yeah. What do you want me to do?'

'Nothing.'

'Nothing?'

'That's what I said. Simply sit in here for ten minutes with the door shut while me and my colleague have a quiet word with the four gents in the corner of the room—about the smoking.'

'Ah, okay.'

'And hand me your mobile. Don't be perturbed. I'll place it on the counter when we leave.'

'But why?'

'You don't need to know why. And one last thing—you've never seen us, and we were never here. Do I make myself clear?'

Harry involuntarily shakes as he comprehends something more sinister at play. 'Yes. I understand.'

'Good lad,' Frank pats him on the arm as he takes Harry's mobile. 'Have a seat and relax. I'll let you know when we're done.'

The two officers amble across the gloomy clubrooms. 'You take the side wall and keep in the shadows,' Frank whispers. 'Rizzo's a coward and will no doubt try to make a run for it.' They split up as Zac melts into the darkness. As Frank nears the men, the low hanging lampshade above the snooker table still obscures their faces. Someone lines up a cue and takes a pot. The white ball clips the black and sends it rolling gently towards a corner pocket. As it nears the drop, Frank picks it up.

'Nice shot. Shame it didn't go in.'

'Oi, what the fuck!' an angry voice yells as Frank and the men finally come face to face. 'Who the fuck are you?' a medium-sized muscular man questions angrily.

Frank spots Rizzo and quickly assesses his other two mates. They're both skinny wasters who could do with a good feed. 'Rizzo, long time no see,' Frank declares with a disquieting smile.

'Mr... Mr F. What are you doing here?'

'That could have cost me the fucking game, you wanker?' growls the muscle man as he approaches Frank.

'I want a word in private with Rizzo. The rest of you have one chance. Leave the club quietly, now.'

'And who's going to make us?' the muscle man snarls as his two skinny mates fall in behind him.

'I am.'

They all laugh, albeit uneasily. 'Yeah, well, how about I crack your skull open?' he says, flipping the cue around, so the butt is poised menacingly in the air.

Frank yanks out the telescopic baton, jerks it down with a click, then whacks it hard into the side of the muscle man's collar bone. He drops the cue and falls to his knees, clutching his shoulder in agony as his acquaintances rush toward Frank.

Rizzo takes off, scurrying along the wall like a rodent. One skinny bloke throws a lightweight punch, which Frank parries away with the baton, following it up with a straight jab to the man's nose. He staggers back, stunned as blood gushes down over his mouth and onto his chin. His fearless mate bolts towards the exit. There's a kerfuffle behind as Frank glances over his shoulder, witnessing Zac grab Rizzo and deftly spin him around, forcing Rizzo's arm up his back. He yelps and stands on his tiptoes to ease the excruciating pain.

Frank returns his attention to the two men in front of him. 'Right, I suggest you two clowns follow your brave mate out of the fucking door. Go on, skedaddle before I really get going.' They both stagger away sideways, then break into an uncoordinated jog as they scamper towards the entrance. Zac is already frog-marching his catch towards the toilets as Rizzo squeals his discomfort.

'Mr Finnegan, what's all this about? I think you've made a mistake.'

Frank strides quickly, catching them up. 'Keep your trap shut, Rizzo, until I say you can open it,' he orders.

Rizzo is slammed into the toilet door and manhandled inside, where Zac releases his arm. He backs away into the corner, cowering, his sunken eyes darting from side to side like a hunted animal.

The harsh fluorescent lighting occasionally buzzes.

A tap drips, resonating off hard surfaces.

Stale urine fights with caustic disinfectant to control the air. It's a stalemate.

Walls with green flaky paint glisten with damp.

A discarded betting slip, cigarette butts, and a dead cockroach decorate the red, tiled floor, grubby, chipped, cold.

'Mr Finnegan, what's all this about?'

'I want a name, Rizzo?' Frank says as he collapses his baton and puts it back in his pocket.

Rizzo holds his hands up in confusion. 'A name? What are you talking about, Mr F?' he stammers.

'Don't play fucking games. I have one of my officers on life-support not a mile away from where we're standing. Are you telling me you're not aware of that?'

'Yeah, yeah, of course I'm aware of it. It's been all over the news, twenty-four-seven. And I'm very sorry to hear it. Nobody should be shot while going about their job, but I don't know what you want from me.'

'Are you deaf as well as stupid? I want a name. I know the circles you move in and someone, somewhere, must have heard a whisper. Now start talking?'

'Honest, Mr Finnegan! I've heard nowt!' he cries, squirming further back into the corner as Frank approaches.

'You're lying! You pathetic piece of low-life scum. A name!' he booms.

'I swear...'

Frank loses patience and nods at Zac. 'When was the last time you washed that greasy, nit infested mop of yours?' he says, gazing disapprovingly at Rizzo's lank, greying locks. 'You never were one for personal hygiene.'

He kicks open a cubicle door as Zac grabs Rizzo by the scruff of the neck, drags him inside and forces his head into the toilet bowl. Rizzo pleads his innocence as Zac pushes at the flush handle. The water from the cistern gushes forth, mingling with frantic gurgling. As the water subsides, Zac yanks Rizzo's head back up and releases him. He collapses onto the floor, and leans up against the cubicle side wall as he coughs and splutters, desperately trying to expel water from his lungs.

'Name!' Frank bellows.

'I... I've heard... noth... nothing, Mr F... swear to God,' he gasps, wiping water and snot from his face.

'Okay, have it your way. Round two.' Zac grabs Rizzo by the collar again and jerks him towards the bowl.

'Wait! Wait,' he screams.

'Go on?' Frank says.

'It's true Mr Finnegan. I swear on my mother's life. Give me twenty-four hours and I'll try to get you a name. Please, I beg you.'

Frank stares down at the quivering mess, then dips his head slightly, as he throws Zac a glance.

'Okay. Twenty-four hours and you better come up with something good, otherwise your life won't be worth living. I'm not in the mood for tiptoeing around the dregs of the earth anymore. The gloves are off. And don't try to hide, Rizzo, because *I will find you.'*

'You have my word,' Rizzo sniffles.

Frank chortles. 'Your word? Do me a fucking favour.' He pulls five ten-pound notes from his wallet and tosses them into the toilet bowl. 'You have my number. A name by tomorrow night and there's another fifty for you. If not... well, let's not go there. Enjoy the rest of your evening.'

3

Both men shiver in the shadows as they press up against a stone wall. A pale creamy glow from a replica Victorian streetlamp illuminates the 199 Steps. The wind whistles through the gravestones of the nearby St Mary's church as distant waves angrily thunder into the East Pier far below. Static up-lights eerily emphasise the ruins of the abbey, standing tall on the top of the hill, as it silently views the unfolding drama.

Frank stamps his feet and claps his gloved hands together. 'It could freeze the barnacles off an Eskimo's plums,' he mumbles, frozen to the core.

'You can't use that word anymore, Frank,' Zac states, rubbing vigorously at his arms, attempting to keep his circulation moving.

'What bloody word?' Frank says, patently confused.

'Eskimo. It's considered unacceptable. It's the Inuit or the Yupik people these days.'

'Stone the bloody crows. I can't keep up.' He glances at his watch. 'What's the name of your snout?'

'Cleavage.'

'Parent with a sense of humour?'

'No. He's a big lad. Got a nice set of man boobs. That's how he got the nickname.'

'Hellfire, there are some cruel bastards about,' Frank says with a chuckle. 'Are you sure he comes home this way?'

'Aye. He lives on the estate at the back of the abbey and that was definitely him we saw, propping up the bar in the Prince of Wales.'

'When did he become your grass?'

'About five years ago. I'm not proud to say it, but I met him in an illegal gambling club.'

'Cards?'

'Aye. Poker. He'd received two cautions and community service for being found in possession of small quantities of speed. Personal use. Then he received a suspended sentence for his third offence. Anyway, you may recall that drugs ring we busted, you know, the one involving the fishermen?'

'Vaguely.'

'Cleavage was involved in that. He's a casual deckhand for the trawlers. Found ten wraps of cocaine on him.'

'He'd become a dealer?'

'Yes. He gave me a big sob story about how he was due to be married in three months' time and he was only dealing to raise money to pay for his wedding. If I had nicked him, he'd have spent his honeymoon in D wing of Durham Prison.'

'You believed him?'

Zac stops rubbing his arms and gazes at Frank. 'Yes, I did. He's a likeable lad. He looks mean and tough, but he's a gentle giant. I told him I'd let him go on the proviso he kept me informed on any illegal activities he heard about.'

'And has he?'

'He's come in handy occasionally. Doesn't even want paying, although I always drop him a twenty.' Zac becomes distracted as he squints down the ancient steps. The sound of good natured, drunken singing drifts to both men on the biting wind. 'I think this is him. He's a happy drunk and likes to think he can carry a tune.'

'You need to put him right on that one,' Frank says as they slink further back into the darkness.

They watch on in silence as a large man with a bushy beard, dressed in jeans, boots, and a black bomber jacket staggers up the steps. His singing is occasionally interrupted as he stops and lets forth a succession of loud belches.

"What shall do we with the drunken sailor, what shall we do with the..." He breaks off again, this time to urinate against the side of the wall.

'Charming,' Frank murmurs.

He zips up and resumes his unsteady climb up the steps. As he approaches the top, Zac and Frank emerge from the shadows and stand directly under the radiance of the streetlamp, their bodies silhouetted and swathed in a ghostly halo. The big man stops and squints.

'What's all this?' he questions in a deep baritone. 'If you boys are looking for trouble, then you've found it,' he says with false bravado.

'It's me, Cleavage,' Zac says in his soft Scottish brogue.

'Zac, is that you?' he quizzes, hand placed above his eyes, salute fashion.

'Aye.'

Cleavage is visibly relieved and laughs nervously. 'You great, big, daft bugger! What are you doing skulking about in the shadows? You fair scared me half to bloody death.'

'Sorry. But it's best if we're not seen together.'

'And what's wrong with the phone?' he asks, his edginess returning.

'Phone conversations don't really impart the full intent of a message,' he says, as he walks towards him and places an arm around his shoulder. 'There's no body language.

I'll walk you to the abbey. My car's parked there, anyway.' Cleavage gazes sideways at Zac's arm, then shoots a tense glance at Frank. 'Don't worry about him, Cleavage. That's my boss. He's here to do my yearly appraisal. Make sure I handle the job correctly.'

They amble up the steps together as Frank falls in behind them, adding further to Cleavage's unease. Zac and Frank look more like Mafia hitmen than genial British police officers.

'I haven't anything for you, Zac. I get most of my gossip off the boys on the boats, but the trawlers haven't been out for two weeks because of the rough seas. I heard about that officer mate of yours who was shot, but I ain't heard nothing. If I had, I'd have been in touch. How's he going, by the way? Is he out of trouble yet? Bad business all round, and what with his missus being preggers, an all.'

Zac doesn't reply, as they walk on in silence, passing the church and the gravestones which jut up from the frigid earth. As they reach the turning circle at the back of the abbey, Zac stops and gently pushes Cleavage up against a wall, as Frank moves in close to his side.

'The thing is, Cleavage. You still owe me. You haven't forgotten, have you?' he says quietly, calmly.

'No... no, I haven't. But I can't tell you owt if I know nowt,' he replies in a tone of resigned desperation.

'I understand that, Cleavage. I suggest tomorrow you go for a wander around town, all the caffs, betting shops, fish market and maybe a pub crawl to finish the day off. You know all the locals. See what you can find out. Just a whisper is all we need. A friend of a friend who knows someone else's brother. I realise it's like Chinese whispers, but sometimes there's a shiny diamond to be plucked from the mire of shite. Just a name, or an address, or someone who thinks they might know who pulled the trigger.' He takes a fifty from his pocket and sticks it into Cleavage's hand. 'A little extra. Call it tomorrow's expenses.' He pats him gently on the cheek and offers him a warm smile before turning on his heels, followed by Frank. 'I'll wait to hear from you!' he calls out as they both near the car.

Cleavage gazes on in quiet dismay. 'Fuck,' he murmurs. 'He's a scary bugger, that one. I'd rather deal with the criminals.'

4

Condensation collects on cold glass. Occasionally, a teardrop forms, growing in size until gravity breaks the surface tension and the droplet bursts, creating a rivulet which carves a streaky path down the window. It pools on the sill. Prisha's eyes wander over the town, gazing at the Christmas decorations twinkling along North Terrace. She can just make out the familiar sight of Whalebone Arch and the red glowing warning light from the distant East Pier.

She pulls the curtains shut, blocking out the icy breeze, which always finds a way around the window frame. Flicking the TV on, she surfs the channels before switching it off and throwing the remote control onto a chair. Pulling her favourite from the bookcase, she slumps onto the sofa and opens the book—Wuthering Heights. Ten fractured minutes pass as her eyes compute the words, but her brain refuses to put meaning to them. For once, the complexities of Catherine and Heathcliff's relationship leaves her numb. She puts the book down, heads to the kitchen, and pours herself a large glass of dry white wine. Closing the fridge door, she gazes upon the colourful postcard and reads the short message on the back, smiling.

'If I'd have accepted your proposition, Tiffany, I'd be in Buenos Aires now. I could be learning to tango or cruising down the River Plate, eating oysters and caviar washed down with the finest champagne. We'd laugh and joke and flirt with handsome men. Instead, I'm here, alone, in cold, wet North bloody Yorkshire, angry, and depressed... and sad.'

The sharp buzzer from the main entrance three stories below gives her a start. She peers into the door monitor and spots the delivery driver already getting back into his van.

'Charming. They don't even announce themselves now. Just dump the food on the top step and bugger off.'

She piles rice up on her plate, then empties a tub of bean sprouts and Mongolian beef into the middle. Using a fork, she tucks into the food with abandon.

'Oh, my! That is good. I needed this.' Feeling re-invigorated, she grabs a notebook and pen. 'No point dwelling on things, Prisha. Let's do something constructive.'

She scribbles wildly and freely into the notebook, making lists and placing abstract ideas onto the pages. At the very top is one word—WHY? Beneath it, a series of prompts and counter prompts. She paces back and forth across her small living room, talking to herself.

'Why would anyone shoot a police officer for a traffic offence? Mental health issues? Out of their heads on drugs? It happens, but it's extremely rare. And what about the gun? This is Britain, not the USA. Guns are hard to come by unless you move in certain circles, which indicates someone with a police record. What about the robbery at the jeweller's shop in Middlesbrough? Not even sure there's a link. No weapon was used, just intimidation. And a stamp... who nicks a bloody stamp? Certainly not a drug dealer or someone looking to make quick money. The report from uniform is sketchy. I need to pay a visit myself and get the facts.'

She stares at the one thing in her notebook which is incontrovertible.

Vehicle - metallic blue Subaru WRX—still not been found. Partial number plate. AF 67.

Her pacing resumes. 'What do we have, Prisha? Not much. Let's say there is a connection between the robbery and the shooting. No, no, no! The rare stamp doesn't add up. Robberies of rare artefacts are usually committed by clever professionals not stand-over men with illegal guns. And why drive erratically and draw attention to yourself, then shoot a copper for a traffic offence? Highway Patrol would have probably issued an on-the-spot fine. I doubt they'd have searched the occupants, and even if they did, and they found a stamp, they'd think nothing of it. Which means what? I don't know! Think, think, think!'

Finishing her meal, she sets the dishwasher going and tops up her wine glass, then returns to her notes. Tapping a fingernail into the coffee table in an agitated manner, she goes over and over her questions. Her eyes close. A deep intake of breath. Her mind discards all thoughts. The deep, soulful vocals of Amy Winehouse drift from the Bluetooth speaker, helping her relax as she sips wine.

The empty glass falls from her hand, lands softly on the carpet, and rolls up against the leg of a chair, creating a gentle clink. Eyelids flutter as she rouses from an exhausting micro-sleep. She picks up the glass and stares at her distorted reflection. Killing the music, she turns all the lights off, pulls the living room door shut, and plods into the hallway. She gazes at the stairs which lead to her dormer bedroom and a cold mattress. Placing one foot on the bottom step and a hand on the bannister, she stops as a thought visits her.

'You've got something to hide, haven't you?' she whispers. 'And whatever you're hiding, it must be something big. That's why you shot a copper. You couldn't risk being taken into custody and investigated further. And if you're willing to shoot a police officer, then it may point to one thing—you've killed before and haven't been caught!'

5

Monday 30th November

Frank is standing at the front of the incident room, ready to hold court. To his side are his trusted allies, Zac and Prisha. In front are four other CID officers drafted in from around North Yorkshire, plus five uniformed officers.

'Thanks, ladies and gents. I realise six-thirty is an early start, especially for a Monday, and I appreciate it. I checked with the hospital a moment ago and DS Cartwright... sorry... Jason, is still on life-support. No change. It's not good news, nor bad news, so let's all keep praying and if you're not the praying type, then keep hoping.'

Worried faces and nods of the head greet his remarks. He shuffles sideways to expose the whiteboard, which is already loaded up with bullet points. He puffs out his cheeks.

'Before I begin, I'm sure most of you have heard about the tragic accident that happened overnight. Two young lads in a stolen car came off the bend on the Ruswarp Bank Road and hit a tree. A fifteen-year-old is in a ward with a few broken ribs and a dislocated hip, but at least he's stable. A sixteen-year-old is in the ICU and from what I hear, it's touch and go if he'll make it. They were both local Whitby lads, so let's also spare a thought for them, and their parents, and hope they both make a speedy recovery.'

It's certainly not a good news day and the oppressive mood only deepens.

'Right, down to business,' he says, pointing at the whiteboard. 'As you can see, we don't have much to go on. We don't know why the gunman shot Cartwright. We don't know if there's a connection between the assailants in the Subaru WRX and the robbery on the jeweller in Middlesbrough two hours before the shooting. All we know for sure is the make and model of the car and a partial number plate, and that the car had two occupants, more than likely male, although even that's not ironclad. After our appeal for witnesses on social media over the weekend, we've had over eighty replies from people who think they saw the car and the occupants. Uniform, I want you to chase up every one of those witnesses and take statements—ASAP. CID officers, I want you to get in touch with all your contacts and see if they've heard anything, no matter how tenuous. It's time to call in some favours. This shooting appears random, but in my experience, very few things are random. DI Kumar has a theory she'd like to expound on... remember, it's merely a theory at this stage, so don't let it throw you off course. DI Kumar.' He holds his arm out towards her.

Prisha steps forward. 'Thanks, boss. As Frank said, what I'm about to say is merely conjecture at this stage. I've been struggling over the weekend as to the whys of this shooting and it makes little sense. As a minimum, the driver of the car may have received penalty points and a fine. Depending on their past driving history, they may have lost their licence, had their vehicle impounded, possibly even incurred a very short prison sentence if it was prosecuted. None of which warrants shooting a police officer at point blank range.'

An unknown face from York CID puts her hand up. 'Ma'am?'

'Go ahead.'

'I've come across many people who have been off their heads on crack and meth who were capable of anything. Then there's the mentally ill who have been released back into the community. I'm just bringing it up, ma'am,' she adds apologetically.

Prisha smiles. 'Yes, I agree. It could be any of those scenarios and I've considered them and have not ruled them out. But those instances are typically rare. My theory... no, more of a thought bubble is this: someone who will shoot a police officer *doesn't* want to be arrested. Why? Because their past may catch up with them—meaning he, or possibly she, has committed a serious crime, or crimes before. What's the worst crime you can commit? Murder. The shooter was desperate not to be arrested. In my opinion, the shooting wasn't random. Once Jason flashed his warrant card at the driver, it set off a chain reaction. Every action has a reason behind it, and it is possible the shooter has killed before. Maybe they are on the run; possibly a recent release on parole; perhaps a killer who has never entered our airspace. We don't know. I just want you all to keep it in mind.'

Her address is abruptly halted as the door to the incident room is flung open. Detective Deputy Chief Constable Martin Overland strides in clutching a takeaway coffee, satchel slung over his shoulder. He's immaculately dressed as usual, his well-manicured goatee beard, and shaved head, offset against large rectangular spectacles. Following behind him is Superintendent Banks, basking in the reflection of the great man's glory. Frank and Zac do well to hide their groans as the rest of the room watch on in expectation.

Overland carefully places his coffee and satchel on a table, then slides out of his bespoke raincoat and looks for a suitable hook to hang it on. Not spotting one in the immediate vicinity, he throws his coat onto another table, in a deliberate carefree manner. He finally fronts the room, after making a slight adjustment to his glasses... his signature power play.

'Team, take ten, and talk amongst yourselves or grab a coffee,' he states with a gracious smile. He turns to Frank. 'I'd like a quick word with you, Frank and DS Stoker and Acting DI Kumar, in Superintendent Banks' office. It won't take long.'

As they all troop out of the room, Frank touches Zac's arm indicating for him to hang back. Zac throws him a concerned look.

Frank leans in and whispers. 'If this is about our little fishing trip last night, then it was all my idea. I commanded you to follow along. I'll take the fall. You were merely following orders from your superior.'

Zac shakes his head. 'No way, Frank. We're in this together. If you go down, we both...'

'Shut it, sergeant. I take the fall. Understood?'

They stare at each other for a moment until Zac nods.

The five officers squeeze into Anne Banks' micro-office. There are only two chairs, and no one takes a seat. Deputy Chief Constable Martin Overland and Superintendent Banks stand behind the desk, side by side. Anne is exhibiting her usual passive-aggressive, cold, grey expression, like a dead fish, whereas Martin Overland is sporting a disarming expression akin to an executioner with a warped sense of humour.

Frank closes the door. 'What's all this about, Martin?' he asks.

'Any breakthroughs, yet Frank?' he replies.

'Not as such, but it's early days and we have a lot of legwork to carry out.'

'Hmm... I see.' He slightly readjusts his spectacles before fixing his attention on Prisha. 'Acting DI Kumar, I don't think we've had the pleasure?'

'No sir.'

He purses his lips and becomes serious. 'You've had a baptism of fire since you joined us from the Midlands.'

'Yes, sir.'

He smirks. 'It's not always like this, I can assure you.'

'So I've been told, sir.'

'I'm sure you have. I believe you have your interview with the Independent Office for Police Conduct at eleven today. Once that is concluded, you are to stand down from active duty on full pay until they have delivered their final report and recommendations. You will surrender your warrant card over to Frank.'

'What? But sir...'

'Don't be alarmed, inspector. It's due process.'

'But sir, that's not fair. I've done nothing wrong. I need to be on this investigation!'

'Whatever led you to believe life was fair, inspector?'

Frank intervenes. 'Martin, DI Kumar is a damned fine officer and to lose her from this investigation...'

Superintendent Banks cuts him off. 'I don't think the deputy chief constable has finished yet, Frank.'

'Thanks, Anne,' he says as they exchange knowing smiles. 'Frank, I'm taking over this investigation as of now. A high-profile case like this needs a senior officer.'

'I am a bloody senior officer if you hadn't noticed—a DCI!' he shouts, astounded at the statement.

'Frank! Remember who you're talking to,' Banks snaps.

'Who's bloody idea is this?' Frank barks ignoring Anne's request. 'Does Gordon Critchley know about it?'

Overland lifts his hand for peace. 'The chief constable has been overseas. As his deputy I have been standing in for him. The decision is mine. The public and the media are always reassured when someone of a higher authority leads a case like this. A police officer has been shot. His life hangs in the balance. We need to be seen as taking this seriously and throwing everything we have at it. If we don't do it for our own, then what chance has the average person got? It's all about garnering trust and confidence.'

Frank wipes his brow with his palm. 'Have you ever even talked to Jason?'

Overland frowns. 'Not that I can remember, but that's not the point.'

Frank is unwilling to back down. 'DS Stoker and I have worked with Cartwright for nigh on ten years. DI Kumar, last week, solved a double murder case with great assistance from Cartwright. Jason was part of my team, my gang, and I run this investigation.'

'Frank!' Superintendent Banks hisses a warning.

Overland nods. Smiles. 'Sorry Frank, but my decision is final. And without wanting to rub salt into the wounds, I'm standing you and DS Stoker down from the case. Emotions are running high, understandably, but in my experience emotion and the efficient running of a major investigation do not make great bedfellows. I'm sure you have plenty of other work to be getting on with.'

Frank is almost apoplectic, but reins it in. 'And when was the last time you headed up a murder investigation? Eight, ten years ago? You're out of touch, Martin. You need someone who's still on sentry duty to run this case, not a bloody glory seeker out to appease the media and put a greasy mitt on the next rung up the ladder.'

'Frank! I won't warn you again,' Anne yells, pushing her fists into the desk.

'That's okay, Anne,' Overland says as he and Anne make their way to the door. Bearing an enigmatic smile he faces Frank. 'I'll ignore the insubordination on this occasion. As I said, emotions are running high, as you've proved. And by the way, I'll be requisitioning your office, Frank.'

'And where am I supposed to bloody work from?' Frank booms.

'You can use this office,' Anne says.

'That's right. Superintendent Banks will act as my second in command on the case,' Overland adds.

The door is gently closed as they exit the office.

Frank tries to pace up and down the office, but he only manages two strides before he faces a badly painted plasterboard wall. He stops and stands sideways on to Prisha and Zac. His bulldog-sized head grows redder and redder by the second. Zac and Prisha exchange worried glances.

Zac makes a move. 'Frank,' he begins gently, 'you need to calm down. Think of your blood pressure.'

Frank ignores the request, his mind a feverish cesspool of injustices. 'That snivelling little shiny shit! He was on my team years ago as a snotty nosed constable. Couldn't find a light-switch in the fucking dark. Oh, but he was good with the top brass and making sure his timesheet and expenses were always in early. Always eager to please those in high places. I don't give a flying fuck about that, though. The fact is, he's not the man for this job and to remove the three of us from the case is a recipe for disaster.' His anger is building, not subsiding. He pulls his warrant card from his pocket and takes a step towards the door.

Zac blocks him. 'Frank, what are you doing?'

'I'm going to shove my badge so far up the clacker of the deputy chief constable he'll be able to read my name as it pops out of his mouth. They've been trying to get me out. Now they have what they want. I'm officially retiring, as of today!'

He pulls at the door. Zac spins around behind him and grabs him in a tight bear hug.

'No, Frank! You're overreacting. Calm down.'

Frank growls menacingly. 'I don't want to hurt you, Zac, but you have three seconds to let me go.'

'Zac's right. Stop and think,' Prisha implores.

'One, two...'

'I'm not letting you do it,' Zac says, bearing a grimace as Frank flexes his muscles.

'Three!' He puffs out his barrel chest, tenses his biceps and jerks his shoulders back, breaking the arm lock as he jabs an elbow into Zac's ribs. The embrace is broken as pain sears through his body.

He staggers backwards. 'Jesus,' he gasps.

Frank turns to apologise. 'Sorry, Zac. But I warned you.' He spins on his heels to head out of the door, only to be confronted by Prisha, her arms splayed out, blocking the exit.

'You'll have to get by me first,' she spits with unyielding determination.

Frank shakes his head, sighs, then gently places his hands under her armpits. He lifts her effortlessly into the air, spins sideways, and deposits her two feet away to his left, her right foot landing in the wastepaper basket. The manoeuvre has left him unguarded as Zac regains his composure and grips Frank in another bear hug from behind.

'We can keep doing this all day,' he wheezes.

'That's true,' Prisha confirms as she jumps back in front of the door.

The tension falls from Frank's body, the wind knocked out of his sails as he realises the stupidity of his intentions.

'Okay. Fine. I submit. Anyone got any bright ideas?' he groans as Zac releases him.

Silence ensues for a few seconds.

'Have you two had breakfast yet?' Prisha asks.

They both shake their heads, beaten, dispirited, and reply, 'No.'

'Then I suggest we head to Miserly Joe's caff. We can order a full English breakfast and fill our veins full of saturated fat and discuss our options. Any takers?' she asks, confident she's on solid ground.

The day is still young, but for the first time, there are three genuine smiles.

6

Frank mops the last of the egg yolk from his plate with a piece of buttered white bread.

'That's me done,' Prisha says as she drops her napkin onto her plate.

Zac eyes the leftover rasher of bacon and slice of fried bread. 'You eating that?'

'No. I'm pogged.'

'Can I?'

She pushes the plate towards him. 'Go for it,' she says as she pulls her warrant card out and slides it over to Frank. He takes a gulp of tea, smacks his lips together and studies the card, before pushing it back towards her.

'You forgot to hand it over and I forgot to ask. After all, emotions are running high.'

Prisha grins. 'We could both end up in hot water over this.'

'Dilligaf,' he replies cryptically.

'What?'

'Do I look like I give a fuck?'

She grins and retrieves her card then slips it away. 'What are we going to do?'

'The three of us will continue searching for the suspect in Cartwright's shooting. Everything else is secondary. Prisha, you head up to Middlesbrough and interview the jeweller. Also, check out nearby CCTV and see if you can get a hit on the Subaru. But bear in mind...'

'... it could be a false lead and have nothing to do with the shooting,' Prisha says, finishing his sentence. 'What are you and Zac going to do?'

'We're hoping we may get some intel later on today.'

'Who from?'

Zac finishes the last of Prisha's discarded breakfast and wipes his mouth on a tissue. 'From our contacts who frequent the seedier side of life.'

Prisha frowns and stares at the battered Formica-topped table. 'I'm not looking forward to the interview later this morning. I feel like I'm the criminal,' she mumbles.

'Ah yes, the intrepid officers from the Independent Office for Police Conduct,' Zac says with a smirk. 'Have you fronted them before?'

'Yeah, just the once. When I was part of the drugs squad in the Midlands, we conducted a raid on a suspected trap house and a uniform got stabbed in his thigh severing his femoral artery. He nearly bled out. Luckily, he survived. The IOPC interview was intense. I went before them feeling guilty and came out convinced I was the one who stabbed my colleague. Why did the super call in the IOPC instead of referring it to our own in-house Professional Standards Department?'

Frank chuckles. 'That's Superintendent Banks for you. Does everything by the book and then some. Anyway, don't worry about the IOPC, it's simply due diligence. They're doing their job. Stick to the version you have in your written report, and everything will be fine. A word of warning though—don't get their backs up. It's yes sir, no sir, three bags full, sir. Show respect and no emotion. Understand?'

'Hmm... I suppose.'

'No! Not bloody—I suppose! Respect and professionalism, get it?' Frank bellows, making the other patrons in the grimy café turn their heads to investigate the commotion.

'Okay, okay. I get it,' she acquiesces, receiving a fatherly smile from Frank.

'Good lass.'

The three of them stand to leave when Prisha has a thought. 'Hey, Frank?'

'What?' he says, holding the door open for her.

'I have no wheels. I can't use an unmarked car as I'm supposed to be standing down after the interview. My car is out of action. It's at the mechanics and he's waiting on a part to be delivered.'

He ponders for a moment. 'Not to worry. I have a spare in a lock-up. It's a classic car. My pride and joy, so you be careful with her. I'll give you the address and you can meet me there about one o'clock.'

She grins. 'Okay. Sounds good.'

As the three of them wander out into the street, Frank emits a deep sigh, which doesn't go unnoticed.

'What's the matter, Frank?' Zac asks, fastening his coat against the cold.

'I'm dreading the sound,' he murmurs, squinting up towards the church and abbey across the river.

'Oh,' Zac says. 'Yeah. I forgot about the bloody bell.'

'What bell?' Prisha asks, confused.

Frank gazes down on her. 'It's an old tradition. If someone dies in tragic circumstances, Saint Mary's ring the bell to alert the townsfolk. Three warning tolls followed by as many chimes as the age of the deceased.'

'Fuck,' she whispers. 'That's ghoulish.'

'Aye, it is that. Anyway, thought it best I made you aware.'

'Thanks... I think.'

7

Prisha shuffles nervously as she finishes her recount of the events leading up to, during and after the shooting. It's about the fifth time she's relived the gruesome details and with each retelling, it becomes a little easier, more distant, as if she's talking about someone else.

The panel of three continues making notes. The lead investigator of the enquiry is particularly frosty and hard to read, like a middle-aged headmistress from a bygone era. Prisha glances around the interview room, the same one she's interviewed suspects in. Now she's on the other side of the table. The three investigators finally place their pens on the table.

'Thank you for your time, inspector. I have a few questions, then I'll run through our process for you. Going back to your statement, when you were in the car, and you heard the gunshot.'

'Yes.'

'You said you were holding your police radio and were about to call through to control that you'd apprehended the occupants of the Subaru on the forecourt of the petrol station.'

'That's correct.'

'But you didn't?'

'No.'

'Why?'

'As I said, the gunshot gave me a start, and I dropped the radio.'

'You then left your car and rushed towards your colleague while the Subaru was still on the forecourt?'

'Yes. But it took off like a bat out of hell before I'd even reached Jason... DS Cartwright.'

'In situations where a firearm is discharged by a member of the public, what should your response have been?'

'Ahem, I should have sought safety and called for armed response.'

'But you didn't?'

'No.'

'Therefore, potentially putting yourself in the line of fire.'

'Well, yes, but it all happened within a few seconds. I wasn't thinking of my safety or the gunman. I was thinking of my colleague.'

'But you agree you didn't follow the correct protocol?'

'I didn't follow police protocol, but I followed human protocol, to rush instinctively to the aid of a friend,' she replies testily, already regretting her snipe.

The lead investigator pulls her lips back and stares at her, eyeballs flitting back and forth over Prisha's face. She holds her gaze for a few seconds before glancing down at her notes.

'From leaving the car to assist your colleague and issuing the instruction to the petrol station attendant to call for an ambulance, how many minutes would you say elapsed?'

Prisha shakes her head, attempting to compute the timeframe. 'Not long, and not minutes. Maybe ten, twenty seconds.'

'Are you certain?'

'No, I'm not certain, but it was a matter of seconds, not minutes.'

'I see,' she says, scribbling notes. 'Of course, we'll be able to ascertain exactly how long it took from the CCTV footage at the petrol station and the logs of the emergency dispatcher.'

'Twenty or so seconds wouldn't have made any difference to the situation,' Prisha states, instantly regretting her words.

'In a life and death situation, seconds *can* count, inspector.' She turns to her colleagues. 'Any further questions?' They both shake their heads. 'I'll quickly run through our process, Inspector Kumar. We shall gather statements from people who witnessed the incident and analyse the CCTV and any dashcam footage from vehicles on the forecourt. We may obtain other documents, including telephone and GPS records, and review policies relevant to the event. And we'll speak with forensics and our own experts to help in the investigation, if required. Any further questions, inspector?'

Prisha is feeling the pressure.

'Yes. How long will all this take? I've been stood down and I want to return to work as soon as possible.'

'By the middle of next week, we will have concluded our investigation. We'll send a copy of our report to your commanding officer and any other interested parties.'

'The middle of next week!' Prisha exclaims, frustrated and annoyed.

'At the earliest. As an investigator yourself, I'm sure you're aware of how time-intensive these things can be. Anything else?'

'No,' she murmurs, rising from her chair, dispirited. She pulls at the door as her fiery temper gets the better of her. She turns. 'I've done nothing wrong, and yet you three have made me feel like I'm the criminal. Well, I'm not! And I won't be cowed by you bastards!'

She receives nothing but cold, blank stares with hints of condemnation.

Shutting the door behind her, she stands in the corridor, experiencing a mixture of emotions... mainly shame.

'You bloody dickhead, Prisha,' she murmurs. 'So much for yes sir, no sir, three bags full, sir.'

Frank lifts the roller shutter door on the garage and flicks a light on. Prisha is still chewing his ear off about her interview.

'It's ridiculous, Frank. I'm all for the police being held accountable. There are rotten apples and incompetent people in every large organisation. But this beggars belief. They were trying to imply that if I'd radioed through instead of running to Cartwright's aid, then somehow things would have turned out differently, which is bullshit! He'd still be in intensive care and on the critical list.'

'Let it go, Prisha. It's a waste of mental and emotional energy trying to solve the complexities of bureaucracy. I gave up years ago. They live in their own private world. You didn't say anything to stir them up, did you?'

She pretends to peer around the grimy lock-up, averting his gaze. 'No, of course not. I did everything by the book, as you instructed.'

Frank's not entirely convinced. 'Really?' he says in a low baritone, eyeballing her intensely.

'Cross my heart and hope to die,' she says, fingers crossed behind her back.

He grabs the corner of a large white sheet and yanks at it. 'Ta dah!' he says, holding his arms out, grinning madly.

Prisha stares at the vehicle. 'What the...'

'What do you think?' Frank asks, admiring his pride and joy, completely misreading Prisha's expression, which resembles that of a stunned mullet.

'Frank, when you said you had a classic car, I envisaged a sports car, an old MG, or Aston Martin. I mean, that's what older men who are going through a mid-life crisis usually waste their money on, isn't it? Does this old banger even go, and more importantly, is it roadworthy?'

Frank is mortally wounded. 'I'll have you know this is a 1968 Ford Anglia 105E Deluxe.'

'Deluxe! Christ, what was the base model like?'

She follows Frank as he wanders around the car, pointing out its special features, of which there are very few. 'Slanted rear window to keep dirt and the rain off. Muted tailfins for aerodynamics. A sweeping nose line.

And look at that styling. Pure 1950s Americana. On a smaller scale, of course.'

'Of course.' They circumnavigate the vehicle until they are standing in front of it. 'Aw,' Prisha says, cooing softly.

'What?'

'It has sad little eyes and a down-turned mouth,' she says, describing the headlights and radiator grille.

Frank scratches his head. 'Aye, I suppose she does,' he replies, humouring her. 'This is the same model of car they used in the Harry Potter films.'

'Oh, my God! You're right. The flying, invisible car.'

'And the same one they used in Heartbeat for many a year. Anyway, jump in and get a feel for her. I've already added you to my insurance, at no cost.'

She slips into the driver's seat, the red plastic upholstery squeaking in annoyance.

'It's only got one wing mirror,' she says with dismay. 'What are its safety features?'

'The brakes.'

'Is that it?'

'It's from 1968. What do you expect? Oh, it has a sash seatbelt.'

Prisha stares disdainfully at the sash. 'That thing would cut me in two if I was involved in a head-on.' She glances at the radio. 'I don't suppose it has Bluetooth?'

'What do you think? AM and FM and you're lucky it has that. The original radio was long, short, and medium wave.'

'What?'

'Never mind. Start her up,' he says, passing her the keys.

After searching for the ignition for a few seconds, she eventually fires the engine. It grumbles and stutters. 'Why is it shaking?'

'It's cold. You need to pull the choke out for a minute.'

'The what?'

'The choke,' Frank says, losing patience as he leans inside and pulls at the choke. 'Think of it as the equivalent of your first coffee in the morning, but for cars.'

'Oh.'

'This was the first car I bought when I turned eighteen. Exact same make, model, and year,' he states with pride. 'Do you know what that meant?'

'You'd been ripped off?'

'No! It meant freedom. Until then I had to go everywhere by bus, train, or shanks' pony.'

'You had a pony? Hell, you're not that old, Frank.'

He shakes his head in dismay at the younger generation and climbs into the passenger seat.

'Shanks' pony means using your legs. My original was a maroon colour. But I must admit, this turquoise look is growing on me. Right, stick her in reverse and drive around the block a couple of times to get used to her.'

Prisha stares at the gearstick. 'Which way's reverse,' she mumbles.

The grating clash of metal on metal reverberates around the garage as Frank cringes, regretting his offer to lend her the car.

'Don't worry about the gears. We'll pick them up on the way back.'

8

The forty-five-minute journey from Whitby to Middlesbrough in a fifty-year-old car is an eye opener for Prisha. With heavy oncoming traffic, and the incessant squally rain mixed with a pedestrian windscreen wiper, she's initially terrified. But, by the time she reaches her destination, she is merely alarmed, not terrified, if a little dry in the mouth.

She parks up and unfastens the sash belt across her lap.

'Bloody death trap,' she mutters, exiting the car and locking up. As she walks away, she stops and peers back at the Ford Anglia.

'Aw... but its sad little face is so cute.'

———◦———

Entering the high street jeweller's shop, she spots an attractive, smartly dressed woman behind the counter, busy polishing a bracelet.

'Mrs Windsor?' she asks.

The woman looks up and smiles. 'Yes? Oh, are you Inspector Kumar, who I spoke with earlier?'

'Yes,' Prisha confirms, flashing her warrant card.

'My husband is in the back doing the books. Please come through,' she says, unlocking a gate to enter behind the counter and display cabinets. 'Garth, Inspector Kumar is here to see you,' she calls out, leading Prisha into a back room.

A grumpy-looking man in his early fifties wearily glances up from his desk. 'Huh,' he grunts.

'I'll leave you to it,' Mrs Windsor says as she heads back into the shop.

Either Mr Windsor has had a hard life or there's a definite age gap between him and his wife.

'Take a seat,' Garth says as he removes his spectacles and rubs at weary eyes. 'I have to say, I'm very disappointed in your reaction time, inspector.'

'Sorry?'

'I was robbed last Thursday lunchtime. A uniformed officer arrived later that day to get the details, and he said CID would arrive Friday. It's now early afternoon, Monday. I informed my insurance company of the theft, but I need a police case file number. It's not good enough.'

Prisha inwardly groans. 'I'm sorry, Mr Windsor, but the police are stretched to breaking point at the moment. We take all crime seriously, and as distressing as your loss is, it's not a life or death situation.'

Windsor grunts and relaxes back in his chair, reflective. 'I heard about the officer who was shot. I apologise. It puts things in perspective. How is he?' he asks, slightly chastened.

'Still on the critical list in ICU.'

'I see.'

Prisha shuffles in her seat and pulls out her notebook. 'The report written up by the constable last week is a little patchy in places. Shall we go through the details of the robbery again, from the beginning?'

'Yes, of course. Last Thursday...'

'Thursday the twenty-sixth?'

'Yes. Last Thursday there was an auction at Broad & Herron Auctioneers in Newcastle.'

'What time?'

'Eleven. There was a special item I've been wanting to get my hands on for many a year—a Two Penny Blue, specifically, an imperforate.'

Prisha scribbles notes, peculiarly interested in the subject. 'A stamp?'

'Yes.'

'Okay. Before you continue, I know nothing about philately. Can you explain in layman's terms what you're describing, please?'

'Sorry. The first official stamp to be produced anywhere in the world was the Penny Black in 1840. They were produced in their tens of millions. The Two Penny Blue was issued a few days after the Penny Black, and being twice the cost, not as many were issued.'

'Which makes them rarer?'

'Exactly. Although, not as rare as you may think.' He pulls a catalogue from his drawer, and flicks through a few pages, then places the brochure in front of her, tapping at an image. 'That's the Two Penny Blue. The exact same one I bought last Thursday.'

Prisha pulls her phone out. 'Do you mind if I take a photo?'

'Be my guest. A used Two Penny Blue isn't worth much—ten, twenty pounds at most.'

'Used?'

'Meaning, it bears a watermark stamp from the sorting office to stop people from reusing them.'

'I see.'

'An *unused* penny blue is worth around a hundred pounds, max.'

Prisha takes a snapshot, then puts her phone away as her eyes scan the catalogue. 'But this one here has a reserve price of thirty thousand pounds?' she adds, pointing at the image.

'It's an imperforate, or an imperfection. It's missing the perforations around the edges.'

'So, a stamp with an imperfection is worth more than one which is perfect?'

'Yes. Because they're extremely rare. The rarer a stamp—the higher its value.'

'Good old-fashioned supply and demand.'

'Precisely.' He points at the stamp in the catalogue again. 'It's not only an imperforate but also missing the white lines above and below Queen Victoria's head. Some collectors refer to it as the—two penny no lines design. The *official* identifying name is the Scott 2. Used, this would fetch seven, eight hundred pounds. Unused, the highest sale price until last Thursday was thirty-five thousand pounds.'

'And you bid on the stamp and won the auction?'

'Yes. I paid forty-five thousand pounds for it. Way above what I intended to bid.'

'How come?'

'By the time we reached the reserve price, there were three bidders left in the game. Myself, in person at the auction house, and two online bidders.'

'People can bid over the internet?'

'Yes. It's all done in real-time.'

'Do you know who the other bidders were?'

'No. Maybe overseas collectors.'

'You still haven't explained why you bid way over the reserve price.'

'I'm a collector, inspector. I'm not obsessed with the stamps I collect, although I do find them fascinating. Their history, the rarity, who the original owner may have been. But I'm not sentimental. There is a method to my madness. I've recently turned fifty. I and my wife's long-term goal is to retire in another five years. We'll sell the business and stock, then buy a chateau in the south of France. Enjoy the fruits of our labours. We have some savings but they're modest and I believe one should always have something in reserve for a rainy day: unexpected hospital bills; a new car; a round the world trip. My collection is a nest egg. At a conservative estimate, at today's prices, it would be worth about half a million. I don't intend to sell it at auction en-masse. I shall dip into it as needs arise. Maybe two or three items at a time. Some people put their money into stocks and shares, others into gold. They can be volatile markets. With rare stamps, the only way is up. They're safe.'

'Sounds like a wise investment. Can we move onto the actual robbery?'

'Of course. Follow me.' He leads her into a stock room full of unopened boxes and various shelves. As he fronts a large steel door, he presses at a monitor on the wall, tapping in digits. It's followed by a few clunks as various locking mechanisms are released. He takes a set of keys and manually unlocks a series of three deadbolts.

'That's some door,' Prisha comments.

'State-of-the art. When I first bought the business, I saw the back entrance as a weak point. Cost me a fortune to have it installed, as has all the security. No one can get in via the back. We've had seven attempted robberies over the last twenty years and never lost a thing... apart from a few smashed display cases. They always come in through the front door during opening hours. I have cameras everywhere, alas, not outside at the back. An error of judgement on my part which will soon be rectified.'

He pushes open the door and they both walk out into grim daylight. Prisha scans the area. There's a large square car park in front of her. To the right is the back entrance to a supermarket. Dead ahead are two large stores. To the left, a row of two-storey office buildings with a to-let sign, and behind, the rear entrances to a row of high street shops.

'Can you show me exactly your movements last Thursday, immediately prior to when you were robbed?'

'Certainly.' Garth Windsor points at a car parking bay only ten feet away. 'I parked in that spot, right there.'

'At what time?'

'I can't be certain, but I'd say it was about 12:30. The auction was held in Newcastle, which is forty-five minutes away. It began at 11 am and the bidding on the stamp was about twenty minutes later. After my successful bid, I transferred money across to the auction house, filled out paperwork, and called my insurance company.'

'How long did that take?'

'About thirty minutes, all up. I then returned to the shop.'

'Who's your insurer?'

'Heritage Collectables. They specialise in antiquities.'

Prisha jots down the details. 'Then what happened when you arrived back here at the shop?'

'I exited the car carrying a small case containing the stamp. I intended to deposit the stamp in my safe.' He spins around and points at the steel security door. 'I was standing right there. I swapped the case from my right to my left hand, pulled out my phone, pressed the security door app, tapped in the code, and waited a few seconds until I heard the mechanisms go through their motions. I then put my phone back into my jacket pocket and was fumbling for my keys to open the three deadlocks when I felt a presence behind me. Spinning around, I was confronted by a large man. He was wearing a full-length puffer jacket, woollen hat, and had a bandanna pulled up over his mouth and nose. Needless to say, I realised I was in a spot of bother.'

'What happened next?'

'He grabbed me around the throat... not aggressively, and he didn't squeeze, but I could sense the power in his hand, in his fingers.'

'And?'

'He said—*I'll take that*, then snatched the case from my hand, turned on his heels and headed towards the supermarket. I dropped my keys about half a dozen times, trying to get them into the lock. I'm not ashamed to admit I was quite shaken. When I eventually got inside, I locked the back door and told my wife to close the shop. Then I dialled 999.'

Prisha glances over to the back entrance of the supermarket and spots the clearly visible CCTV cameras. *Hmm... odd.*

She continues. 'Did he run towards the supermarket?'

'No. He walked.'

'Fast, slow, edgy?'

Windsor considers the question thoughtfully. 'I only had two quick glances over my shoulder... but he walked at a normal pace. Not fast, but not ambling.'

'A normal shopper going about his day?'

'Yes, I suppose you could phrase it like that.'

'The emergency call you made was logged at 12:37 pm, nearly seven minutes after the robbery?'

'Yes, I suppose so.'

'Seven minutes is rather a long gap?'

'I was shaken up. My wife made me a cup of tea to calm my nerves before I rang. It's all a bit of a blur.'

'Hmm... so, when the assailant grabbed you outside, did you offer any resistance?'

'You say that as if it were a failing on my part, inspector. There weren't many people about. Plenty of cars, but not many passers-by. I instinctively knew I was no match for him, and as painful as it is to lose an artefact worth forty-five thousand pounds, it pales into significance compared to losing your life or being seriously injured.'

'Yes, you're right. I apologise. I didn't phrase my question correctly. There was no intention to apportion any blame.'

'Apology accepted.'

'Let's focus on the assailant. You say he was big—do you mean tall?'

'Sorry, no. I meant muscular, overdeveloped. Like a body builder. Height wise, he wasn't much taller than me, and I'm five foot ten.'

'So, possibly five foot eleven, max?'

'Yes.'

'Any distinguishing features you can recall?'

'No. he was fully clothed and all I could see were his upper cheeks and eyes. Although...' he pauses, reflects.

'Go on?'

'His bandanna... it was, how can I put it... full.'

'Meaning he could have had a beard?'

'Yes. And his eyes. They were a piercing blue colour, and his pupils were dilated, almost like he was on something.'

'Hmm... I see,' she says, furiously making bullet points in her notebook. 'But definitely not aggressive, well, apart from placing one hand around your neck?'

'No. He appeared calm.'

Prisha chews a few thoughts over before asking her next question. 'Which hand did he use to grab you with?'

'His left.'

'And what was his right hand doing?'

'Erm... I'm not sure... wait, yes, that's right... his right hand was sort of out of view until he grabbed the case from me.'

'Out of view?'

'Yes. Hovering behind his back.'

'Christ,' she murmurs.

'Has that some significance?'

'Possibly. He may have been reaching for a weapon until he realised you weren't going to put up a fight.'

'Hell,' he mumbles staring at the ground, realising the significance. 'I made the right decision then.'

Prisha regains her thoughts. 'I think you did. You've been very patient and helpful, Mr Windsor. I'm sorry we didn't get such a detailed report last Thursday. The detective constable who initially interviewed you will be spoken with.'

'Oh, please... I don't wish him any trouble. I admit he was a little distracted, but he said he was getting married last Saturday then flying out to Cambodia on Sunday for a two-week hiking trip with his bride. I'd hate for him to get the sack.'

Prisha offers a reassuring smile. 'He won't get the sack, Mr Windsor. The worst he'll suffer is a roasting from a grumpy DCI. Sloppy police work needs to be nipped in the bud.' She hands him her card. 'If you recall anything else, no matter how insignificant, then call me. It's sometimes the little things that lead to the breakthrough. By the way, do you recall his accent?'

A bin lorry enters the carpark, and reverses, its guttural diesel engine and incessant beeping drowning out their voices.

'I'd say he was native to these parts,' Windsor shouts above the din.

Prisha bends in. 'Sorry? I didn't get that?'

'I said he was local!'

'A Teesside accent or Yorkshire?'

'Hard to say. He only said three words.'

Their strained, staccato conversation is rudely interrupted as two young boys whizz around the corner on e-scooters. They're laughing, joking, fighting with each other. Distracted, they take a tumble, their scooters slamming into the side of a parked car.

Prisha yells at them. 'Oi, you two! Those things are illegal for kids of your age!'

They laugh and give her the V sign. 'And wot you going to do about it... bitch-face?'

Infuriated, she flashes her badge at them. 'I'm a police officer and I can arrest you!' she screams.

'Ha-ha! You can't arrest us. We're both under ten. Nowt you can do about it... pig, bitch!'

They both pick themselves up and zip off, throwing expletives and finger signs at Prisha. In two minds whether to chase after the boys, or conclude her interview, she decides on the latter as the rubbish truck lumbers its way to the far side of the carpark, making hearing a little easier.

'Little bastards,' she mutters. 'They know the law better than I do. Those e-scooters are a bloody menace.'

'And that is why, inspector, my wife and I intend to retire to the South of France. In distance, it's not too far away. In attitude, it's a hundred years in the past. People still have respect. There's none around here. The country has gone to the dogs. I blame...'

Prisha cuts him off, being well versed in these fruitless conversations many times before.

'You said the assailant was fully clothed, his face partially covered, but from your description he was extremely muscular, with distinctive blue eyes, and possibly a beard. Bearing that in mind, had you noticed anyone who matched his description hanging around, or entering the shop, prior to the robbery?'

Garth pouts and thinks. 'No. Being a jeweller, I have an eye for detail, and I certainly can't recall anyone who looked like that. Not a typical customer.'

'What about when you were at the auction house?'

'No.'

'I see. Just a few more questions, Mr Windsor. Can you give me an approximation of his age?'

Windsor shuffles restlessly. 'I'm sorry, but as I've explained, his face was covered, and it was all over in a flash.'

'I understand. But was he a youth, an old man?'

'If I were to hazard a guess, I'd say somewhere between late teens and early fifties.'

'That's a thirty-year age gap?'

'As I said, it happened in seconds and his face was covered. I'm trying my best, inspector.'

'Yes, I know you are. Whoever stole the stamp obviously knew it's value and significance. This doesn't sound like a random opportunist attack.'

'My thoughts entirely.'

'Do you know of any dodgy collectors or scam artists?'

He emits a wry laugh. 'The entire country is full of them. It seems half the population prefers to spend their time making money illegally rather than hold down a lawful job. Everyone wants to get-rich-quick these days. It's like a disease.'

'How easy would it be to resell the stamp?'

He ponders. 'It obviously couldn't be resold at a public auction, as whoever took it won't have the papers of ownership and authentication. But on the black market, it would be very easy to sell to another collector. And that's another thing, the value of the stamp will have risen by at least ten per cent overnight.'

'How come?'

'Around five years ago there were eight known Scott 2s.'

'Unused, Two Penny Blues, missing the perforations and the two white lines?'

'Correct. Unfortunately, one was destroyed in a fire, and another was stolen during transit to an exhibition in Italy. That left six authenticated Scott 2 penny blues in the entire world. Hence, why the value has soared recently.'

'Back to supply and demand.'

'Yes. Now there are five. Once I inform the philately societies around the world of the theft, then the remaining penny blues will increase in value. Whoever stole my stamp is now in possession of an artefact worth at least fifty thousand pounds. Not a bad payday, by anyone's reckoning.'

She puts her notebook away and pulls her collar up against the cold. 'Thank you, Mr Windsor. I'll keep you updated of any progress, but stolen stamps are not normally the remit of CID. We have an Economic Crime Unit that deals with serious fraud and money laundering. I'll liaise with them regarding the best way to move forward.'

'Yes, I understand. And thanks for your assistance, inspector.' He hands her his business card. 'Here are my details. As mentioned, I will require a case file number... for insurance purposes.'

She takes the card and slips it into her pocket. 'Not a problem. I'll text through the case number sometime tomorrow, and if the insurance company wishes to speak to me directly, then tell them to contact me on my mobile number, not the station number.'

He smiles gratefully until a frown suddenly forms. 'By the way, the officer who was shot, did you know him personally?'

'Yes. We're on the same team.'

'Good grief.'

'Goodbye, Mr Windsor.'

9

Prisha is standing behind the supermarket manager in his office as he trawls over the CCTV footage. She glances casually around the bland, windowless room. It reminds her of Superintendent Banks' office, if a touch bigger.

'Are you sure it was Thursday at 1:30 pm, you were after?' the manager queries.

Prisha stares down at the bald spot on the back of his head and silently curses.

'I said 12:30.'

'Oh, that could explain it. And it was definitely last Thursday?'

'Yes,' she replies, looking over his shoulder at the screen, which is rolling grainy footage of the car park to the rear of the supermarket.

'I don't see anyone matching the description you gave me. But I can see Everest having a sneaky gasper behind the bins.'

Prisha squints at the screen. 'Everest?'

'Yeah, the short, stubby git skulking in the shadows. See?' he says, tapping the screen. 'I might just run the tape back and see how long he was outside for. He's paid to stack shelves, not loiter near the dustbins smoking. It's also a no smoking area. It's hard to get the staff these days. People think it's a dead-end job, but it's not. There's a career path if you care to follow it. I started at age fifteen as a stacker and now, thirty years later, I'm deputy assistant manager.'

'You're the deputy to the assistant manager?' she queries.

'Yes.'

'Third from the top?'

'No fourth. The assistant to the deputy manager is above me, although we share similar roles.'

'Christ, I thought the police was top heavy.'

'Then there's the area manager, district manager, and regional manager, which is my ultimate goal. That's the position that wields the most power. Oh, yes... the power. I'll shake logistics up once I'm in charge. A new broom.'

Prisha refocuses on the computer monitor. 'As interesting as the hierarchy of supermarkets is, do you think you could hurry things along a little?'

'The whole thing needs modernising. Too many outdated practices. For example...'

Prisha, not renowned for her patience, is becoming exasperated. 'Mr Bunting, can you please focus on the description of the man I gave you?'

'What, oh, yes. Sorry. Last Thursday about 1:30.'

'No, 12: 30! For crying out loud. Rewind back to 12:15 then scroll forward.'

'No need to shout, inspector. I'm trying my best.'

Fuck! If this is your best, I'd hate to witness you on an off day.

'I'm sorry. It's been a stressful week.'

'Ha! Don't talk to me about stress. Yesterday I had a crate of baked beans go missing. I mean, how can a crate of baked beans simply vanish? Same thing happened six months ago. I suspect there's a black market for stolen baked beans.'

Prisha's hands are now hovering behind his neck, ready to throttle him. She catches a figure walk into view on the screen.

'Wait! Stop there,' she shouts, startling the manager. 'Go back a little.'

The manager dutifully obliges, and rewinds the footage, then slows it as a man comes into view, entering the back entrance from the car park.

'He looks like your man,' the manager mumbles as he scrolls the video back and forth.

'Can you zoom in?'

'A little,' he replies.

The well-built figure is wearing a puffer jacket and a woollen hat, but his face is hard to distinguish. He disappears as he passes beneath the camera.

'Do you have a camera directly inside the back entrance to the store?'

'Yes. Give me a moment.' The manager clicks his mouse and another view pops onto the monitor. This time the clarity is better as he zooms in. 'He fits your description. Bandanna pulled up over his face. But he's not carrying a small case.'

'No. Probably stuffed it into his jacket. Okay, can you track him through the store and see where and when he exits?'

'Sure thing.' The manager effortlessly flicks from camera to camera as it tracks the man heading directly across the store to the front entrance and exits the doors. The outside camera picks him up, climbing into a car and driving off.

'Go back a bit and zoom in on the vehicle's number plate,' Prisha commands, squinting at the screen.

'Sure.'

The footage zooms in as Prisha experiences a tingle through her body. 'Got you, you bastard!' she shouts as she pulls her notebook and pen out. 'Metallic blue Subaru WRX. Number plate AFX 967. Go back again and zoom in on the passenger side.'

The footage is grainy, but there's definitely another figure sitting in the passenger seat.

'That's the best shot I can get,' the manager apologises.

'No, that's fine. You've done a great job.' She taps a finger against her lips. 'What's their game?' she ponders aloud. 'They're not the getaway driver. Weren't involved in the robbery. So why sit there in the car?'

'Maybe his wife or girlfriend?' the manager suggests.

'I've heard of doing things together to cement a relationship, but that's ridiculous. No, there's a reason they're there, but I'm not sure why. Okay, well thank you very much. Can you gather all the relevant footage and drop it onto my USB stick, please?' she says, pulling the micro-USB from her keyring and handing it to him.

'No problem. It will take me about fifteen minutes, though.'

'Fine. I'll grab a coffee and call back. Oh, and can you zoom in on the man and print out a snapshot?'

'I can, but the quality won't be great.'

'I understand. It would still be useful, though. And once again, thank you so much. You've been a great help.'

'My pleasure. It beats trying to locate a missing pallet of baked beans.'

10

Prisha is experiencing that special feeling. It only happens when things begin to fall into place. Like a game of Cluedo, where initially you're stabbing in the dark, pure guesswork. Then something clicks, and your mind hones in. Tiredness and lethargy are quickly banished, and you feel alive. For her at least, it's the best feeling in the world.

Before setting off to pay a visit to the auction house, she calls Frank.

'Prisha, what have you got?'

'An ID on the man involved in the assault and robbery outside the jewellers. CCTV footage of him getting into a car; and an ID on the car—a metallic blue Subaru WRX. Number plate AFX 967. I'm heading to the auction house where the stamp was sold last week. Then I'll head back to Whitby.'

'Great work, Prisha. I'll get Zac onto the number plate right now. As you're not supposed to be on the job, you obviously can't come back to the station, so meet me and

Zac in The Granby at six. It's usually nice and quiet and they have a log fire at this time of year. We can go over our notes together there.'

'Where's The Granby?' she asks, still not familiar with every watering hole in Whitby.

'Walking distance from your place. Halfway down Skinner Street.'

'Okay. Any other developments?'

'Not that I've heard. See you later... oh, how is Beatrice treating you?'

'Who the hell is Beatrice?'

'The car, the Ford Anglia?'

'You have a name for your car?'

'I do. She has a personality.'

'She certainly does. Old, draughty, noisy, and slow... and bloody dangerous. Yes, I think Beatrice suits her.'

'You be kind to her. Treat her gently and she'll reciprocate.'

'Bye, Frank.'

———— ◦•◦ ————

The auctioneer gazes at his laptop. 'Ah, yes, here we are. Lot 9, last Thursday. A Scott 2. Unused, Two Penny Blue from 1840. An imperforate with missing white lines. Reserve price, thirty thousand pounds. Sold for forty-five thousand to Mr Windsor. Quite unexpected. But that's auctions for you.'

'I've already interviewed Mr Windsor about the robbery, and he said once the reserve price was met, there were only three bidders left in the auction, including himself. Is that correct?'

'Technically no. In reality, yes.'

'Can you explain?'

'A bidder can drop in and out at will. But the truth is, as an auction progresses, the number of bidders dwindles until the final bid.'

'Apart from Mr Windsor, can you tell me who the other bidders were?'

'Certainly.' He taps at his keyboard. 'That's right, I remember now. They were both online bidders. One was an auction house in the United States, the other was Mr Alfred Dunn of Staithes, North Yorkshire.'

'I'll need Mr Dunn's address and phone number.'

'Certainly.'

'And before Mr Windsor won the final bid, who was still bidding?'

'Let me see,' he says, squinting at the screen. 'The auction house from the States dropped out at thirty-eight thousand and the last bid from Mr Dunn was at forty-four thousand.'

'Are you aware if Mr Dunn and Mr Windsor know one another?'

The auctioneer chuckles. 'Oh, yes. They know each other all right.'

'Friends, acquaintances?'

He offers her a wry smile. 'They were mutual acquaintances until they fell out with each other about three years ago.'

'Over what?'

'Mr Dunn is an avid collector. He buys antiquities because he has a love and fascination for them. Mr Windsor, on the other hand, buys them as an investment. That's not to say he doesn't appreciate them, he clearly does. But his interest is predominantly financial.'

'Yes, he said as much to me. The falling out?'

'As I said, about three years ago there was a much sought after pair of cuff links up for auction. They once belonged to Hermann Goring. If you're unaware, he was Commander-in-Chief of the Luftwaffe during the war,' he adds in a rather patronising manner, assuming anyone under the age of fifty would not have heard the name Hermann Goring.

'Yes, I'm aware of who he was. The falling out?' she prompts for the third time, becoming impatient.

The auctioneer coughs realising his faux pas. 'Mr Dunn specialises in Second-World-War memorabilia and mentioned the cuff links were coming up for auction to Mr Windsor. Once again, Mr Windsor outbid him.'

'How much did they go for?'

The auctioneer frowns. 'I'd have to check back through my records,' he says, tapping at his laptop.

'Ball park figure will do.'

'From memory, I think the reserve prices was twenty-five thousand and I believe Mr Windsor paid thirty thousand for them. He has much deeper pockets than Mr Dunn.'

'And that caused the rift?'

'Yes, they had a big blow up right here in this room. I had to separate them.'

'Hell! All over a pair of cuff links once worn by a Nazi,' she murmurs.

'They were quite exquisite, inspector,' he replies, incredulous at her remark.

'Okay, back to last week. I believe Mr Windsor settled his account with you after the auction for the stamp?'

'Yes, in full. He's well known and respected at this establishment. An honourable gentleman, as is Mr Dunn.'

'I see. I'd like to look at your CCTV footage of the auction and any video footage you may have of outside.'

'Certainly. That's not my area of expertise, but I'll introduce you to our extremely efficient secretary. I'm sure she'll be able to help.' They set off across the auction room towards a set of small offices.

'Oh, one last thing; would the online bidders know who won the auction?'

'No. All they can see is the item for sale. And they can obviously hear my auction chant to keep track of the highest bids.'

'And what about the bidders who were here in person? Do they know who the online bidders are?'

'No.'

Prisha takes the slower, scenic route along the coast to visit Mr Dunn. She passes by Marske, Skelton, and Easington before the GPS on her phone tells her to turn off the main road onto Cowbar Lane. The car rattles along the narrow road at the edge of the cliff, offering expansive and magnificent views of the coastline. The road tapers into a single vehicle track and rapidly descends. As she rounds a bend, her eyes feast on the tiny, picturesque fishing village of Staithes.

'My God! This is delightful. Now I know why I came to North Yorkshire. I can put up with all the crap just to witness places like this. I could live here. It's only twenty minutes from Whitby.'

She parks the car outside an old, stone fishing cottage with a terracotta tiled roof, and windows and doors painted in dark blue. It overlooks a beck that runs out to the sea. On the other side is the main town with its narrow, cobbled lanes. The rain is back in sporadic gusty bursts as the daylight prematurely fades. She glances at her watch. Nearly five. She's not even sure what she's doing here. It would have been far simpler to have phoned Mr Dunn, but she prefers to meet people of interest face to face and see if her senses pick anything up. She raps on the front door, then waits as she gazes down to the beach. The door creaks open and she's confronted by an elderly gentleman with grey hair and ruddy jowls. His expression is a mixture of surprise, maybe even concern.

'Yes?'

Prisha flashes her card. 'DI Kumar. North Yorkshire Police. Are you Mr Alfred Dunn?'

'I am. How may I help you?'

'It's about the auction last week in Newcastle. I believe you were an online bidder for a rare stamp?'

'Yes, that's right.'

'Can I come in for a moment?'

He shuffles backwards as he points the way to the living room. 'Of course. Go through and take a seat. I was just about to pour myself a cup of tea. Would you care to join me?'

Bloody tea! They live off the stuff up here. 'Yes, that's very kind. Black, no sugar with a drop of cold.'

As he walks to the kitchen, she enters the living room and takes in the surroundings. Two built-in bookshelves surround the fireplace, packed to the gills with books and magazines. On the walls are numerous paintings, most of them depicting idyllic English scenes from a bygone era. Three on each wall, all perfectly aligned in neat rows, apart from one which is slightly off kilter. The room is cosy and tidy, with an imitation coal fire built into the chimney. She doesn't notice any family photographs. Browsing the bookshelves, she pulls out a few books. Memoirs and biographies, crusty tomes on ancient civilisations, hardbacks on various campaigns during World-War-Two. She's already formed an impression of the type of man Mr Dunn is.

He enters the room carrying two cups as Prisha accepts the drink and flops down into a shabby old Chesterfield couch.

'Do excuse the mess, inspector. Old bachelors are not the most fastidious of people.'

'You should see my place at the end of the week. Hell of a mess,' she lies, to put him at ease. 'I like the paintings,' she says, nodding towards them.

'Ah, yes. One of my many passions. Turner and Constable are my favourites. There's something about the late 18th century romanticism landscape painters which I find fascinating. The way they capture the sky is unique. It would have been a blissful era to have lived through. No electricity, no cars, no damned mobile phones.'

'No antibiotics, no running water, no National Health System, no votes for women. If you had money, it may have been blissful, but I dare say for most people it was a bloody tough old grind, year in year out.'

'Ahem, yes, well... you're here to talk about the auction?'

'Yes. The stamp sold last week at the Broad and Herron auction house was stolen not long after the auction finished.'

'The Two Penny Blue?'

'Yes.'

'Good lord! I hope whoever bought the stamp had it insured.'

'Yes, it's insured.'

'That's terrible news but I don't see how I can help, unless you suspect I stole it?' he says with a croaky laugh.

She stares at him as she sips on her tea. 'I believe you're a collector, Mr Dunn?'

'Yes, I am. Coins, stamps, and memorabilia from World-War-Two, mainly.'

'I take it you're retired, but what was your previous occupation?'

'I was a professor at Durham University for thirty years.'

'What did you lecture in?'

'Museum and artefact studies.'

'The auction last Thursday finished at 11:20 am. What did you do after that?'

He places his cup down on a side table. 'I drove to Durham and caught up with an old friend of mine who also used to work at the university. We had luncheon together.'

'And your friend can verify that?'

His eyes narrow as lines flex across his forehead. 'Yes, of course. I can give you his number. You really do suspect I was involved in the robbery, don't you?' he adds with incredulity.

'I'm investigating anyone who had a motive to steal the stamp. You were obviously keen to get your hands on it as your top bid was forty-four thousand pounds. That's a lot of money. You must have been disappointed to miss out?'

He chuckles, timidly. 'I'm not sure how the stamp was stolen, inspector, but as you can see from my demeanour, I'm no cat burglar.'

She employs a device picked up from watching Frank in play. Stares, unblinking, emotionless. Holds his gaze for a few seconds until he's uncomfortable. Then, a sniff, pursed lips, as if she doesn't believe him. The next is her own ruse. 'Hmm...' More silence as she glances at her notes and takes a sip of tea. 'What's the most valuable piece in your collection, Mr Dunn?'

'I have a Penny Black block of four, unused, which I purchased for eighty thousand pounds about a decade ago.'

'What would it be worth today?'

'Possibly double.'

'Where do you keep your collection?'

'I have a safety deposit locker in York where the most valuable items are kept.'

She takes another swig of tea and stands up. 'Thanks for your time, Mr Dunn.'

'Is that it?' he asks, surprised.

'Yes. For now. I'll be in touch if I have any further questions. Oh, wait.' She pulls out the poor-quality photograph obtained from the supermarket CCTV and hands it to him. 'Do you recognise this man?'

He fumbles his spectacles on and studies the image. 'No. I'm not sure anyone could discern who it is from this photograph.'

'It's not the best. He's about five-ten. Solid, well-built, possibly a body builder. Distinctive blue eyes, local accent.'

He hands the photo back. 'Sorry inspector. I can't help you. I take it this is the man who stole the Two Penny Blue?'

'We believe so.'

He escorts her to the door. 'I hope you find the stamp. I'm guessing the chap who was robbed is most perturbed, despite it being insured.'

Who said he was robbed? I said the stamp was stolen.

'He's rather stoic about it,' she replies, pulling open the door. 'Oh, your friend's telephone number...'

Again, a flicker of astonishment. 'Yes, of course. Let me get a pen.' He disappears back into the room and returns a few moments later with a stub of paper in his hand containing a name and number.

'Enjoy the rest of you day,' she says. 'You live in a beautiful spot.' As the door closes, she scurries across the road and jumps into the car as fast as she can. Pulling her phone out, she stabs at the numbers. 'Come on, come on...' she urges. The familiar, engaged tone greets her. 'Damn it!'

11

Zac pulls up outside the address and gazes upon the modern bungalow on the outskirts of Scarborough.

'Nice looking pad,' he mutters. 'That would be worth a few bob.' He saunters up the garden path and knocks on the door. As he waits, he notices a next-door neighbour eyeing him suspiciously from his garden. Zac nods and smiles, then raps on the door again.

'He's not home,' the man grizzles as he ambles towards Zac, a spade slung over his shoulder. 'What are you after him for?'

'It's a private matter,' Zac says, turning around as the older man gives him the once over.

'Oh, aye,' he replies, his words dripping with scepticism.

Zac pulls out his warrant card. 'A private police matter,' he says. 'Have you any idea when Mr Platt will be back?'

'Shouldn't be long now,' he says cryptically, in a deadpan Yorkshire brogue.

'How long is long? A minute, an hour?'

'Could be. Then again, it could be a day or two.'

'And do you know where he is?'

'Maybe I do. Maybe I don't. Done summat wrong, has he?'

'Not as far as I'm aware. I'm making enquiries into an ongoing investigation he may be able to help us with. Now, either you know where he is, or you don't?'

He pulls his flat cap off and scratches at his balding nut. The man loses interest and turns around to tend to his garden. 'Works in't east.'

'Newcastle, Norwich, Aberdeen?' he calls after him.

'No, yer daft bugger. Middle East, on the rigs. Like a say, he'll be home soon, right enough.'

'Thanks. You've been a great help,' he says, with a hefty dose of sarcasm.

As Zac hops into the car, he glances in the rear-view mirror as a Black Cab parks up behind him. A muscular man jumps out, says something to the driver, then goes to the boot and pulls out a huge khaki holdall. He waves at the driver then saunters up the garden path, acknowledging his verbose next-door neighbour. There's an exchange of words between them and the man peers in Zac's direction with a concerned frown.

Zac takes a seat in the tastefully decorated lounge room as Daniel Platt faces him from across the room.

'What's it all about?' Platt asks.

'You're the registered owner of a metallic blue Subaru WRX with the numberplate AFX 967.'

'Aye, what about it? Oh, hang on, I know what this is about,' he says, clearly annoyed.

'You do?'

'Yes. It's about that bloody bypass and their stupid HOV rules, isn't it? I know for a fact there are no speed cameras on that section of the dual carriageway, which means someone's grassed me up. Well, it's my word against theirs, so you're bloody stuffed,' he adds angrily.

Zac screws his face up. 'What? No, no. It isn't that. Your neighbour said you work in the Middle East, on the rigs?'

'Aye. Two on, two off.'

'Months?'

'They're hardly likely to fly me out there for two weeks, are they?'

'You look fit. Do you work out?'

'Yep. Twelve-hour shifts, so it leaves a bit of time on my hands. Not much to do on a rig apart from watching the telly. I spend a good hour in the gym every day.'

'You've obviously just finished your latest stint. Where and when did you land?'

'Last week. Wednesday. Flew into Heathrow.'

Zac's ears prick up. 'Last Wednesday, the twenty-fifth?'

'That's right.'

'Six days ago. Where have you been since then?'

'London.'

'With family?' Zac asks, intrigued.

'No. Not family.'

'Then what?'

Platt huffs and pushes back into his chair. 'I take it you've never worked in the Middle East?'

Zac shakes his head. 'No.'

'Money's good, I'll give it that. But it's tough on a man. No smoking, no drinking, and no women. You're the detective. What do *you* think I was doing in London?'

'Wine, women, and song?'

'Exactly. A few beers, then a couple of girls from a legit upmarket escort agency, a nice meal, then who knows. I treat the ladies well, and they reciprocate... if you know what I mean. I always give them a generous tip. I'm a creature of habit, Sergeant Stoker, always have been, even as a lad. I did a few years in the army, which I guess reinforced those traits. I spend the week before I leave for the Middle East with my ex-missus, her partner, and my son in Pudsey.'

'Leeds?'

'Aye. I have a bit of quality time with my lad, and it gives the ex-missus a break. We all get on fine. Even get on well with her new fella. We both support the Bradford Bulls. There's no animosity between any of us. Some people may find it odd, but it was a mutual split. But that bloody Stanningley bypass is a nightmare. Worst idea the council ever came up with, and they're not short on bad ideas. This *is* about the HOV, isn't it?'

Christ! I couldn't get a word out of the neighbour, yet this guy suffers from verbal dysentery.

'Mr Platt, let me start from the beginning as we seem at cross-purposes.'

12

The pub is quiet. A few patrons drift in after a hard day's work, but the weather is lousy, and most people seem to have headed off home for the night. The open log fire crackles, offering comfort and warmth, as the three officers sit down around a table.

Frank and Zac take a welcoming draught of ale as Prisha goes through her notes, interspersed with her own conclusions and theories.

'And that concludes Mr Windsor's version of events,' she says, as she takes a sip of her gin and tonic.

'You said that as if you don't believe him,' Zac says.

'Did I?'

'Yes.'

Prisha pulls her chin back. 'I didn't mean to. There's no reason to doubt him. He's a respectable businessman who was robbed of a valuable stamp. His story stacks up, confirmed by the supermarket CCTV showing the man matching the description of the robber.'

'Sorry,' Zac says with a shrug. 'It was the inflection in your voice. I must have misread it.'

'What about the auction house?' Frank interjects, eyes swivelling from Prisha to Zac and back again.

'Again, Mr Windsor's account rings true. He won the bid, settled his account, signed some papers, then collected the stamp and proof of ownership. He made a ten-minute phone call, I assume, to his insurance company, then left the rooms and got back in his car.'

'And the times match from when he left the rooms and arrived back at the shop?'

'Yes, pretty much.'

Frank picks up the printout of the suspect provided by the supermarket manager and studies it. 'So, our suspect is five-ten, five-eleven. Piercing blue eyes. Possibly has a beard. Is built like a brick shithouse and has a local accent, but we're not sure if that means a Teesside accent or a typical Yorkshire accent.'

'That's right,' Prisha confirms.

'The accent is ropey,' Frank adds, stroking the stubble on his cheek.

'How'd you mean?'

'There must be fifty slight variations on the Yorkshire accent. You only have to travel twenty miles in any direction, and you can notice a difference.'

'That's true,' Zac says. 'Although, it narrows it down. At least we know he's not a foreigner, or southerner, or scouser.'

'Aye, better than nothing, I guess. Did you tell Windsor we think this guy shot Jason?' he asks Prisha, tapping at the photo.

'No. Because at the time of speaking to him, it was still a very tenuous connection. I didn't want to muddy the waters and set the rumour mill going.'

'Good. And what about this Alfred Dunn you went to see? What's his story?'

'Retired professor. Bachelor in his late seventies, early eighties, I'd guess. Lives in Staithes. Has a keen interest in stamps, coins, and World-War-Two memorabilia. He dropped out of the bidding at forty-four thousand.'

'Was he at the auction?' Zac queries.

'No. He was bidding online. There were only three bidders after the stamp had reached its reserve price: Windsor, Dunn, and an auction house from the States. But interestingly enough, Windsor, and Mr Dunn used to be mutual acquaintances until they had a falling out a few years back when Windsor outbid Mr Dunn for a pair of cuff links once owned by Hermann Goring.'

'Hermann bloody Goring!' Frank says with surprise.

'The one and only,' Prisha responds with a wry laugh. 'Anyway, I asked Dunn for his whereabouts at the time of the robbery, and he said he met up with an old colleague in Durham for lunch.'

'Hang on,' Zac begins, 'the stamp was stolen about 12:30, right?'

'Yes.'

'And the bidding for the stamp started at 11:20 and lasted how long?'

'Six minutes, max,' Prisha says, taking a sip of her gin and tonic.

'And Dunn lives in Staithes, which is about an hour's drive to Durham.'

'Aye,' Frank says, joining the dots. 'It's tight. To get to Durham by 12:30 he'd have needed to be in his car straight after the auction finished. Mind you, he hardly fits the description of our mugger, does he?'

Prisha waggles her lips from side to side. 'No, but he could have hired a heavy. When I left, he gave me his friend's number, the one he said he had dinner with. It took me less than thirty seconds to get into my car and place a call, and guess what?'

'Engaged?' Frank suggests.

'Precisely. I think Mr Dunn was giving his friend a heads-up.'

'Or maybe Dunn's friend was on the line with someone else,' Zac says. 'You've a very suspicious nature, even for a copper,' he adds with a chuckle.

She ignores him. 'Anyway, when I got through, sure enough, his friend vouched for Dunn. Said he met him at 12:30 and they parted at around 2:15.'

Frank finishes the dregs of his pint and wipes his mouth on the back of his jacket sleeve.

'Dunn is a retired professor. He doesn't sound like the type to hire a heavy to nick a stamp.'

Prisha taps her pen on her lips, pondering. 'Because he's a professor?'

'No. Because he's retired and clearly comfortably off. Those professors earn a good crack. And if he's a bachelor, then he probably lives a frugal existence.'

'I'm sure even ex-academics can succumb to revenge. Anyway, I don't think the stamp was stolen because of its value. It was stolen because of what it is...a rarity. And who knows the lengths an obsessed collector would go to? Those with an above average intelligence typically commit white collar crime. He was most concerned the stamp was insured. It could be his middle-class guilt gnawing away at him. After all, it's a so-called victimless crime. The only one to lose out is the insurance company, and they elicit little sympathy from the public.'

'And rightly so,' Zac says.

'There you go. You proved my point. And another thing, back to the car. Who the hell is that sitting in the front seat? What if it was Alfred Dunn? What if he paid a knucklehead to commit the robbery, and wanted to be there to collect the stamp right away?'

'Nah,' Zac begins. 'I can explain the mystery person in the car.'

'You can?' Prisha asks.

'Yep. It's a mannequin dressed up as an old lady.'

Prisha and Frank both pull perplexed expressions.

Zac places the refills on the table and smiles as he takes his seat.

'Bloody tease,' Prisha grumbles, with a slight smile.

'What?' Zac says.

'Keeping us on tenterhooks. Go on then, explain the mannequin.'

'The registered owner of the Subaru is one Daniel Platt, who lives in a very tidy bungalow on the outskirts of Scarborough. He's an oil and gas platform operator who works on the rigs in the Middle East. Two months on, two months off. He arrived back in London last Wednesday after finishing his two-month shift.'

Frank grimaces. 'Wednesday? That was the twenty-fifth. The day before Cartwright was shot.'

'Aye, but hold your horses, Frank. Before he sets off for the Middle East, he spends the last week with his ex-wife and son. They live in Pudsey, West Yorkshire. While he's there, he drives his son to and from school each day. To get there, he takes a dual carriageway known as the Stanningley bypass. During rush hour, it operates a system called HOV.'

'What the hell's that?'

'High Occupancy Vehicle.'

'Meaning,' Frank quizzes.

'It means only vehicles with *more* than one occupant can use the outside lane, colloquially known as the fast lane. It's a scheme designed to encourage carpooling and reduce overall traffic on the road. I've done some research, and it's a bit of a white elephant and the locals hate it. There are no speed cameras on the bypass, so any breaches of the system have to be monitored by uniform on patrol. There's only been eighty fines in the last five years, so the whole thing is a bit of a failure.'

'Ah, I get it,' Prisha says. 'Mr Platt puts the mannequin in the front seat to beat the system.'

'Yep. He says it was his son who first suggested the idea, as his mate's dad does the same thing. Anyway, Platt thought it would be a bit of a giggle and went along with it. That explains the mystery passenger. As for his car... well, on the day he leaves for work he drives to Leeds and Bradford airport, parks up in the long-stay car park, catches a flight to London then a long-haul to Riyadh. When he returns, he spends a few days in London letting his hair down, then catches a flight back to Leeds and Bradford. Anyway, today his flight was cancelled because of some technical issues, so he jumped in a Black Cab to drive him home.'

'That wouldn't be cheap,' Frank says.

'The oil company pays for all his travelling expenses, as long as he has a valid receipt.'

'And have you checked if the car is still at the airport?'

'Yes. I rang West Yorkshire police and asked them if they could send a patrol to have a look in the car parks. They did and said there's no car there matching the description or the number plate.'

'CCTV from the airport?'

'I'm onto it, but it's going to take a while. The car could have been stolen on the day of the shooting, or it could have been nabbed two months earlier when Platt caught his flight. That's potentially sixty days of footage to scroll through. The airport said they don't have the resources to commit to it so they're going to make a copy and send it to us.'

'And what about this Platt character?'

'Seems legit. Although he is a sizeable lad. Got all the big guns. Works out while he's offshore.'

'Height?'

'About five-ten. But I'd say his eyes were grey, certainly not piecing blue.'

'Eye colour can change dependent on the lighting,' Prisha chips in.

'True,' Frank says. 'Beard?'

'No, but they're easy enough to get rid of. And he has a strong North Yorkshire accent. But to be honest, I don't think he's our man.'

Frank scratches his cheek. 'Does he have a record?'

'No.'

'Have you checked out his story?'

'He showed me his passport, flight ticket stub, and hotel receipt. Everything tallies with what he told me.'

'He could have arrived back Wednesday, checked into the hotel so there's a record of him being there, then made his way up to North Yorkshire.'

'Then randomly steal a stamp, drive erratically back to Whitby in his own car, pull a gun and shoot an unarmed officer?' Zac says with an element of scepticism.

'Aye. It's implausible, but not impossible. We don't know the exact circumstances of anything yet. Just keep an open mind.' Frank necks down half of his pint in one hit and smacks his lips together. 'Okay, let's summarise. We haven't got a lot, but we have something: a description of the driver of the stolen vehicle and our stamp thief.'

'Erm, not technically, boss,' Prisha says. 'There was no actual CCTV of the robbery. The supermarket cameras only extend to the edge of the car park. I tried all the other buildings and although some had cameras, all were pointing straight down over their own entrances.'

'There you go again,' Zac comments.

'What now?'

'You implied Windsor wasn't telling the truth.'

'No I didn't.'

'You said there is no CCTV footage of the robbery, and yet we have Windsor's account of the theft and a description of the robber.'

'If you want to get pedantic, Frank *inferred* we have a description of the stamp thief. He based that on facts. I was merely pointing out that a witness statement from a victim is not a fact. It's their interpretation and recollection of events, which as we all know from experience, is not always factual. CCTV footage is factual.'

'Christ, you've lost me,' Zac concedes. 'The question is, do you believe Windsor or not?'

'I have no reason to doubt him.'

'Is that a yes or a no?'

'It's neither. I'm impartial. A disinterested party until evidence can sway me.'

'Fuck me,' Zac groans.

'Okay children, stop the squabbling,' Frank says, intervening.

'She started it.'

'No, I did not!' Prisha bristles.

'Oi, oi, oi! Enough!' Frank commands. Silence ensues as Prisha and Zac throw each other dirty looks. 'That's better. Right, any further points either of you wish to discuss?'

'Not really. Oh, that reminds me,' Prisha says, picking up her pen and scribbling in her notebook. 'I need to text through the case file number to Windsor for insurance purposes.'

Frank turns to Zac. 'Tomorrow, it may be worth calling Mr Windsor's insurance company. Let's check the stamp was insured, and at what time.'

'Aye, will do. What's the name of the insurers?'

Prisha flicks through her notes. 'Erm, Heritage Collectables.'

Frank is becoming restless as his stomach rumbles. 'Anything else?'

'Yes,' Prisha says.

'What?'

'Any updates on Jason?'

'No. Still in ICU. No change in his condition. I'd like to pay a visit, but it's mainly family and close friends who are allowed in. I could hardly be called a close friend, could I? I've bawled him out a few times over the years, which I now feel terrible about. Not that he didn't deserve it,' he adds with a wistful air.

Zac rolls his large hands around his pint glass. 'Aye, well, I was no saint. He can try your patience. I'm sure we're all experiencing an element of guilt.'

'Yes,' Prisha says as she turns away and stares into the glowing embers.

Frank pushes his chair back. 'Right, I best get back to the station and give an update to Overland. It will not be pretty considering we're not supposed to be working on the case, but I don't give a damn. I shout louder than he does. Wish me luck.'

'Frank, what do you want me to do tomorrow, bearing in mind I can't access anything?' Prisha asks, concerned she might have to spend the day at home twiddling her thumbs.

'Hmm... not sure yet. Let me have a think on it and I'll call you tomorrow. You can keep Beatrice until your car's back on the road. How are you getting on with the old girl?'

'She's growing on me... like a scab.'

'Hilarious. I'll see you two later.'

As Frank makes his way to the station, he ruminates on what Martin Overland's reaction will be. He realises he's playing a dangerous game, which could backfire at any moment. All it takes is for Overland to make a call to Garth Windsor and the truth will be out and he and Prisha could face disciplinary action. He needs to tread lightly and pull off a subtle charm offensive. Overland is a ruthless careerist, but he has one chink in his armour—his ego.

13

Overland listens on in silence, his chin resting on clasped hands, as Frank gives him his update. A knot has formed in his stomach as he attempts to suppress his anger. He's in charge. There is a chain of command, a hierarchy. That's the way things work. And yet, here is Frank Finnegan, the gruff, old Yorkshire stalwart, calmly explaining he's disobeyed his orders. There's not a hint of regret or shame in Frank's demeanour. In fact, quite the reverse.

Frank finishes his roundup of the day's events and drops the USB drive onto Overland's desk... technically, Frank's desk.

'The CCTV footage from the supermarket is on there,' Frank says, nodding at the USB. 'I suggest you get someone to upload it onto the system ASAP and get prints of the suspect distributed to all officers. See if anyone recognises him. Then get a clip of the footage out on social media and send it to the news outlets. You may still make the later bulletins tonight if you're lucky.'

Overland finally speaks, calm, measured. 'Frank, we've known each other a long time and I want you to be brutally honest with me. Do you think I'm suffering from an undiagnosed cognitive disorder?'

'Not that I'm aware of, Martin.'

'I seem to recall issuing you specific commands early this morning. I stood you and DS Stoker down from the investigation. Did I imagine that?'

'No.'

'Phew! Then I'm not going mad after all. Which brings me to my next question: why?'

'Why what?'

He erupts into barely contained fury 'Why have you and Stoker deliberately disobeyed my orders?' he yells.

Frank is unflinching. 'Calm down, Martin. It's not what it looks like. And Zac wasn't involved. These were leads that me and Zac were already exploring. I took today to clear up all the loose ends and hand them over to you. A line in the sand, as it were. You know what it's like when you pass a lead onto someone else. It gets forgotten about and pushed to one side. Everyone wants to reinvent their own bloody wheel.'

'So today, you drove to Middlesbrough and interviewed this... this jeweller, a Mr, Mr...'

'Windsor. That's correct. The original report was a little vague. I wanted to clarify a few points, and it paid dividends.'

Overland is torn. Disobeying a direct order is a disciplinary offence, albeit, discretional. But Frank is well liked and respected by the rank and file. To discipline him would damage morale in the team, and morale is already low. It would paint Overland in a bad light. An over-officious pen-pusher, whereas Frank would be seen as a victim. And yet... to not punish him undermines Overland's authority, something he can not allow to happen. It's a game of chess and Frank has made his move. A stalemate. He desperately tries to think of a way out of the situation that would save face for both men, particularly for himself.

Frank leans forward and offers a warm smile. 'Martin, why are we fighting with each other? We have one of our own in ICU. God only knows if he'll pull through, and if he does, what sort of state is he going to be in? You've seen the surgeon's report. The bullet grazed his heart and took out a fragment of his spine. If he survives, he may never walk again. Why are we wasting time butting heads instead of catching the bastard who did this? We need to get this man off the streets and behind bars for everyone's welfare. I have a suggestion.'

'Go on,' Overland says, softening as Frank gently pushes open a door for both men to walk through.

'Can we not work together on this? I've policed this area of North Yorkshire for most of my professional life. I know it inside and out, the villains, their haunts, the plays they make, the scams they pull. I live and breathe the underbelly of the place. By shutting me out, you're losing your greatest weapon. The officers you've brought in are on top of their game, I acknowledge that... but they're not from around here. You *need* me and Zac back on the team, and, once Prisha is cleared of any wrongdoing, she needs to be brought back into the fold. Can I be forthright?'

Overland relaxes back in his chair. 'I'm listening.'

'You're heading up this op. The media are already losing faith. The public tide is turning against us. Without my team, how long do you think it will take to catch the gunman? Six weeks? Six months? Never?'

Overland crosses his arms. 'Your point?'

'Let me catch the bastard. I'll run the day-to-day operation and you run the public relations side of things. I take my hat off to you, Martin. I'm afraid I've never been good with the media. I take their questions personally, as though it's a direct attack on my integrity. It gets my hackles up. That's why Anne fronts the media these days. She's good, but she's not a patch on you. Martin, you possess a certain gravitas mixed with authority in just the right amounts. You engender trust. You know how to deal with the MPs, councillors, and the shock jocks on the radio baying for blood. What you provide, Martin, is reassurance.'

Overland experiences a measure of pride in himself. It's true—he is a good front man. Even so, disobeying an order needs to be dealt with. 'That's all very well, Frank, but...'

Frank interrupts, as if reading his thoughts. 'I apologise for going against your wishes, Martin, but I *really* was tying up a loose end.' Both men relax back and gaze at each other reflectively. 'The chief constable will be retiring next year. And you're his natural successor. If this case were to drag on and on, it would reflect poorly on you. However, if we catch our gunman in a timely manner, then it would be another feather in your cap.'

Overland considers the implications. He knows Frank has massaged his ego, offered an apology, then finished it with a worst-case scenario. But he has a point. And more importantly, it offers both men a way out. Despite this, Overland's ego cannot let Frank walk out of the office thinking he's gained the upper hand.

'I tell you what I'll do, Frank,' Overland says, adjusting his spectacles. 'I'll consider your position overnight. Act in haste, repent at leisure has never been my way.'

Frank smiles, rises, and pushes his seat underneath the desk. 'Right, I've said my piece, and it's time I was away. My wife will wonder where I am. Night, Martin. And think about what I've said. United we stand, divided we fall. After all, we are all on the same side.' He walks out of the office and gently closes the door behind him.

Overland strokes at his goatee beard, then leaps from his seat, gently opens the door and peeks through the crack as he watches Frank saunter through the incident room, casually engaging with the five remaining officers.

'Night Abigail. By the way, how's that young lad of yours doing? Is he over the colic yet?'

'Yes, Frank, I'm finally getting an unbroken night's sleep. Thank Meera for her tips. They really worked.'

He chuckles. 'I'll tell her, don't you worry. Night Gavin. I see United won at the weekend. I still don't think they've the team for a top four finish, though.'

Gavin guffaws. 'We're on a roll now, Frank. We've hit our stride.'

'We'll see. Night Toby. The Rhinos aren't going too well this season. It's time they lifted their game. We don't want the Grand Final to be won by one of those buggers from across the Pennines again. It was Yorkshire who invented Rugby League. It's only fair we should lift the trophy occasionally.'

'I couldn't agree more, Frank.'

'Night, Ashley. By the way, how's your mother doing? She broke her leg ice skating, didn't she?'

'Aye, that's right. She's on the mend now, though.'

'Tell her from me, she must be wrong in the bloody head, ice skating at her age. She must be eighty if she's a day.'

'Seventy-four, actually, Frank.'

'Oops. Don't tell her I said that. She must have had two milk rounds as a lass. Anyway, give her my best.'

She laughs. 'Will do. Night, Frank.'

'Damn him,' Overland murmurs, closing the door. 'He has the bastards eating out of his hand.' He sits and twiddles at his goatee.

What has he got that I'm haven't? Why don't my officers interact with me in that way?

'Okay Frank, the people's person. I'll let you and your sergeant back in. It offers me a few other options should I need them. If the case is resolved quickly, then I take the glory. If it isn't resolved in a few months, then I can publicly remove you from my team. The action will imply you are the reason for the failure and buy me more time. You may think you've outmanoeuvred me, Frank, but I play a long game.'

14

Frank stacks the plates in the dishwasher as Meera washes the pans.

'Best damned shepherd's pie you've ever made, love,' he says slamming the door shut and hitting the start button.

Meera chuckles. 'You say that about every meal I make.'

'It's true. You get better and better.'

As she rinses a pan, she stares at him, concerned over the lengthy account of his day and his chat with Martin Overland. 'You're walking on thin ice Frank, and it worries me. You've never done anything like this before.'

'Like what?' he says, wiping the kitchen table down.

'Lying to your superiors. Going behind their back. Disobeying orders. It's not only you I'm worried about but also that young woman, Prisha. You should have taken her warrant card and told her to go home and wait it out. If you're found out, it could be a serious black mark against her name. Did you think of that?'

He stops cleaning and grunts. 'Hmm... yes, I did. There was no coercion on my part. She was more than willing. Anyway, if it blows up, I'll take the blame. I'll say I ordered her to keep on working. She might cop a slap on the wrist, but that's all.'

'And what about you?'

'I dare say they'd ask me to go quietly. Anyway, stop worrying, Meera. I gave Overland a way out for both of us. He's not a stupid man. I'm sure he'll make the right decision.'

'And if he doesn't?'

'Then I have an ace up my sleeve if the shit hits the fan.'

'What ace?'

'The chief constable himself.'

'Gordon Critchley? What's he got to do with all this?'

Frank throws the dishcloth into the washing-up bowl full of dirty water, much to Meera's annoyance, then flicks the kettle on. 'Tea?'

'Please,' she says, retrieving the dishcloth and giving it a good rinse under the tap.

'Gordon Critchley owes me one.'

'You're not filling me full of confidence, Frank. Go on, although I'm dreading to hear it.'

Pulling two cups from a cupboard, he drops a tea bag into each one.

'I've never told a soul this story before. It was many years ago, and I'd recently transferred from uniform to CID. I was probably about a year into my role. Gordon Critchley was my inspector. He was a rising star destined for the top. Always driven, keen, a bloody good copper, but political, too. Knew who to keep on his side and who to distance himself from. Anyway, I'd noticed a change in him over a few months. His first wife had left him, and it hit him pretty hard. He began working late and drinking on the job. I was on the graveyard shift, and I'd come back to the station after failing to nab a car thief. It was about ten at night. As I pulled up, I noticed Critchley heading across the car park. He was smashed. Had the wobbly boot on. He gets into his car and starts the engine. I went over to him and told him it wasn't a good idea—drink driving. He ignored me and attempted to fasten his seat belt, unsuccessfully. I pulled the keys from the ignition and dropped them in my pocket. He fell out of his pram. Began shouting and hurling abuse at me. Said I'd spend the next two years on crossing duty. He staggered from the car, and unexpectedly threw a punch, which hit me on the jaw. Being an ex-boxer, you'd have thought I'd have seen it coming. Bloody hurt as well. The fighter in me wanted to give him a belting, but I didn't. He realised what he'd done and apologised and slumped back into the driver's seat. I got in the passenger side and sat next to him. Then he opened up. Told me all his woes. I listened with a sympathetic ear. After he'd finished, it was like a load lifted off his shoulders.

The day before, I'd been working on a domestic abuse case. The wife wouldn't press charges. Her old fella had booked himself into Alcoholics Anonymous, and she wanted to give him another chance. It gave me an idea. I told Critchley he was at a crossroads in his life. He could go left, or he could go right. One road would lead to ruination and disgrace, the other to great things. If he wanted to take the road to salvation, then I suggested his first destination should be AA. Get himself off the booze. Then everything else would fall into place.'

The kettle clicks off and Meera pours the boiling water into the two cups. 'You're an enigma, Frank. Did he take your advice?'

'Yes. After a few weeks, he was back to his old self. Ended up getting a divorce, then found a new love. There was no stopping him. He flew through the ranks until he ended up as chief constable.'

'And you'd use that incident against him to save your own skin?'

He frowns at her. 'No, of course I bloody wouldn't. What kind of man do you think I am?'

'I'm not sure anymore. You've told me a few things tonight that I never thought I'd hear.'

Frank sighs. 'When one of your team is shot, then you do things you wouldn't normally do. Yes, I bent the rules, but for the right reasons. That's the bloody problem with this job: sometimes your own people tie your hands behind your back instead of focussing on getting the bad guys off the street.'

'And what about the chief constable?'

'As I said, *if* things blow up, then I'll make a personal call to him and explain my actions and the reasons behind them. I'll also make damn sure Prisha's name is cleared. We have a deep mutual respect for each other, me and the chief constable. When you save a man's life, you create a bond.'

Meera drapes her arms around him and kisses him on the forehead. 'There's never a dull moment with you, is there?'

'Would you prefer the quiet life?'

'Yes, actually, I would,' she says, pulling away and picking up the sugar bowl.

'Two sugars in mine, love.'

'Don't push it, Frank. One. And while I'm on the subject...'

'Here we go,' he murmurs under his breath.

She places the fourteen-day pill storage box down in front of him. 'You've been forgetting to take your angina tablets. You've missed the last two days. I specifically bought this box so you wouldn't forget. It's even kept next to the damn kettle. First thing in the morning when you make your brew, take a tablet!'

'Sorry. I'll take two now to make up for it,' he replies sheepishly as he opens a compartment.

She snatches the box, removes one pill, and hands it to him. 'It doesn't work like that. It's a measured medication. Sometimes, Frank, it's like living with a child!'

———◦———

Meera is engrossed in a reality TV show about farmers searching for a wife, much to Frank's chagrin.

He stands up and slips into his coat. 'I can't watch this crap.'

'Where are you going?' Meera asks, distracted, her eyes glued firmly to the TV screen.

'I'll take Foxtrot for a walk around the block.' The dog, on hearing his name, jumps from his spot in front of the fire and sits obediently at Frank's feet as he attaches the lead. 'Right, I shouldn't be long,' he says, but receives no response from his wife. Gazing at her, he repeats his statement. 'Meera, I said I won't be long.'

She gives him a half-hearted wave, still engrossed with a pug-ugly farmer, and his woes at not finding a bride. 'Okay,' she murmurs.

He makes his way to the door. 'Then again, I might call in at number fifty-two and make passionate love to Mrs Davies.'

'Fine.'

'And Mr Davies too, if he's there.'

'That's nice dear.'

'If I'm not back by next Friday, call the police.'

'Will do.'

He walks down the garden path as fine sea spray tickles his face and a stinging wind off the beach numbs his hands. He stops and pulls his gloves on.

'I tell you what, Foxtrot, if this weather front keeps up, I think we could be in for some snow. First day of winter tomorrow so it could be right on cue. Christ, it could freeze the tits off a mother superior. Come on lad, let's lift our pace and keep warm.'

Man and dog complete a twenty-minute circuit and head back to the comfort of a warm fire and sexually frustrated farmers. As he nears the front gate, his mobile rings. He pulls it out and stares at the name.

'About bloody time,' he mumbles, as he hits the answer button and saunters across the road to a nearby bus shelter. 'Rizzo, what have you got?'

'Mr F, is that you?'

'Of course it bloody is. You rang me, remember? Do you have a name?'

'No, Frank.'

'You disappoint me, Rizzo.'

'Hang on, I may have something else for you.'

Frank and Foxtrot shiver in the bus shelter, which provides zero protection from the bitter conditions. 'Get on with it! My gonads have shrivelled to the size of sultanas.'

'I was talking with my business associate...'

'You mean your dealer?'

'Now Mr F, don't be like that.'

'Speed it up, Rizzo.'

'He mentioned a burnt-out car.'

Frank instantly forgets the cold and his anesthetised limbs. 'Whereabouts?'

'He didn't know. He'd heard about it from someone else.'

'What bloody good is that to me?' he snaps.

'Chillax, Frank. I'm getting to it. There's a card game tonight, starts at midnight. The guy who mentioned the car is going to be there.'

'Address?'

'Sorry Frank, I can't give you that. If anyone found out, I could be a dead man.'

'If you fuck with me, Rizzo, you will be a dead man. I told you last night... I'm not in the mood.'

'I'm not fucking with you, Mr Finnegan. Hear me out. I'm going to the card game, but I need to be careful. I can't just ask him where the car is. It would raise suspicions. I thought I'd give it a couple of hours and once the drink and weed has kicked in, I'd bring up the subject of the copper who was shot. See if that starts any tongues wagging.'

'Okay, I'm liking this.'

'Just one thing though: I'm a bit short.'

'That's what smoking does to you as an adolescent—it stunts your growth.'

'No, what I mean is, I'm short in the money department. I have enough dough for the game tonight, but it means me possibly losing the rest of my dole money, and my benefits don't drop into my account until Friday.'

'Meaning you want me to fund you for the rest of the week?'

'I need to eat, Frank.'

'You obviously have little faith in your poker game. Okay, how much?'

'A hundred should cover it.'

'A hundred! You're taking the piss, Rizzo. What do you live off: fillet steak and caviar?'

'I have overheads.'

'Fuck me. Okay, get me the place of this burnt-out car and if it's a match, then I'll drop you a ton. But only if it's the suspect's vehicle.'

'I can't guarantee it is, Mr F.'

'No, and that's why I can't guarantee you a hundred. If it's not the car we're looking for, I'll buy you a dozen tins of alphabet spaghetti. That should last you until Friday and maybe help with your spelling. I'd hate to see you fade away. There's not much of you to begin with.'

'Okay. I'll be in touch. Probably safer to text you. Not sure when, though.'

'Fine. Oh, and Rizzo?'

'Yes?'

'Watch your back.'

A hoarse chuckle drifts down the line. 'You know me, Frank. I'm a wily old dog.'

Frank puts his phone away and scurries across the road and into the heat of the house. The domestic dilemmas of desperate agronomists still transfix Meera.

'She's a raunchy one that Mrs Davies. Tied me up and poured golden syrup all over my naked body, then licked it off.'

'Oh, good. I'm pleased for you.'

'I'll put the kettle on and make a brew, shall I?' he says, throwing his coat onto the back of the couch.

'A, huh.'

'No sugar for you and ten for me.'

'That would be lovely.'

15

Tuesday 1st December

The incident room could hardly be described as a cauldron of excited activity. The early morning start has led to most officers hastily chugging down hot coffee hoping to kick-start their lethargic nervous systems. Everyone is still wrapped in their winter overcoats, a testament to the antiquated heating system of the building.

Frank and Zac wait impatiently in Anne Banks' micro-office, wondering if they'll get the call from the deputy chief constable to attend the 6:30 morning brief.

'I'll bet you a tenner he blanks us,' Zac says.

'Thought you'd given up gambling?' Frank replies, checking his phone for about the tenth time.

'I have. Still no news from Rizzo?' he asks.

'Nah. Bloody little scrote. You know about these things: how long can an illegal card game take?'

Zac pushes his hand through his long dark locks and blows out air. 'I've known some that went on for twelve hours or more.'

'Strewth! I don't want to call him. It could put him in an invidious position.'

'A what position?'

Frank glances bleary eyed at him. 'A tricky position.'

'Oh.'

The desk phone rings and Frank snatches at the receiver. 'Yes. Yes. I see. No, of course not, Martin. I'll run everything past you first. Good. You won't regret it, Martin. We'll be there in two shakes of a bee's dick.' He hangs up and beams at Zac.

'Good news, I take it?'

'Sure is. We're back on the investigation.' Both men rush to the door.

'What did he say?'

'Don't go off half-cocked. Keep him up to date. Run everything by him. Don't talk to the media... that's his job. And follow orders, not our own whims and fancies. Tosser! I've nearly forty years' service under my belt. You'd think I was some snotty nosed cadet straight out of training.'

'Are you going to do as he asks?'

'Pig's arse, I am. I'll let him think I'm playing by his rules. But as I said before, Martin Overland couldn't find a gobstopper in a jar full of toffees.'

Zac grins. 'Nice one, Frank.' They march down the corridor together.

'You heard from your snout, Cleavage, yet?'

'No. I'll call him after the morning brief.'

Frank pauses outside the door to the incident room. 'Remember Zac, humility, obedience, and respect. That's what Overland expects. Let's not disappoint him, even if it's only to fool the prick.'

'Gotcha.'

Overland is standing next to a large whiteboard holding court. Frank is slightly behind and to his left.

'Morning team,' Overland begins, as ever looking more like a sales rep for a designer menswear company than a copper. He receives a few dispirited grunts. 'Before I begin, I'd like to welcome back onboard DCI Finnegan and DS Stoker.'

Compared to his morning greeting, the response is rapturous, with claps, hoots, and whistles as everyone comes alive. Frank blushes, not that he's a particularly humble man, but he feels it's a tad embarrassing for Overland. The last thing he wants is for Overland to think he's a threat. Zac grins from the back of the room as the noisy approvals taper off. 'Frank, a few words?' Overland gestures.

Frank takes a step forward. 'I've kept abreast of all your reports and despite your efforts and long hours, we've still not made much headway in finding the gunman. Do *not* be disheartened or discouraged. I've worked many cases like this over the years, maybe not one so close to home, but still. Sometimes it can feel like you're in an underground labyrinth in the pitch black, wading through mud, not sure which way to turn. When you get a lead, it turns out to be a blind alley. When you think you have a suspect, they have a watertight alibi. When someone calls you anonymously and gives you a name, it turns out to be a crank caller. Believe me, I've had them all, and then some. But you keep on keeping on, digging, probing, asking questions, querying every little aspect. Then bang!' He slaps his palm hard on the whiteboard, making everyone start. 'Someone from the team has something. A name, a place, a fingerprint, suspicious activity. It could be anything. That's when we reap the fruits of our labour, that's when things escalate quickly. Remember this: the darkest time of night is the hour before dawn. Oh, and one last thing before we start: talk, talk, and talk some more about every aspect of the investigation with one another, morning, noon, and night. Talk in your dinner break, tea break, outside having a gasper, going up and down the stairs, in the car even in the bloody toilets. You may mention something which means nothing to you, but one of your fellow officers suddenly pricks up their ears. Okay, down to brass tacks, let's take a butcher's at what we have so far.'

A few moments ago, ten lethargic, downcast officers were staring at a whiteboard, and a man with a goatee beard they didn't believe in. Now, a swell of energy and enthusiasm fills the room as Frank sets about his business.

Frank finishes his briefing with a quick recap, using a ruler to point at the bullet points on the board.

'You all have a photograph of the man caught on CCTV after the stamp robbery at 12:30 last Thursday. This guy is now a person of *significant* interest. We need to find him and find him quickly. To me, he doesn't look like the sort of guy who collects stamps in his spare time, but who knows? He obviously knew the value of the stamp. Which means he's an opportunist and is hawking the stamp around various dealers hoping to be paid cash for it, or more than likely he was paid by someone else who knows about stamps. To rule out the first scenario, I want four officers to ring around every stamp dealer, known collector, antique shop, and auction house in North Yorkshire, and see if anyone has walked in offering the stamp for sale. Not very glamourous work, I know. If you draw a blank, extend your search to East and West Yorkshire.'

He stops for a quick drink of water. 'Next: I want three uniformed officers to visit every gymnasium, council leisure centre, and boxing club within a thirty-mile radius of Whitby. Any place that could have weights, make a call, and ask questions about our mystery man. The photo is not brilliant, but we know he's about five-eleven, has piercing blue eyes, possibly a beard, although he may have shaved that off by now, and is built like a brick shithouse.'

PC Kylie Pembroke puts her hand up 'Frank, is he a local?'

'Yes, Kylie, we think so. The jeweller said he was local. Although, he wasn't specific about the accent. I think it best to keep an open mind and assume he has a northern accent. And he was also vague about the age—anywhere from late teens to early fifties.'

His last statement is met with a chorus of groans.

'So, we're after a well-built male with a northern accent aged between eighteen and fifty with blue eyes. That narrows it down a bit,' a wag from the back comments.

Frank holds his hands up in defence. 'Yes, I know. It's not much to go on, but it is what it is. And listen up, if any of you think you may have an ID on our suspect, then report back to me or DCC Overland. Do not approach him. I don't want any heroics. We all know what he's capable of. Next, the weapon. Using the bullet removed from DS Cartwright, ballistics believe the pistol used in the shooting is an original Luger 9 mm P08. The Luger was German made and used extensively during World-War-Two. Ballistics don't just pull this shit out of thin air. Interpol has an extensive database on firearms called the Firearms Reference Table, so we can be confident, if not certain, the gun identified is on the money. I want two CID officers on this. Again, ring around all the antiques shops, auction houses and go back over burglaries over the last twelve months. Think of where a weapon like this may have come from—a country house, a stately home, a museum. There could even be a connection to the army. Think like a criminal who wants to get their hands on a firearm. Where would you get one from? Any questions? Good. Now split yourself off into teams, and work to your strengths. If there's any bickering about who's doing what, then I'll come around and knock your blocks together. Understood?'

There's a chorus of good natured "Yes, Frank," followed by excited chatter and a rush of activity.

16

Frank pushes open the door to his temporary office and stands back as Zac wheels the trolley in containing a bar fridge.

'Where do you want it?' Zac asks.

Frank gazes morosely at the limited space. 'Good question. Not a lot of options are there? It either sits on the desk or on top of the filing cabinet.'

'I'd suggest the cabinet. It's not a good look having a bar fridge perched on your desk. People may form the wrong impression and think you have an eating disorder, i.e. you're a greedy bastard.'

Frank chuckles as he helps Zac lift the fridge into position on top of the cabinet, then plugs it into the power outlet. 'Okay. That will have to do.'

'Why did Overland want it out of your office?'

'He says the buzz gives him a headache.'

'He gives me a headache. Hasn't he got better things to worry about? Talking of food, I haven't had breakfast yet. What about you?'

'No. I'm famished,' Frank replies, as his stomach growls.

'I'll do an egg and bacon butty run. One or two?'

'I should only have the one.'

'So, that means two?'

'Aye. Go on then.'

'On my way,' he says, darting out of the doorway.

'He's a good lad. I'd be lost without him.'

Prisha is sitting on the sofa in her cosy flat as the rain beats at the window. She taps at the image of Frank's smiling face on her phone.

'Prisha, I was just about to call you.'

'It's seven-thirty, Frank. I've been waiting.'

'There's been a few developments. Me and Zac are back on the team. I'm leading the main investigation and Overland is heading up the public relations side of it.'

Prisha experiences a rapid onset of FOMO. 'Oh, I see. That's a turnaround,' she says trying to mask her feelings.

'I had a chat with him last night and I think he saw the error of his ways. Oh, I have some news. Ballistics have identified the firearm used in the shooting as a German made Luger.'

'An original or a replica?'

'Original, though how the hell they can tell is beyond me.'

'So, what have you got for me to do?' There's a pregnant pause, and she fears the worse.

'Not much, really.'

'Not much really, or nothing?'

'I've already allotted all the tasks to the team.'

'I see. A team I'm no longer part of,' she says, her contempt obvious.

'Now Prisha. It's no time for bruised egos. It's out of my hands. Why don't you go for a run and let off a bit of steam?'

'Don't humour me, Frank. I'm not a child. I feel useless.'

'I can understand how frustrating it must be for you, but we both need to tread carefully. If Overland gets wind that you're swanning around doing police work, then the shit's really going to hit the fan.'

'Please, Frank, there has to be something I can do?'

He sighs. 'Listen, it's a dynamic situation and if anything crops up where it's safe to use you, I'll be straight on the blower, yeah?'

'Fine.'

'Actually...'

'Yes?' she says expectantly.

'You could pay a visit to see Jason.'

'Oh.'

'What?'

'Yes, I suppose I could, but I'm not sure I'm ready for that. Any updates on him?'

'No change. Still in an induced coma. Anyway, I'll leave it with you. Your choice. Got to go.'

Hanging up, she stares out of the window at the stormy sea hammering the west beach.

'Bugger it. I'll wrap up and go for a walk. I can't stay in here all day. It will drive me insane.'

Frank is feeling bad about Prisha. She's done nothing wrong but has been temporarily ostracised by correct police procedure. He doesn't ruminate for long as his desk phone rings.

'DCI Finnegan,' he says.

'Frank, it's me, Gordon.'

'Gordon?'

There's a throaty laugh on the other end of the phone. 'Gordon Critchley, your chief constable.'

Frank sits upright. 'Gordon! How are you? I was speaking with Meera about you last night.'

'I thought my ears were burning,' he says with a friendly chuckle.

'I was telling her what a damn fine detective you used to be.'

'That's nice to hear. Frank, I apologise I haven't called sooner. I spoke with Superintendent Banks immediately I heard the news about DS Cartwright, but I've been overseas on a fact-finding mission. Waste of bloody time. Just got back to Northallerton today and thought I'd ring up to see how you're going.'

'I'm okay. Keeping busy. There'll be plenty of time for soul searching once we've caught the bugger.'

He spends the next ten minutes giving the chief constable the latest on the investigation, during which Zac returns with breakfast. Frank tips his hand up and down, indicating he'd like a fresh cup of tea. Zac scowls as he takes his raincoat off and gives it a good shake, showering Frank in water droplets. He departs the office as Frank rubs water from his face.

'Thanks for the update, Frank, although I am receiving daily reports from Martin. How are you two getting along, by the way?'

'Bit frosty to start with, but I think we're now both playing to our strengths.'

'He's a damn fine spokesperson. Handles public relations very well. Knows how to get the message across and smooth the feathers of disgruntled MPs and councillors. Listen, I've got to dash, but if there's anything you need, you only have to say the word, and I'll ensure you get it.'

'Thanks, Gordon...' Frank knows he shouldn't ask, but he's not a man to die wondering. 'Actually, Gordon, you may be able to help.'

'Go on.'

'It's a delicate situation and I fully understand if...'

'Get on with it, Frank. It's not like you to beat about the bush.'

'My officer, DI Kumar, has been stood down pending the findings of the IOPC.'

'Yes, I'm up to speed with the case.'

'They indicated to her they wouldn't complete their report until the middle of next week at the earliest. They have a backlog, apparently. I realise they're an independent body and there can be no police interference on the outcome of their investigation, and nor should there be. But I was thinking if someone from a senior position could ask them to expedite the matter, whatever their conclusions, then I could get one of my best officers back on the case.'

'Are you that desperate for more officers? I can certainly arrange for more resources to be drafted in?'

'No. We have a small but experienced team.'

'Then why the rush to get DI Kumar back?'

'Because she has a nose like a bloodhound. She's good. Gordon. One of the best and I've worked with some outstanding coppers in my time. And I also think it will be beneficial for her mentally... to be active, take her mind off past events.'

'Is she emotionally and mentally stable?'

'She hasn't been formally assessed, but she's as tough as old boots. Professional to the nth degree.'

'Hmm...' The line goes dead for a good ten seconds as Frank unwraps his first butty, but resists taking a bite. 'I tell you what, Frank. I know a couple of people in the IOPC. I'll call one of them in an informal capacity and explain the situation. See if there's a way they could prioritise their process. I can't promise anything, and I'm certainly not going to throw my weight around. And another thing, if she is cleared of any wrongdoing, then she must pass a psychological assessment before returning to work. Tell her to get that done as soon as.'

'Understood.'

'Anything else?'

'No. I appreciate the call.'

'Yes, well, I should have called sooner. My prayers are with Jason and his family. We must catch up sometime, Frank.'

'Yes, we should. Maybe when we've put this one to bed.'

'Indeed. And Frank, catch the bastard who did this.'

'I intend to, Gordon.'

Frank hangs up and taps at his desk, sporting a wry smile before the aroma of bacon brings his attention back to his breakfast.

'Right, sunshine, time for you to take a ride into my stomach!'

———✦———

The two officers munch on their bacon and egg rolls and devour them in record time. Frank takes a slurp of tea and rinses his mouth, then throws a glance at the clock on the wall.

'Another thirty minutes and you can ring the insurance company, Zac. See exactly what time Garth Windsor insured his precious stamp. Let's make sure his story adds up.'

'I know. I haven't forgotten. Prisha's right about you—you're a micro manager.'

'Just a friendly reminder.' His phone pings. 'Eh up, message from Rizzo. About bloody time. I'll read it to you.'

"Mr F. Done my dough big time. Took a while but someone eventually brought up the shooting. The guy I told you about said he heard from a mate there's a burnt-out car in Cock Mill Woods, not far from the beck, bordering a ploughed field. P.S. Need money for food."

'Aye, you'll have to wait, Rizzo,' Frank says, leaping from his seat as Zac slips into his damp overcoat. 'Let's go Zac, things are happening.'

17

Prisha parks Beatrice in the hospital car park, quickly locks up, then makes a mad dash for the entrance, her raincoat covering her head as the volley of hailstones smash into the ground.

After spending ten minutes signing in, filling out a form, and being lectured by an acute care nurse with an abrupt manner, Prisha, kitted out in PPE, is finally ushered into the critical care unit. She stares dolefully at the lifeless body of Jason, as the beep beep of the ICU monitor transmits an emotionless message.

'Ten minutes, inspector, and that's all. We normally only allow one visitor per day and Mr Cartwright's wife is due in this afternoon.'

'Yes, I understand. Can I speak to him?'

'Of course,' she replies tersely. 'But don't question him about what happened.'

'Can I hold his hand?'

'Yes, as long as you're gentle. Right, I'll be back in ten minutes.'

She takes a seat, unsure whether to speak. Reaching out, she touches his hand and instinctively recoils but doesn't know why.

The clock ticks.

Finally, she cups his hand in hers. It's warm, soft.

'Hi, Jason, it's me, Prisha. How are you doing? That was a silly bloody question, wasn't it? We, erm, we're making some progress on the investigation, but old starchy knickers said I wasn't to talk about it, so I won't. The weather's turned to shit. Cold, wet, dreary. I received a call on Friday night from the vice-captain of your darts team. What's his name... Gary Oldham, or Oldman. Anyway, he said the boys intended to forfeit the game on Saturday night considering what's happened. I gave him a right earful. I said it would be the last thing you wanted and that they better show up and play, otherwise they'd have me to answer to. Then, early Sunday morning, about three o'clock, my bloody mobile goes off. Scared me to death. I was fast off. It was your mate, Gary, again. He was well pissed. Thought I'd like to know they won the game... sorry, match. Which means, one more win and you're through to the nationals. I suppose you already knew. I'm sure your wife has told you, or maybe she hasn't.'

She gazes with dismay at the various tubes attached to his body as a glut of emotion rises to the surface.

'I'm really sorry, Jason. If I could swap places with you, I would in an instant. If we'd set off from Settle five minutes sooner, or later, you wouldn't be lying here now. If we hadn't taken the scenic route back to Whitby, you wouldn't be lying here now. If I hadn't spotted the car at the petrol station, or if I'd let highway patrol deal with it... you wouldn't be lying here now. I feel so guilty.'

She sniffs but holds back the tears.

'You remember the darts medallion you gave me, the first one you won all those years ago? I threw it into the sea. You said I could. Some people believe that places, buildings, objects can absorb feelings and emotions from humans. I'm not a new age hippy, but I think there could be something to it. Sometimes when I go into an old building, a church, or a museum, I pick up a sensation. It's like a vibration of someone's past life, as if they've left an imprint of themselves behind. I know it sounds crazy. That's why I threw your medal into the sea. When I held it in my fingers, I could feel your joy and spirit. Part of you was embedded in that little metal disc. I wanted to set it free. To let it be washed out to sea where it could live on forever.'

She spots the nurse through the glass, who lifts her hand up and taps at her watch, then lifts a finger in the air, indicating one minute remaining.

'It's time for me to go. Your nurse, Eva Braun, has just given me the finger. Keep fighting, Jason. Never give in. Think of your unborn child. You're a dad now and you need to be around for her or him, although I think it's a girl.' She leans forward and kisses the back of his hand. 'I miss you. Come back to us when you're ready.'

Buttoned against the cold, and woollen hat pulled down over her ears, she strolls along the concrete walkway past the brightly coloured huts on the west beach. The tide is out, and the rain has fizzled to nothing more than a fine drizzle. Climbing the steps at Battery Parade, she notices the café is closed.

'Damn.'

Strolling along the promenade, she pulls her phone out and sees a text message from Frank. She opens it up and reads it out.

"Had a word with the chief constable. You need a full psychological assessment before returning to work. His words not mine. Get yourself booked in today if possible.

No promises, but you may be returning to work sooner than you think."

She groans at the prospect of another session with the shrink but experiences a shard of excitement about returning to work. Glancing up, she realises she's standing outside Fun City, the amusement arcade. On the spur of the moment, she heads inside, exchanges a two-pound coin for a cardboard cup full of old two pence pieces and spends half an hour playing the various retro arcade games. Her favourite is the Grand National, where five horses race against each other to the sound of galloping feet. Another is the Penny Falls where she drops coins into a slot, and they fall onto a horizontal moving platform. It's the first time in her life she's ever been inside an amusement arcade, and she can now see the attraction.

She makes her way to the old town on the east side of the river and enters a cosy café on Church Street. The smell is delightful as she walks in. The place is empty apart from a woman behind the counter who is busily unloading a batch of muffins into a glass display cabinet.

'Are they straight from the oven?' Prisha asks.

'Aye, love. Still warm.'

'Oh, yes. I'll have a latte and a cinnamon muffin, please.' She hands her money over and takes a seat at a table near the window, then rings her psychologist, leaving a message on the answering machine. The woman soon arrives with her coffee and muffin.

'This weather's no good for business,' she complains, then promptly disappears out the back.

She devours the warm muffin in no time and relaxes back as she sips on her coffee. Her eyes rest on the deserted street outside as she mulls over her thoughts. She's not sure whether the visit to see Jason has made her feel better or worse, but then chastises herself.

It's not about me, it's about him. Who knows, maybe he could sense my presence or even hear my words?

A solitary figure, walking briskly and carrying a leather case, comes into her peripheral vision. At first, she takes no heed, idly watching the elderly man stride down the street towards the cafe. Something kicks in. Recognition.

'Purely coincidence?' she mutters to herself. 'You know what Frank would say. No such thing as bloody coincidence,' she says in a low growl, performing a good impersonation of Frank. Quickly finishing her coffee, she zips her coat up, dons her woolly hat and steps outside, deliberately bumping into the man.

'I'm terribly sorry,' she says, most apologetically.

'That's quite all right, dear.'

'Oh, it's you, Mr Dunn,' she declares, offering him a thin smile.

At first, he's puzzled. Then a nervous frown takes up residence. 'Ah, inspector...'

'Inspector Kumar. We spoke yesterday.'

'Yes, of course. Any developments on the stolen stamp?'

'We have a few lines of enquiry we're investigating. Can't say too much.'

'No, of course not. Well, I must be...'

'Are you here on business or pleasure?'

'Pardon?'

'In Whitby. Business or pleasure?'

'Erm, neither. I was visiting my... sister. She's not been too well of late.'

'Oh dear, nothing serious, I hope?'

'No. She sprained her ankle and can't get out, so I delivered her some groceries. I really must be going. I have a doctor's...'

'Of course. Sorry to have kept you,' she says, moving out of his way.

'Good day, inspector.'

'Goodbye Mr Dunn.' She watches him scurry away. 'You lying little toe rag,' she murmurs.

18

The wood is a narrow band of greenery that follows the contour of the beck. On the south side of the beck is a large, ploughed field.

'Hell,' Zac says. 'This is going to be a bugger to access if the car is in there,' he groans.

'If it is, then there has to be a path or track.'

'We've had a lot of rain since last Thursday, though. It could be a quagmire.'

Frank opens the hatch of the car and retrieves his Wellington boots. 'Only one thing for it,' he says, balancing precariously on one leg as he kicks a shoe off and jiggles into a boot. 'I don't see your boots in here, Zac?'

Zac winces and gazes down at his new Nike trainers. 'Fuck.'

'You weren't a boy scout, were you?'

'What?'

'Always be prepared,' Frank retorts with a chuckle.

'That's what I like about you, Frank.'

'What?'

'Oops... it's slipped my mind.'

They trudge along a path through the wood, Frank happily splashing in puddles and mud, whilst Zac attempts to walk along the fringes, on damp grass, his feet already soaking wet, and his new trainers covered in sludge.

'This path is wide enough to get a car down, but I haven't spotted any tyre marks yet,' Frank notes.

Zac attempts to leap across a large pool but doesn't quite make it. His back foot disappearing into the mire. His top lip curls in disgust as he lifts his leg out and shakes it. Frank chuckles away to himself.

Zac glares at him. 'When I was twenty, I had a choice of two careers: join the police or go to university and study to become a marine biologist.'

'I think you made the right choice, son. You get seasick in the bath.' Frank becomes distracted as his eyes spot something. 'Hello, hello, what have we here?' he says as he crouches down and inspects the trail. 'Tyre mark, unless I'm very much mistaken.'

'Come on, let's get on with it,' Zac says, lifting his pace.

The track meanders along for a good mile until the trees thin out and abruptly end. Standing at the edge of the wood, Frank and Zac survey a grassy clearing.

'I don't see a bloody car,' Zac moans. 'Are you sure your man Rizzo isn't winding you up?'

'Would you want to live off alphabet spaghetti for the next three days?'

Zac grimaces. 'What?'

'Never mind. Rizzo said the car was in the wood, near a beck and opposite a ploughed field. There's the beck, there's the field, and there's the bloody wood behind us,' he says, pointing at the landmarks. 'Get your GPS out, Zac, and let's scan the area from above. See exactly where we are.'

As Zac pulls his mobile out, it slips from his hand. Akin to a juggler, suffering with an acute case of the DTs, coupled with an involuntary bodily twitch, he repeatedly grasps and fights with the phone in mid-air until it inevitably drops into the mud with a gloopy splat.

'Fuck it!' he yells.

'Not your day, is it sunshine?' Frank chortles, sporting a mischievous grin.

'Piss off!' He delicately retrieves the phone, wipes the mud from it, then taps at the screen.

Frank leans in to take a peek at the terrain on the screen. 'Aha! I've got it,' he says, having a eureka moment.

'If it's contagious, keep it to yourself,' Zac grumbles.

'We're at the wrong bloody end of the wood. We started at the halfway point. We should have gone the other way,' he explains, tapping at the aerial shot. 'Come on, look lively,' he says setting off at a cracking pace back the way they came.

'Wonderful, just bloody wonderful.'

They both stare at the burnt-out wreck.

'Looks like the body of a Subaru Impreza or WRX to me,' Zac declares as he edges closer to the vehicle.

'Hmm... I agree. No number plates. The bugger obviously removed them. See if you can lift the bonnet. We'll have to check the vehicle identification number.'

Zac stares at the blackened hull and crumpled bonnet. The front of the car is perilously close to the banks of the babbling stream. 'Why don't you lift the bonnet?' he replies indignantly.

'Isn't it obvious?'

'No.'

Frank pulls out his warrant card and flashes at him. 'Detective chief inspector, that's why. It trumps a sergeant.

No point having a dog if you're going to bark yourself. Now stop dithering and lift the bloody bonnet. I have the VIN number somewhere,' he says, searching his pockets.

Zac stands at the front of the car, his back to the stream. He slides his hands under the bonnet, searching for the latch unsuccessfully. 'Can't seem to...' he grimaces, catching his fingers on something sharp.

'Stop buggering about, Zachariah. Put some effort into it. A big strapping lad like you should be able to yank that bonnet up with a bit of brute force.'

'It's jammed fast. I can't get a good purchase.'

'Nonsense. Grab the edge and give it a good old yank.'

Zac grips the bonnet and attempts a powerful heave. As he does, his feet lose purchase with the slimy, wet grass and he slides backward into the stream, the freezing water rushing over his knees. 'Great,' he mumbles, staring at Frank.

Frank shakes his head in obvious disappointment. 'What the hell did you do that for?'

'Because I had an overwhelming desire to do so. I fancied a wee paddle. Just the right weather for it,' he says, staring up at the ponderous sky above as the drizzle turns to rain.

'Look on the bright side, your trainers will be clean,' Frank replies with a chuckle.

'Ever thought about a career in stand-up comedy?' Zac replies, unsuccessfully attempting to exit the angry torrent of water.

Frank pulls the driver's door open, crouches, and fumbles about under the steering wheel. There's a click and the bonnet shudders.

'Well, well! I'll go to the foot of our stairs! The bonnet release mechanism still works despite the fire. Who'd have thought?' Frank says, scratching his noggin. 'Right, stop playing silly buggers, Zac. Lift the bonnet and I'll read the engine number out. Let's see if it's a match.'

19

The aroma therapy diffuser bubbles away, emitting a comforting scent of lavender into the room. Exotic unlit candles adorn the mantelpiece above the fireplace. A Dreamcatcher hangs from a lamp in the corner, and a small modern bookcase is stacked with enough self-help books to give Doctor Phil an erection.

Prisha is resting uncomfortably on a large beanbag, which almost swallows her up, making her feel like a child. She glances at the clock on the wall, then back at her psychologist—Donna, who is sitting on a beanbag opposite her.

I know she means well. She's doing her best to delve into the dark recesses of screwed up minds, but the fact is, that face of hers could do with a good slap. She has a permanent expression of maudlin pity on her dial. Even when I crack a joke or make a witty remark, the only change is that her left cheek twitches slightly. My God, that irritates me! I feel sorry for her husband. Imagine having sex with her? Just as

*you reach climax, you gaze down into that mush, and those
big, puppy dog eyes, pitying you. Christ!*

'Prisha? Prisha?'

'What? Oh, sorry, what was the question again?'

'You drifted off. Do you do that often?'

Only when I'm bored to tears. 'No.'

'It could be a sign.'

'A sign of what?'

'Your mind running away from the horrors you've
witnessed over the last few months. Could it be that?'

Oh, please! Do me a favour. 'No. I was just wondering
what to have for my dinner.'

Another commiserative stare. 'Okay, you're doing well.
Not long to go. Have you grieved yet?'

'He's not dead.'

'You can grieve for people who are living. They don't
have to be dead. We've established you have this ability
to compartmentalise. To separate your working life from
your personal.'

'Yes.'

'How do you do that in practical terms?'

'When I walk into my flat on a night, I take out my
warrant card and drop it on the table. That's me done. DI
Kumar clocking off for the day. Next morning, I pick up

my ID and put it in my jacket pocket. That's me clocking on for the day.'

'And the incident involving Jason, do you think about it often?'

'Not really. I feel a certain amount of guilt that it was him instead of me who was shot.'

'That's a natural reaction. What about any physical manifestations? Waking in a hot sweat, night terrors, nervousness, anxiety?'

'No. None.'

'What about self-harm?'

'No.'

'Anger, retribution?'

'Oh, yes. I'm angry with the bastard who stood me down from my job. And angry with the panel of snooping pen-pushers who interviewed me to see if I was at fault.'

'I meant about the person who shot Jason?'

'Oh, I see.' She pauses and ponders. 'You know what, at the moment, he's almost like an abstract figure, not real.'

'Interesting. Go on.'

Oh fuck! Open the door just a crack and she's all over you like a cheap suit. You should know better by now, Prisha. 'Well, that's it.'

'You don't wish him harm?'

'If I do, is that a good or bad thing?'

'It could be either, or neither.'

What the hell does that mean? Don't ask. 'Like I said, he doesn't seem real to me at the moment.'

'Hmm...you may be dehumanising him, stripping him, and yourself, of any emotion. Your mind's way of dealing with distress?'

Give me a break! 'Oh, yes. You could be right. I never thought of that.'

'Right, well, I think we're done for today. I will need to see you again regularly. Say once a week until the end of January. Of course, my surgery will be closed over the Christmas period for three weeks, unless you become desperate.'

Bite your tongue, girl, and God bless Christmas. 'Ok. No worries. What's the prognosis, doctor? Are you going to pass me fit to return to work?'

Donna stands up and opens the door. 'Yes, with one caveat.'

'Which is?'

'I want you to meditate for twenty minutes twice a day. Let all thoughts go. Can you do that?'

Of course not, you beanbag loving, dippy-hippy, nosey, puppy-eyed windbag! 'Yes. I think it's a wonderful suggestion and I'm grateful you spent twenty minutes teaching me how to meditate earlier. It will become part of my daily routine for the rest of my life. I can't thank you enough.'

She offers Prisha another ghastly, compassionate, caring smile. 'I'm glad to have helped.'

Prisha resists one last urge to give her an almighty slap across the face and bids her farewell.

20

Frank enters the incident room and smiles. It's deserted apart from PC Kylie Pembroke, who is busy on the phone. A near empty room means his team is out on the streets gathering potential intelligence. He gazes through into his old office but doesn't see DCC Overland. Giving the thumbs up to Kylie, he departs and heads to his shoe box.

A few moments later, there's a gentle tap on the door.

'Come in, my office is always open,' he says, in good spirits after the discovery of the vehicle. He looks up from his phone. 'Ah, Kylie, what can I do for you?'

A tad nervous, she pulls up a chair. 'Thought you might want a quick update.'

'Good idea. By the way, we've found the car out at Cock Mill Woods.'

'Yes, I heard.'

'Charlene Marsden and her forensic team are there now, although it's doubtful they'll get anything from it. All burnt-out.'

ELY NORTH

'Is Zac still there?'

Frank laughs. 'No. Nipped home to get changed. He got a little wet.' He relaxes back in his chair and peers at the young PC who he has a soft spot for. 'How long have you been a PC now, Kylie? Two, three months?'

'Three months, tomorrow.'

'And how long were you a special constable?'

'Just over a year, sir.'

'Already got plenty of experience under your belt, then. Nice to get a pay packet each month, though, I bet. And you've obviously finished university. You were studying archaeology, weren't you?'

'Yes, sir.'

'And how did you go?'

She blushes slightly. 'Ahem, fist-class honours, sir,' she almost whispers.

'Excellent! Don't be embarrassed about it. You need to shout from the rooftops and let everyone know. Give it two or three years in uniform, then put in for a transfer to CID. We're always on the lookout for bright young officers like yourself.'

'I'll bear that in mind, sir.' She shuffles uncomfortably as there's a slight pause in proceedings.

Frank detects her awkwardness. 'Okay. Any fresh leads?'

'That's what I wanted to talk to you about. You've probably not heard yet...' she says, hesitantly.

'Heard what?'

'Deputy Chief Constable Overland sent two officers over to Liverpool.'

'Why?'

'The deputy chief constable thinks he's had a breakthrough?'

'Does he indeed? And where is he?'

'He nipped out for lunch.'

'And what's this breakthrough?'

'He was going through a list of offenders recently released on parole, looking for anyone who matched the suspect's description.' She pulls out her notebook and flicks through the pages. 'Patrick O'Donoghue, thirty-four years old, five feet ten. Keen bodybuilder when he was inside. Released on parole from HM Prison Risley, Warrington, last Tuesday, a week ago.'

'Risley is a category C prison, low-risk offenders. What was he in for?'

'He attempted to rob a betting shop.'

'What with?'

'Ahem, a battery powered chainsaw.'

'Strike a bloody light! Not the sharpest tool in the shed, pardon the pun. And what happened?'

'The chainsaw died. He'd forgotten to recharge the battery.'

'It just gets better.'

'He escaped but handed himself in the next day. Got sent down for four years. Served two.'

'Any other history?'

'No.'

Frank leans back in his seat, perplexed. 'What's Overland playing at?' he murmurs.

'That's what I thought, boss.'

'Does Donoghue have a beard?'

'I rang the prison and spoke to a guard. He said when Donoghue left last week, he was clean shaven. And he has a Scouse accent.'

'I've known some hairy buggers in my time, but I've never met a man who could grow a bushy beard in two days. I've met a few women who could, but never a man. Right, well, thanks for the heads-up.'

———◇———

Zac places the parcel down on Frank's desk and peels back the butcher's paper to reveal four golden, crispy, battered haddock, a mountain of chips, and two tubs of mushy peas and curry sauce. He pulls a can of shandy from his pocket and hands it to Frank.

'You know how to suck up to the boss, Zac. Where did you get them from?'

'Trenchers.'

'Nice.'

As they tuck into their lunch, they discuss the latest development initiated by Martin Overland.

'I don't get it, Frank. This Donohue guy doesn't fit the bill at all, apart from he's pumped himself up whilst inside.'

Frank drops a fleshy, succulent piece of fish into his mouth and chews thoughtfully before taking a swig of shandy.

'Had me puzzled... for about ten seconds. You see, Zac, you have to understand people's nature, and why they do the things they do. Humans are creatures of habit and it's very hard, if not impossible, to change your personality. Overland looks the part. He's tall, lithe, works out. Sports a manicured beard, trendy haircut, crisp shirts with waistcoat, shiny shoes. Smells like an aftershave factory. He walks with an air of confidence, authority. He's cut a niche for himself over the years. He looks like a modern thinking, get ahead copper. Someone the public automatically trust. He was born for public relations, either that or a politician. He can speak for twenty minutes and actually say very little. Oh, it sounds good, but it's all weasel words to deflect questions or criticism. It's worked very well for him, that's why he is where he is.'

'That doesn't explain why he's pulled this guy in for questioning.'

'You don't know him like I do. It's been six days since Cartwright was shot. It's been all over the media. Just last night, I watched the news as they ran a quick update on it. The reporter ended by saying—and the police still have no idea who or where the gunman is—as though we're sitting around doing nothing.'

'We are,' Zac chuckles.

'An army marches on its stomach,' Frank replies as he scoops up a forkful of mushy peas. 'Superintendent Banks fronted the media twice before Overland came onboard, but the public are restless, concerned, frightened.'

'Are you saying this is all a publicity stunt by Overland to allay the fears of the public?'

'Possibly. Once he has the suspect back in Whitby, he'll call a media conference and put on a calm, assured, measured performance of a man in charge, getting things done. The public will breathe a sigh of relief and it will buy us a few more days without the media scrutiny.'

'And waste a lot of man hours which could be better spent.'

Frank dabs at his chin with a tissue. 'Exactly. Alas, it's a necessary evil these days, placating the public. Right, anymore for anymore?' he says grabbing the edges of the fish and chip paper.

Zac stares at the empty wrappers. 'There's nothing left, and you had way more chips than me.'

'Quit your whining.' Frank scrunches up the paper and drops it into the bin. 'Right, down to business. Let's go over our notes. Okay, we have the vehicle. We have a description and video footage of our primary suspect. What are we missing?' he queries Zac, offering him the chance to put his thinking cap on.

'Motive—we don't know why he shot Jason. We have a theory. He couldn't risk being arrested because he may be implicated in a prior serious crime he's not been associated with.'

Frank squeezes past the desk and stands at the whiteboard with pen in hand. 'Can you think of any other reasons?' he asks as he divides the whiteboard into two with a thick black line down the middle.

'Could be mentally unstable. Possibly a psychopath who hates coppers. Or possibly having a bad day... a bust up with the missus, or denied access to see his kids, and he wanted to take it out on the world. Jason could have been simply unlucky.'

'Good. What else *don't* we know?'

'Where does the stamp fit in? Without wanting to stereotype people, philatelists aren't typically bodybuilders who rob people, then shoot an unarmed officer in cold blood.'

'I agree,' Frank says, jotting down notes. 'What else?'

'A stamp of that value being hawked around would immediately raise suspicions. I'm sure by now it's common knowledge amongst collectors.'

'Meaning?'

'He was possibly put up to it. Someone paid him to steal the stamp, obviously someone who knew its value. Which brings us back to collectors of rarities.'

'And why do we suspect this guy lives locally?' Frank probes.

'He was coming back from Middlesbrough to Whitby on the A171. That's the main road to Whitby, Scarborough, possibly Filey... and all places in between. If you wanted to go anywhere else in the country, you wouldn't use that road. Also, the car was dumped at Cock Mill Woods. Only someone who knew the area well would know about that place. It's hardly a renowned beauty spot.'

'Correct.'

Zac scrunches his face up. 'There's two things I don't get, Frank.'

'Go on.'

'First, he calmly conducts a robbery and nicks the stamp, cool as a cucumber. Then he drives erratically back to Whitby and pulls out a gun. What happened during that car journey to change his demeanour?'

'Split personality? Drugs? Steroids?'

'Aye, snorting a few lines of methamphetamine, mixed with steroids, could produce paranoia and aggression,' Zac says, contemplating the scenario.

'You said two things?' Frank prompts.

'Yes. He was nearly back in Whitby. Why stop to fill a stolen car up with petrol when you're nearly home?'

'Hmm... Good point. If he was paid to steal the stamp, then at some point he'd have needed to hand it over. Maybe the instigator lives further afield, or possibly in a remote location without public transport.' Frank taps the marker pen on the whiteboard. 'Let's build a character profile. What does he do for a living, if anything?'

'Bodybuilders eat a lot of food, typically protein, meat. They also take a lot of supplements, protein shakes, maybe steroids, and they'd probably have a gym membership. Those things cost money. Even if he's on benefits, I'd say he has supplemental income.'

'Maybe part-time or casual?'

'Yes. That way, he has plenty of time for the gym. The serious guys are there every day, sometimes for a couple of hours.'

'And if you were a bodybuilder wanting part-time work, where would you look? A kindergarten assistant? A carer at a nursing home? Stacking shelves at a supermarket?'

'No. Door work—security. If I'm going to spend all that time and money building my buns, then why not use them? And it's a good way to pick up the girls and earn a little extra if you're into dealing drugs.'

Frank smiles. 'Good lad. And where do we find security?' he says scribbling on the board.

'Just about everywhere these days.'

'Focus.'

'Erm, nightclubs, pubs, shopping centres, concerts, sporting events.'

'We've watched the CCTV footage a dozen times. What age bracket would you put him in? And don't say between twenty and fifty.'

Zac sucks air in through his teeth and pulls at his beard. 'Tough one. Definitely not old. He moves freely, with no sign of pain. No stoop. He has a—don't mess with me—swagger. He's definitely filled out, meaning he's not an adolescent. But it's still a tough one.'

'Gut instinct?'

'Late twenties to early thirties.'

'What else?'

'He did the robbery solo. Possibly a loner. Either prefers his own company or is socially awkward.'

'Or deliberately avoids making relationships?'

'Possibly. If he has a past which he doesn't want to reveal, the best way to protect it is to keep yourself to yourself.'

'Good. We're working on the theory someone paid him to steal the stamp.'

'Yes.'

'Where would a loner bodybuilder meet a collector of antiquities?'

Silence, as both men try to join invisible dots.

'I have nothing,' Zac murmurs.

'No, me neither. Okay, let's look at what we have.' He stands back and studies the bullet points on the board. 'Local body builder. Possibly employed on a casual, part-time basis as a security guard, door man, bouncer. Reclusive by nature or possibly deliberately. Aged mid-twenties to mid-thirties. Has a northern accent, distinctive blue eyes and possibly a beard.' Frank rubs at the grey strands on his head. 'But what is the connection between a muscleman and a bloody stamp collector? That's the key.'

'Could be related. Father, brother, uncle.'

'Can't rule it out, but it doesn't smell right to me.'

'What about Alfred Dunn? Do you think he could be involved?'

Frank grimaces. 'Possibly, but again, where's the connection? Retired professors and psychotic bodybuilders rarely move in the same circles. Right, get an officer to ring around all the businesses in the north of England that hire out security. Start locally then broaden out. Then take a uniform with you and visit the local pubs and shopping malls. See if someone recognises the photo or the description of our suspect. Security typically work in teams. He may have partnered someone at some point. In fact, take PC Pembroke with you. It will be good experience for her. She's lacking in confidence. Let's bring her out of her shell a bit.'

Zac stands up and pushes his chair under the desk. 'Righto, boss.'

'And Zac, did you check with Garth Windsor's insurance company about what time he insured the stamp?'

'Yes. He insured it on Thursday at 11:30.'

'Okay, good. That's one less thing to worry about. Windsor is kosher.'

'Except, he insured it for sixty-thousand pounds, not forty-five.'

Frank raises one eyebrow. 'Did he indeed? Then he's going to be fifteen grand up on the deal. Having said that, it's not unusual for antiquities to be over insured. I mean, who truly knows their real value and what someone would pay for them? And Zac?'

'Yes, Frank?'

'Good work, and thanks for the fish and chips. My shout next time.'

21

Zac and PC Pembroke split up and spend a fruitless three hours trailing all over Whitby, showing the grainy photograph to landlords and security personnel on duty at the numerous supermarkets. Dispirited, Zac wanders over to a seafood kiosk on the promenade and orders a tub of cockles.

He hands his money over to a familiar face who notices his countenance.

'I take it you haven't caught your man yet?' Anton Joseph asks in his deep Caribbean accent.

'No. He's a bloody mystery,' Zac says, liberally dousing the seafood with vinegar and pepper. 'Here, look at this. Recognise him?' he quizzes, handing the photo over.

Anton studies the photo intently and grimaces. 'It's not the greatest photo. It could be anyone.'

'Five-ten, muscular, blue eyes, northern accent.'

Anton hands the photo back. 'Doesn't ring any bells. How's Jason going?' he asks, familiar with most of the officers from the station, who are regular patrons.

'No change.'

'We must thank the Lord for small mercies.'

Zac checks his phone again, hoping a message may have dropped in from his informant, but he's disappointed. He's left several messages for Cleavage over the past twenty-four hours, but all have gone unanswered. 'Hey, Anton, you know Cleavage, don't you?'

'I do.'

'I've been trying to get hold of him and all I get is his voicemail.'

Anton laughs. 'He was away at sea. I saw the trawler he was on leaving yesterday morning as I was setting up.'

'*Was* at sea?'

'Yes. I noticed it sail back into the harbour about an hour ago. They're probably unloading their catch right now.'

Zac spots PC Pembroke heading his way and waves to her. She scurries across the road, patently discouraged.

'No good?' Zac prompts, spearing three cockles with a toothpick and dropping them into his mouth.

'No. Even tried the amusement arcades and bookies.'

'Good thinking, Kylie. And?'

'Nothing. We could be wrong, you know, about him living or working in Whitby.'

'Yes, we could. But it's the logical place to start looking and work our way out from here. I guess the next move must be Scarborough, but it's getting a bit late in the day now,' he says, checking his watch. 'What are you having—cockles, mussels, whelks?'

'Ugh, no. I'll have two fish sticks, though, please.'

They stroll on together towards the lower harbour and the fish quay, where vessels unload their catch. He spots Cleavage in the distance.

'Okay, Kylie, I'll see you back at the station.'

'Where are you going?'

'To see a man about a dog.'

'Oh, I get it.'

He hangs back as Kylie heads off. Once she's safely out of sight, he heads towards the fish quay as Cleavage finishes a conversation with the skipper, who hands him an envelope. They shake hands and Cleavage turns to walk away but stops as he spies Zac leaning against a railing. Removing his woollen hat, he drags his large fingers through his bushy hair and gives a sideways nod to a row of shops on the other side of the road, then sets off. Zac trails behind and follows Cleavage into the bookies.

'Shit,' he murmurs. 'Hello gambling, my old friend.'

Most people would find the inside of a bookies rather unpleasant. Mainly inhabited by older males from the lower echelons of society, it harbours a heavy musk. It's a smoke-free zone, but enough stale tobacco odour clings to the fabric of cheap clothing worn by the customers to imbue the tiny space with an unforgiving funk. And... it's late afternoon. Last race of the day in England, which means fetid alcohol fumes mingle with stale sweat, smoke, and cloying desperation. Win back the money they spent at the pub, or on weed, or meth, or... well, whatever.

Zac breathes it in. To him it's an elixir. He's lived as a gambler for many a year. The buzz of the win will overrule logic every time. Gambling's a mug's game... right? But still... when your horse comes home at fifteen to one, or when you throw your cards onto the table with three kings, the feeling is better than any high you can experience from drugs.

The shop, if it can be called that, is ultimately a bank from which you deposit frequently but rarely withdraw.

Ten men stare at a massive TV screen on the back wall as the penultimate race enters its climax.

Cleavage is busy at the back counter, head down, hastily scribbling away. Zac sidles over and picks up a half-stub pencil, then grabs a betting slip. Neither man acknowledges the other.

Zac takes a furtive glance around at the men gawping expectantly at the screen. Some are open-mouthed, eyes on stalks as the field of horses round the last bend. Others rub nervously at their faces. A large, overweight man slaps the side of his buttock, urging the jockey to use the whip with more abandon.

'Come on, yer bastard, come on! Get in there!' he pleads, his forehead sweaty with excitement.

'Well?' Zac whispers.

Cleavage remains intent on the job at hand. 'Give me a minute. I've had a red-hot tip for the last race. I'm putting a ton on Prometheus. Twenty-to-one.'

Zac picks up a discarded racing guide from a newspaper and scans the statistics. 'It's a handicapped Maiden race and your horse is carrying an extra seven pounds in weight,' he says with an element of incredulity, forgetting his primary mission.

'So?'

'It's been pissing it down for a week. The track is rated Heavy.'

'I'm telling you, it's a winner. A deckhand on the boat has a mate that works at the stables. The horse is a shoo-in.'

'Yeah, right. If he's so good at picking winners, then why is he working at the stables?' Against his better judgement, the urge to place a bet is growing.

There's an eruption of cheers and curse words as the current race ends. The large man appears shellshocked as he slowly rips up his betting stub. He turns and stumbles from the shop, muttering to himself.

'She's gonna bloody kill me. She'll skin me alive.'

Zac experiences a pang of sympathy, having been in the same predicament on more than one occasion. And yet, the itch grows.

Don't do it Zac. You've not had a bet in months. Don't throw it all away. I'm just playing a part. It would look suspicious if I walked out of here without placing a bet. I'm only doing it as part of the pretence. Ten quid, twenty quid, that's all. Then never again.

He studies the guide a second time and makes an informed decision, then jots his selection onto the slip and follows Cleavage to the counter. Cleavage pulls money from his envelope and passes a hundred pounds and his bet through the window opening. Zac hands his betting slip over along with a fifty-pound note. Both men retreat to the back of the room.

'Did you back it?' Cleavage asks.

'No. I went with Yosemite Sam at eight-to-one.'

'You'll regret it.'

'Tell me about it. I've tried ringing and texting you.'

'Yeah, sorry about that. Been out at sea for twenty-four hours and my phone was dead.'

'You couldn't recharge it?'

'Left my charger at home. I have an iPhone and all the other lads have Samsungs.'

'Do you have a name for me?'

'Yes and no,' he says, staring at the TV screen as the channel flicks across to a different race meeting. 'It's all Chinese whispers, though. A friend of a friend whose mate's sister overheard someone in a pub.'

'I understand.'

'A guy called Riley worked as a bouncer at a nightclub. Apparently, he was overheard talking about this headbanger he once worked with on the door. A real loose cannon.'

'Who's the suspect? Riley or the headbanger?'

'The headbanger.'

'No name?'

'No.'

'And what about this Riley... is that his first or last name?'

'Sorry, I don't know. Like I said, he used to be a bouncer and plays rugby. That's all I have, and it's all third hand information. Probably just gossip.'

'Not a lot to go on.'

They fall silent as the horses bolt from the starting gates. After only three minutes, both men depart separately from the bookmakers. One is on a high, the other bitterly disappointed and regretting his actions.

22

Frank lifts the receiver and stabs at a number. The phone is answered instantly.

'Yes, boss?' PC Pembroke asks.

'Kimberley, I've just had a call from Charlene Marsden from forensics. They lifted several prints from the bottom of the steering wheel. She's sending them through in the next few minutes. Whatever you're doing, put it on hold and run a match. Let's see if we can put a name to our man.'

'Will do. Oh, and Frank?'

'Yes,'

'You may want to switch your TV on. The deputy chief constable is about to front the media.'

'Is he indeed?' Frank murmurs as he hangs up.

———◇———

Frank leans back in his chair and dunks a gingernut biscuit into his mug of tea as he squints at the tiny TV screen mounted on a side wall.

'I always enjoy a good yarn,' he murmurs as he quickly positions his mouth under the biscuit, evidence of his overzealous dunking.

Frank recognises the conference room as headquarters at Northallerton. Microphones line the front of a long table as Martin Overland strides purposefully into shot. He's accompanied by a young, uniformed female officer, who's merely there as decoration. Taking a seat, he opens a leather bound A4 notepad in front of him, fixes the cameras with a resolute gaze, then begins.

'I'm Detective Deputy Chief Constable Martin Overland coordinating the investigation into the attempted murder of Detective Sergeant Jason Cartwright last Thursday, the twenty-sixth of November. I'm here today to inform you we have arrested a person of significant interest in the case and that individual will be helping us with our enquiries.' He pauses for effect as cameras whir and click. 'I'd also like to say that despite most people feeling shocked and devastated at the shooting of an unarmed police officer, occurrences such are these are extremely rare. I understand the public is rightly concerned and requires answers. I'd like to reassure everyone that my Major Investigation Team is working around the clock to get justice for DS Cartwright and his family. We implore anyone with any information to contact our hotline or call Crimestoppers, where you can leave information anonymously. Any questions?'

A disembodied voice, off screen, calls out. 'Can you give us more details about the person arrested? Is it a man, woman, age, ethnicity?'

'The person in question is a thirty-four-year-old Caucasian male who was recently released on parole. I'm not at liberty to say any more than that.'

In typical fashion, a volley of questions resonates around the room.

'Have you found the weapon?'

'Was he working alone? I've heard reports there was someone else in the car with him?'

'Deputy chief constable, are you a hundred per cent certain you have the right man?'

Overland raises his hand to quell the volley of demands.

'We are still searching for the pistol, and at this point in time, we believe the gunman was working alone. During an investigation as large as this, it's not uncommon to bring many suspects or witnesses in for questioning, if only to eliminate them from our enquiries. Right, ladies and gentlemen, I thank you for your time and I will keep you informed of any further developments.'

Frank hits the remote for the TV and the screen goes blank. He pulls out another gingernut and dunks it repeatedly in his tea as he cogitates.

Waste of bloody time, but at least he's given the impression the investigation is moving forward, which it is, but certainly not to the point where we are in a position to arrest anyone. As long as Overland keeps out of my hair and doesn't waste too many resources, then I can live with it.

As he lifts the soggy biscuit to his mouth, the end breaks off and plops into his cup.

'Bugger it!'

23

Prisha taps her card on the payment terminal, then collects the tray of drinks and navigates the busy throng of patrons as she heads back to the table. Frank and Zac grab their pints, and take thirsty glugs of the brown creamy liquid.

'Some good news and some not so good,' Frank begins as Prisha takes her seat. 'Charlene's team recovered a couple of good fingerprint lifts from the inside of the steering wheel. The bad news is I had Kylie run them through the database.'

'No match?' Zac predicts, pessimistically.

Frank frowns at the interruption. 'There was a cold hit. We have a fingerprint match on the database, but no name attached to it.'

'Where and when?' Prisha prompts, sipping her gin and tonic.

'Last April, there was a break-in at Stonygarth Hall. It's a country estate not far from Middlesbrough, belonging to Lord and Lady Ashton.'

'What was stolen?'

'World-War-Two memorabilia: SS insignia, a Hitler Youth dagger, and a signed copy of Mein Kampf by that bloke with the funny moustache.'

'Charlie Chaplin?' Zac sniggers.

'Can you two be serious,' Prisha scolds. 'This could be our breakthrough,' she adds reflectively.

Frank sips on his pint, then wipes his top lip on the back of his sleeve. 'Yes, and no. Whoever left their prints at Stonygarth Hall is not necessarily the gunman, and even if he is, then we're still none the wiser to who he is. Which means tomorrow, Zac, you need to pay another visit to our offshore worker, Daniel Platt. Ask him to come in voluntarily for fingerprinting.'

'And if he refuses?'

'Arrest him.'

'On what charges?'

Frank huffs. 'Burglary. Maybe Mr Platt has a keen interest in old German war mementos. If his fingerprints match, then there's a pretty good chance he's our thief, but not necessarily our gunman. Did you check out his alibis?'

'Yes, I rang the offshore contractor he's employed through, and all the details match with what he told me; the time he arrived in London, the hotel he stayed at, the taxi back home.'

'Okay, but keep digging. Platt may be hiding something. He could have lent his car to a mate or a relative and is covering for them. What about the CCTV footage from the airport?'

'Came through mid-morning. I have a uniform on it, but it could take days to trawl through that amount of video.'

Prisha records details in her notebook. 'Who was the officer in charge of investigating the burglary at Stonygarth Hall? Maybe there's something they overlooked in their report. It could be worthwhile having a word with them.'

Frank winces. 'That will not be possible anytime soon. The investigating officer was Cartwright.'

'Oh,' she replies, saddened by his reply. 'I went to see him today,' she adds as the other two exchange concerned glances.

'And?' Frank probes.

'And nothing. He looked so peaceful, as if he was simply asleep.'

'I suppose he is, in a way,' Zac says.

'We had a chat.'

'We?'

'Yes... we. I'd tell him something, and he'd laugh and make a silly comment or a joke, you know, the way he did.' Frank and Zac stare at her like she's mad. She glares at them. 'Not literally,' she snaps. 'I talked, and he replied, in my head.'

'Oh,' they both say with relief.

'Zac,' Frank begins, 'give Prisha your latest.'

'We did a personality profile earlier in the day and reckon our gunman could be a security guard of some sort. Me and Kylie trailed all over Whitby earlier. Pubs, clubs, supermarkets, showing the photo of the suspect to landlords and security personnel. Not a sausage. Having said that, the photo is next to useless. However, I managed to get my hands on Cleavage.'

Prisha snorts her drink down her nose and coughs, pulling out a tissue. 'I beg your pardon?' she finally quizzes.

'Big Bob, he's my informant. Nickname is Cleavage,' he says using his hands to push his pecs together. 'He really should have some support for those puppies. Anyway, it's a long shot, but someone called Riley, a rugby player, used to work as a bouncer at a nightclub. He mentioned a guy who he thought was capable of the shooting. A real loose cannon, volatile.'

'And?' Prisha asks, less than impressed with the intel.

'That's all Cleavage had.'

'I hate that crap,' Prisha states. 'Innuendo, gossip, half-truths, armchair detectives. It muddies the waters and chews up police time.'

'Hang on,' Frank says, stroking the condensation from his pint glass. 'A rugby player named Riley?'

'Yes,' Zac says, finishing his pint.

'Was Riley his first or surname?'

'Not sure. Why?'

'Many years ago, after I'd given up boxing, I took up rugby union for a few seasons, until a broken leg ended my career. I used to play with a young fella named Keith Miller.'

'And?'

'Haven't seen him for years but I bumped into one of the old rugby gang a few months back and they mentioned that Keith Miller's son was one to watch out for... you know, an up-and-coming star on the rugby pitch. If my memory serves me correctly, I think he said his name was Riley.'

'Riley's a common first name for young boys these days, boss. But not for older men,' Prisha says.

'No, it's not,' Frank replies, absorbed with his thoughts. 'Okay, leave that one to me, Zac,' he says, collecting the empty glasses. 'Father and son usually keep it in the family.'

Prisha shakes her head as Frank heads to the bar. 'What does that mean?' she quizzes Zac.

'It means whichever club the father played for; the son will typically play for the same team. Keep it in the family?'

'Okay, I get it.'

24

The winter night is cold and raw, with a chill whipping in from the sea. A squally breeze whistles past the steel uprights of the floodlights which illuminate the needle-like drizzle. Frank locks up his car and breathes deeply as the familiar smell of Deep Heat liniment transports him back to a time long ago. Gruff male Yorkshire voices bark orders and encouragement to one another as the players on the glistening grass go through their practice drills, apparently oblivious to the inclement weather.

He spots a familiar face kneeling down on the touchline next to a dugout, applying a bandage to a player's thigh. Wandering over, he keeps one eye on the drills the players are going through on the field. Groans, yells and the occasional expletive are accompanied by the slap of bodies slamming into one another. The player receiving treatment rises gingerly to his feet and limps back to where the action is. The trainer administering the treatment stands and is about to head back to the sanctuary of the dugout when he stops and stares at Frank as he wanders towards him.

'Well, I'll be! Frank bloody Finnegan,' Keith Miller guffaws.

The two men shake hands and give one another a warm, friendly slap on the back. 'Keith, it's been a while,' Frank says, smiling.

'A while! I haven't seen you down the ground for over seven years. You used to be a regular for the home games. What happened?'

'Bloody paperwork and chores around the house. That's what happened. I usually call in at the station on Saturday morning to tidy up loose ends and by the time I get home, Meera has a list of jobs for me to attend to.'

'Come into the dugout, away from the cold,' Keith says. 'And how is Meera?'

'She's just dandy. Always on the go. Keeps me on my toes. And how is your missus?'

'Jenny's doing fine. We're grandparents now.'

'Congratulations, Keith. How many?'

'Just the one at the moment. Little Rosie. She just turned seven last week. The apple of my eye, Frank. Jenny dotes on her, as do I.'

'I remember your lad, Riley. Is Rosie his?'

'No. She belongs to my daughter, Scarlet. You probably don't remember her as she rarely came to the games. Single parent, of course. She shacked up with a bad 'un in her late teens. Bloody little wanker he was... is. He got our Scarlet up the duff and buggered off. Last I heard, he was serving ten in Armley prison for dealing, and assault and battery. If he shows his face around here again, I'll be serving up my own version of assault and battery.'

Frank chuckles. 'You always had a bit of a short fuse, Keith. You spent more time in the sin bin than you did on the pitch.'

'Aye, well, I've mellowed now.'

'Sounds like it.'

Keith reflects. 'It's true. Since Rosie came along, I've had a new perspective on life. With grandkids, you can take the time out to enjoy them. When my kids were young, I was too busy working and playing rugby, and drinking. A lot of wasted time that I now regret. I see Rosie as my second chance. She comes first.' Keith pulls a flask from a backpack and pours the contents into two grubby cups. 'Hot coffee with a drop of whisky in it, Frank. Keep the cold at bay.'

'Ah, just the ticket. Cheers,' Frank replies, gratefully accepting the offering.

Keith takes a swig and sighs. 'I heard about your officer, Frank. How's he doing?'

'No change. Still in ICU. Not looking good, but we can but pray.'

'What's the world coming to? Shot in the chest for a bloody traffic offence. I blame the judicial system. They're too soft. The criminals these days get a slap on the wrist and are out on the street again after a few years. It's not right. Anyway, what brings you up here on a training night? It's certainly not my barista skills.'

Frank takes a sip of the bitter liquid and grimaces. 'No, it's not. I actually wanted a word with your lad, Riley.'

Keith is wary, on guard. 'Riley? He's a good lad, Frank. Never been in trouble with the law. What's this all about?'

'Calm the farm, Keith. I'm hoping he may be able to help me out. I heard on the grapevine he worked with a guy who may be of interest to us in connection with the shooting.'

'Oh, I see. He's said nowt to me about it.'

'Which one is he?' Frank asks, surveying the players as they practice a scrummage.

Keith points. 'Tall lad, loose forward, giving all the orders. He's captain, and he's only twenty.'

'Hell, he's a big lad. Last time I saw him, he was a skinny little kid.'

Keith chortles, obviously proud of his son. 'These last two years, he's taken it very seriously. He's at the gym every day. Eats like a horse, but not the rubbish we used to eat. He has a strict diet: chicken, rice, lean beef, pasta, a mountain of greens. He doesn't drink, well, not much. Doesn't smoke. No drugs. He's really come on. Even had some of the big boys from League sniffing around.'

'Really?'

'Aye. Scouts from Leeds and Wigan were at our last home game. He's got all the moves, Frank. He's fast, a great ball handler, goalkicker, can rally the troops.'

'A natural born leader.'

'He reminds me a bit of you in your heyday, before the broken leg.'

Frank laughs. 'I don't think I was ever that good. And I certainly didn't follow his strict diet regime. It was pie and peas and six pints of bitter after a game for you and me.'

'Aye. True enough. It's all changed now. The young kids really know their stuff when it comes to diet and fitness. I'll call him. Riley!' he shouts, cupping his hands together. Riley glances over his shoulder as Keith beckons him over.

The strapping lad jogs languidly towards them with an authoritative confidence belying his years.

'What's up, dad?' he asks.

'Riley, this is Frank Finnegan. DCI Frank Finnegan.'

Frank holds out his hand. 'Pleased to meet you, Riley. I hear you're a rising star?'

The young man laughs. 'Don't know about that. Just getting my head down and doing the basics right. Dad's told me a lot about you over the years. Reckons you could have made the big time if not for a broken leg.'

'Nah! He's building me up. I was never that good. Anyway, the professional life of a sport star can be very short. Ten, fifteen years if you're lucky and don't burn out or have a serious injury. The life as a police officer can be a good forty years or more. You do the maths.'

Riley nods. 'So, what can I do for you?'

'You obviously know one of my officers was shot last Thursday on the outskirts of Whitby. I heard a rumour you have a theory of who it could be?'

Riley stiffens and throws a glance over his shoulder at his teammates in the distance.

'Maybe. But who told you that?'

'I'm a detective inspector... remember?'

Keith steps in to halt the impasse. 'You're not in trouble, Riley. Frank's a good man and anything you tell him will be in the strictest confidence. Isn't that right, Frank?'

'Correct,' Frank confirms.

Riley relaxes. 'Look, Mr Finnegan, it's just a feeling, like you said, a theory.'

'Go on?'

'Last year I was earning a bit of extra money working Friday and Saturday nights on the door of Strangers Nightclub in Scarborough, during off-season. For about two months, there was a new guy who stepped in for any of the regular doormen who couldn't make it for whatever reason. His name is Wayne Barber. He was a real nutjob. Despite what most people think, security is there to diffuse tension, stop potential fights. It's not like the old days. Everyone has a camera on their phone and CCTV is everywhere, so you can't risk putting a foot wrong, no matter how much some pricks try to wind you up.'

'In what way was this Wayne Barber a nutjob?'

'He'd look for trouble. Was a bit too handy with his fists. And he was a racist, sexist pig and hated the police. Had this thing about Hitler and Nazi Germany. Obsessed with it. Said the British and Americans should have joined forces with the Germans to finish the job off. I assumed he was talking about the Jews and the Russians. Also kept quoting stuff from the Bible. And he was definitely on something; meth, speed, crack, and, I suspect steroids. Only five-ten, five-eleven tall, but he was massive. I know what it's like to try to gain muscle once you've reached your natural maximum potential. Even with the best diet and proper training and recovery, your return on investment is ever diminishing. That's when you know a guy is injecting steroids. They just keep on getting bigger and bigger with the same amount of effort. That's not the way it works if you're clean. And he had a smell about him.'

'Sweat?'

'Yeah. A faint smell of sick. That's always a good indicator someone is on the roids. Too much testosterone comes out in their sweat.'

'What colour were his eyes?'

'Brown.'

Frank's heart sinks. 'Are you sure?'

'Yeah. He's sort of dark, you know, swarthy in a Mediterranean way. Black wavy hair combed back. To be honest, he gave me the creeps and I don't spook easily.'

'No, I can imagine. Why did he scare you?'

Riley's puzzled face paints a picture. 'Apart from him being a knobhead and shit at his job, there was something *off* about him.'

'Off?'

'Yeah, weird. As though he had a past, a bad past. Whenever I asked him about America, he'd change the subject.'

'Why did you ask him about America?' Frank asks, puzzled.

'Because of his accent. He's a Yank. A sort of New York accent, although I'm not an expert.'

'Shite,' Frank hisses, his balloon clearly deflated. 'Okay Riley. Thanks for your time.'

'Not a problem. Good to meet you,' the lad says as he jogs back to his teammates.

Keith stares at Frank. 'Not who you're after?' he predicts.

'No. He doesn't fit the description of our prime suspect, but we'll check him out all the same. I take it Riley worked through an agency?'

'Yes, Black Knight Security, based in Leeds.'

'Right Keith, good to see you again. Give my best to Jenny and thanks for the coffee,' he adds as he swallows the last of the bitter brew and hands the cup back.

'Aye, and good to see you. Why don't you come to the next home game a week on Saturday, and we'll have a proper catch up?'

'Maybe I will, depending on how things pan out.'

'Oh, yes. Sorry, I wasn't thinking.'

'No need to apologise, Keith. Life goes on... doesn't it?'

25

Wednesday 2nd December

Prisha skips down the steps, panting hard, as icy sleet stabs at her body. Jogging at a steady pace, she quickly passes from Church Lane onto Church Street, barely a soul in sight. She takes a shortcut through the old town square and emerges near the swing bridge as the red flashing lights indicate their intention. She slows her pace and walks towards the barrier as it inexorably drops into position, blocking ingress and egress. The heavy throb of a diesel engine mutes the sound of the bridge hydraulics as a trawler chugs down the river heading towards the harbour and open sea. She stoops, placing hands on knees, sucking in air.

A bell tolls—deep, sombre, full of foreboding. It resonates across the ancient fishing town with a diminishing after echo, adding a macabre sense of apprehension.

It takes Prisha by surprise as her subsiding heartbeat explodes upwards.

Three times the bell tolls… then stops.

Oh God, please no. Let it be a mistake or a call to prayer, anything. Please don't ring again, please!

Glances at her wristwatch—7:05 am.

The trawler chugs by the open bridge.

Four deckhands line up on the starboard side, staring up towards St Mary's Church high on the hill.

The bell tolls again… then again, and again… this time in short, three second bursts.

She thinks of Jason, then of the teenage boy involved in the road accident.

How old was he? Sixteen, I think Frank said. Please let it be him.

Nausea overwhelms her. She can't believe what she wished for and is repulsed by her thought.

No! What about his parents and siblings? But what about Jason's unborn child and his broken-hearted wife?

It's an impossible choice, not that she can have any bearing on how many times the bell rings. She mentally counts the chimes.

Bile rises in her stomach.

The deckhands remove their woollen hats in their right hand, and in unison, clasp them over their hearts.

One more peel of the bell as it reaches sixteen.

Please, let that be the last!

Seventeen, eighteen.

On and on the agony goes.

She drops to her knees as watery vomit spills onto the road.

The bridge whirs back into position, straddling the River Esk. Warning lights flick from red to green.

As life ends, life continues.

The bells toll as they will until they've pealed forty-four times—the exact age of DS Jason Cartwright. Prisha curls up in a ball, her hands clasped over her ears in a futile attempt to stop the hateful sound.

Frank stares at his reflection, less than impressed.

'Nearly sixty years we've been together, and forgive me for saying so, but I'm getting a little tired of gawping at you every morning. You don't improve.'

Meera calls out from the bedroom. 'Are you talking to yourself again, Frank?'

'No love. I'm talking to my shadow.'

'Daft old man. He's getting worse,' she mutters to herself, pulling her tights on.

Frank taps the safety razor on the side of the enamel sink, shakes the water loose, and places it on his upper left cheek. Slowly, he pulls the razor downwards.

His hand involuntarily twitches at the echo. A nick. Blood.

He grabs a paper tissue and dabs at the stain.

'Did you hear that, Meera?' he calls out, concerned.

'What?' she yells back, slipping into slacks.

'A bell?'

'It's blowing a gale outside. It's probably the guy-ropes attached to the flags banging against the steel posts.'

'No,' Frank murmurs to himself. 'It was deep.'

He resumes shaving, alert but not alarmed. He'd have received a call if something had happened.

A second toll.

He grabs a towel, quickly wipes suds from his face, and races into the bedroom.

'Frank, what the...'

'Shush,' he says, pulling up the window as an icy arctic blast blows into the room.

'For God's sake, Frank, close the bloody window!' his wife yells.

'Shush,' he repeats, head jutting out into the dreary morning light.

It arrives again, a third time. A deep chime of an oversized bell, distant, but distinct from any other sound.

'No,' he whispers.

'Whatever is the matter with you?' Meera laments, becoming ever more anxious.

Silence.

'Frank shut the bloody window. You're letting all the heat out.'

He pays no heed. head still protruding from the opening, despite the bitter wind.

It begins.

The toll of the bell.

In three second bursts.

He slams the window shut and stares at his wife, eyes on stalks. 'Where's my phone?' he demands.

She's frightened. 'Downstairs on the kitchen table where you left it, recharging,' she whispers, realising what's happened.

'Get it.'

Meera makes towards the door but halts as a rapid, familiar vibration, followed by Frank's upbeat ringtone, drifts from the kitchen below.

'Oh, please God, no!' he cries as he drops to his knees, in a stupor.

He sobs as his wife falls to his side, embracing his bulky frame.

She rocks him from side to side in her arms.

'Let it out, Frank. Let it out,' she gently murmurs.

———◇———

Zac slaps four slices of white bread down on the countertop and liberally spreads butter over them. He tops them with cheese slices, then abruptly stops as he gazes around the kitchen.

'Tomato? No. It will go soggy.' He pulls open the fridge door and searches for pre-packed sliced meat but finds none. Slamming the door shut, he spies the tub of cheese slices again and a bottle of tomato sauce. 'Fuck it! That will do.' He wrestles with clingfilm and, after the third attempt, drops the boys' lunch into two sandwich boxes. 'Fruit?' he mutters, staring at the empty fruit bowl. 'Damn.' He fumbles in the mystery cupboard where his wife keeps things which are foreign to him: baking powder, bi-carb, essences, vanilla pods, mace, cardamon, carraway seeds, proving agent. 'I've seen her put them in here. Now where are they... ah, yes.' He pulls a packet of raisins out and quickly drops a handful into two small tubs, then clicks the lids down.

He marches to the bottom of the stairs, cups his hands, and calls out.

'Boys, time to rise and shine. You have thirty minutes to wash, dress, make your breakfast, and catch the bus!'

Silence.

He repeats his commands—louder. 'Did you hear what I said?'

Grumbling drifts down the stairs, a sure-fire sign the boys are awake.

Back in the kitchen, he pops a coffee pod into the espresso machine.

'Christ, this is not working,' he mumbles, reflecting on the fact his wife elected to do nightshift to earn extra money.

The boys amble downstairs, slightly dishevelled.

'Okay, Thomas, Sam, you're old enough to make your own breakfast. Now get to it.'

'Dad?' Tom asks.

'What?'

'Where's my football kit? I've got a game after school.'

'Did you wash it as I showed you?'

'Yes,' he replies with blinking eyes.

'Did you hang it over the radiator to dry?'

'No. I hung it out on the line.'

'And there's your answer. Get your breakfast. I'll grab your gear. Twenty minutes in the tumble dryer should have it dry.'

'Thanks, dad,' Tom says as he scoots into the kitchen.

Zac steps out onto the patio and scans the various items of clothing on the line. He spots the football kit and starts to unpeg it.

A sound startles him, releasing a glug of adrenalin into his veins. He glances at his watch.

'No,' he murmurs, having heard the bell many times before. It rings twice more and ends. He quickly pulls the rest of the football kit from the line, drops it into the basket, and turns to head back inside.

The bell resumes as the reckoning begins.

He pulls open the sliding patio door as his boys enter the living room, bowls full of cereal. Zac stands mute, rooted to the spot as he silently counts, hoping and praying it's someone else.

The boys bicker with each other, unaware of the saga playing out.

At forty-four peals, the bells cease.

Zac drops the basket of washing onto the floor with a bang. His sons notice his demeanour.

'Dad, are you all right?' Sam asks.

'Not really,' he replies, eyes closed.

The boys place their cereal on the table and edge towards him.

'Dad, what is it?' Tom says, perturbed at his father's drawn features.

'Come here, lads. Give your old dad a hug. He needs one.'

They both embrace him as he drapes his arms around them.

'You're not old, dad,' Tom says.

'I'm older than I should be. I've just aged twenty years.'

26

The Incident Room is silent, apart from a few sniffles. The team, made up of people of all ages, is haggard. Long hours and neglect of one's own needs can do that. But so can death. Bloodshot eyes, chaperoned by grey droopy bags beneath them, stare out in disbelief and incomprehension. Everyone knows... there, but for the grace of God, go I.

Superintendent Anne Banks is at the front of the room, flanked by Frank and Martin Overland. Prisha, who has been granted a temporary security pass, is standing with Zac to the side of the big guns.

Anne Banks is known as a fair officer, if obstinately dour, humourless, and lacking any sort of empathy. Emotion is an unnecessary intruder in her life, and she's made sure all entrances to her inner sanctum are secure... at least until today. Her face is drained of any colour, unless grey can be considered a hue. She fidgets with a sheet of A4 paper as she clears her throat and swallows hard.

'Okay team, I understand how difficult this is on everyone. Before I hand over to Frank, I want you to regain your composure and listen carefully to what I'm about to say. It may seem harsh, even thoughtless, but despite our loss, things still need to happen.' She pauses and takes a sip of water. 'I've spent the last thirty minutes on the phone with the Chief Constable Critchley and prior to that I visited Amanda Cartwright, Jason's wife. The funeral for Jason will be this Friday at 1 pm.'

Gasps and quiet murmurings follow her statement. She raises her hand.

'I know forty-eight hours is short notice, but this decision is out of our control. It's Amanda's wish to expedite the funeral. I assured her we would do everything in our power to ensure a fitting send-off for our fallen colleague. Which means most of my time over the next two days will be preoccupied with the arrangements. For the rest of you, however, you must continue with the investigation with professionalism and dedication and find Jason's killer. Let his death not weary you, nor dull your appetite for justice. Instead. let it galvanise you. I will keep you up to date with the funeral arrangements as they fall into place. All attendees will be expected to be dressed in full uniform for the church service. For the wake, please change out of your uniform if you plan to attend. Frank?' She says, holding out her arm in his direction.

Frank steps forward, head down, trying to keep his fragile emotions in check.

'Ahem, now's not the time for a eulogy so I'll only say a few words,' he says, gazing into the corner where Jason used to sit, invariably with his feet on the desk, reading the sports section of the newspaper. 'Most of you will have worked with Jason in some capacity over the years and grown to appreciate his many foibles. Everyone has their quirks because we are all different. We're human. It's a bloody tough job we do and although our families and partners try to understand what it's like, they can never truly know what we go through. I believe most of the public hold the police in high regard, but there'll always be those who hate us for whatever reason. Coming in to do your job knowing there are people out there who wish you harm is always there in the back of your mind. That's why we stick together, help each other out, watch each other's back. We are a family. I know we rib each other and take the mickey. It's our way of dealing with this shitshow called life. But the next time you notice someone is feeling down, take a moment to lend a friendly ear. Sometimes that's all it takes. And remember, everyone needs a pat on the back every now and again.'

His eyes fall onto the empty chair in the corner, as he swallows hard, then takes a deep breath.

'Right, let's get down to business. The suspect we were holding in custody overnight, Patrick O'Donoghue, has been released without charge.' He notes the raised eyebrows and shakes of the heads. 'However, there's been some fresh developments in the last twenty-four hours, so heads up, chests out. DS Stoker will take this morning's briefing. Over to you, Zac.'

The room is silent as Zac pins two photos to the cork evidence board and attaches post-it notes below them, with two names neatly written out.

He taps at the first photo. 'Daniel Platt, thirty-three years old, a local man. He's five-ten and muscular, with grey-coloured eyes. Apologies for the quality of the photo, but it was lifted from his Facebook page. Platt is a platform operator who works on the rigs in the Middle East. He arrived back from his latest shift last Wednesday but was apparently in London at the time of the shooting on Thursday. His alibi seems to stack up. He is, however, the registered owner of the Subaru WRX involved in the incident. Yesterday, we located the burnt-out wreck of the car in Cock Mill Woods, about three miles from here. Luckily, forensics lifted some fingerprints from the vehicle. We ran it through the database and got a cold hit—we have a match, but no name attached to it. The fingerprint is identical to the one we lifted from a burglary at Stonygarth Hall, a stately home on the outskirts of Middlesbrough. Last April, during an open day, three items were stolen from a glass cabinet. Earlier this morning, I called Mr Platt and asked if he'd come into the station to give his fingerprints. He duly obliged and... his prints don't match the one from the car or the burglary.'

A few groans go up as the team become restless.

He taps at the second photograph. 'This is Wayne Barber. Take a good look at him. Not the bonniest looking bugger you'll ever lay eyes on. The head of a bulldog and the neck of a rhino. Like a failed experiment in genetic modification.'

'Zac!' Superintendent Banks chastises.

'Sorry, Ma'am. Wayne Barber worked as a security guard, mainly as a doorman, for about six months. Black Knight Security, a company based in Leeds, employed him. Black Knight operates like a contractor, their personnel as sub-contractors. In other words, it's a way for them to minimise the red tape and their tax obligations. The sub-contractors submit a monthly invoice and Black Knight pay them. It's then up to the sub-contractor to meet their tax and insurance obligations. I'm sure you're finding all this very interesting, but bear with me. There is no record of Wayne Barber with the Inland Revenue. The taxpayer reference number on his invoices is false, as is his home address. We're dealing with an invisible man, which makes tracking him down very difficult.' He taps at a photo on the board again. 'The security company emailed through his mugshot earlier but remember, it's over two years old. Last night, a bouncer who occasionally worked with Barber gave us some intel. According to him, Wayne Barber is a scary individual. He has a fascination with Hitler and the Third Reich, possibly uses steroids and other drugs and... hates the police. He's another big lad and similar height to the assailant who stole the stamp and drove the Subaru.'

Excited murmuring ripples through the room.

Zac holds his hand up. 'However, he has brown eyes and is American, possibly a New Yorker, whereas the man we're after has distinctive blue eyes and has a northern accent.'

The muted excitement dissipates as quickly as it materialised.

A hand goes up at the back. 'Excuse me, sergeant?' a young, fresh faced police constable says.

'Yes, PC... sorry I forgot you last name?'

'PC Dinkel, from York, sir.'

'Go ahead Dinkel.'

'Is it possible he put on a false accent and changed the colour of his eyes?'

Frank steps forward. 'Yes, it is possible, but is it plausible? We don't want to fall into the trap of manipulating the facts to suit our case. The truth is, Platt is on the *periphery* of our radar, whereas Wayne Barber is a little closer to the centre. We need to find Barber to question him, if only to eliminate him from our enquiries. It's conceivable the killer has not yet entered our airspace.'

'Boss,' PC Pembroke calls out.

'Yes, Kylie?'

'What about the bank where Black Knight deposited Barber's money?'

'Good question. Zac chased that up earlier. A Barclays Bank in Whitby. The account was closed two months ago.' He notes the dispirited faces in front of him. 'On the bright side, we have a decent photo of Barber so that should help us in locating him. Right, I want you lot out and about showing the photo to every man and his dog. I believe Martin will hold another media conference this afternoon?' he adds, looking at Overland.

'That's correct, Frank. I believe this time the coverage will be nationwide.'

Frank does well not to roll his eyes. 'There will be a collection bucket doing the rounds for Jason's wife. Please give generously. And lastly, there's a vigil for the next four days as St Mary's church. The doors will be open from six until ten on an evening if anyone wishes to attend and offer a prayer or just spend a minute of two in contemplation.'

PC Pembroke raises her hand. 'About the man we had in custody... O'Donoghue?'

'What about him?' Frank says.

'Why was he released?'

'I'll let Martin answer that one,' he replies, resisting a smile.

Overland coughs. 'O'Donoghue was released because his alibi checked out.'

'Where was he at the time of the shooting, sir?' PC Pembroke persists, much to Overland's embarrassment.

'He was at a local police station in Warrington, checking in as part of his parole conditions.'

Muted sighs and a definite "fuck me drunk" from the back of the room ripples through the air.

27

Prisha slopes down the steps in a stupor. The normal hustle and bustle of the station is missing. Jason may not have been the brightest copper on the force, but he was well liked for his amenable nature and jokey manner.

She drops her temporary security pass on the counter as the desk sergeant offers her a weary smile.

'Have you heard when you're back on duty, ma'am?' he asks.

Prisha stares at the floor. 'What? Oh, no. Next week sometime. If they clear me of any wrongdoing,' she replies, clearly distracted.

'You'll be right. They're just dotting the I's and crossing the T's.'

'Yes, yes... I know. Just doing their job as everyone keeps reminding me. By the way, what's this vigil thing they're holding at the church? It sounds archaic.'

'Not really. The church doors will be open, and you can go inside and make a small donation and light a candle. That's about it, really.'

'Oh, I see. I imagined a horde of weeping locals holding burning crosses whilst speaking in tongues.'

The desk sergeant does a half-laugh. 'No, at least not anymore. We're quite sophisticated up here in the north.'

'Hmm...'

Walking past the train station, she follows the path along the river until she spots a bench and takes a seat. Numb, confused and feeling nauseous, she wonders what to do to fill her day as the drizzle falls. There are so many places she wanted to visit and explore. Old country estates, historical churches, glorious walks through unspoilt hamlets. Today, none hold any appeal. A seagull diverts her attention as it tries unsuccessfully to pull at discarded fish and chip paper crammed into a bin. Eventually, it prospers, and a handful of chips and scraps fall onto the pavement as the paper blows into the river. Immediately, a swarm of birds descend, fighting and squawking angrily at each other as to who should have the spoils. Scarcity can bring out the most undesirable traits in people, as it does in seagulls, she thinks to herself. Her thoughts drift back to the previous evening in the Grandy pub, the information about the fingerprint and this morning's briefing about Wayne Barber.

'There's only one way out of this funk, Prisha, and that's put your thinking cap on and get back to work. Frank doesn't hold much store with Wayne Barber, but there are some interesting threads. He has a fascination with the Third Reich. The fingerprint from the car matches the fingerprint from Stonygarth Hall where Nazi paraphernalia was stolen. And the shot which killed Jason came from a German made Luger pistol. That's enough clues in my book to warrant further investigation. And who else collects World-War-Two artefacts—Alfred Dunn. I'm no use to anyone lolling around maudlin over events. It's time for action. Two cinnamon donuts and a strong black coffee will get you going.' Almost leaping from her seat, she sets off at a brisk pace along the promenade.

***

Mr Dunn is surprised to see Prisha standing on the step as he opens the door.

'Inspector, we meet again so soon,' he says, removing his horn-rimmed spectacles. There's no immediate invitation to come inside, so Prisha forces the issue.

'May I come in?'

It would go against his upbringing and sense of decency to refuse. 'Yes, of course. I apologise. I forgot my manners for a moment. Tea?'

'No thanks.'

He ushers her into the cosy living room.

They both take comfortable seats opposite each other. 'How can I help?' Dunn asks.

'I'm hoping to pick your brain. When I was here last, you said you collected memorabilia from the Second-World-War.'

'Yes, that's correct. I occasionally hold lectures on the subject.'

'Lectures?'

'Yes. Specifically, the rise of the Nazis, their propaganda machine, and their use of symbolism in their flags and uniforms.'

'And where do you hold these lectures—at the university?'

He chuckles. 'Good heavens, no. The university is too politically correct to allow any mention of the Nazis these days. They would be fearful of being accused of fostering and perpetuating extreme right-wing ideologies. No, I hold my lectures in museums, village halls, libraries or occasionally in private residences.'

Prisha is puzzled. 'People invite you into their homes?'

'When I say private residences, I mean stately homes, country houses.'

Her ears prick up. 'Stately homes?'

'Yes.'

'Have you ever held one of your lectures at Stonygarth Hall, belonging to Lord Ashton?'

He lifts a bushy eyebrow. 'Yes, I have. Lord Ashton and I have been friends... acquaintances, for many years.'

'Do you recall a robbery from last April when several artefacts were stolen?'

'Yes, I do. Most disturbing.'

'Hmm... I see. Sorry, I veered off topic. Where were we?'

'You were asking me about my collection and lectures?'

'That's right. How long do your lectures typically take?'

'I think two hours is a sweet spot, with an intermission for tea and biscuits at the halfway mark. After the lecture, I display some of my collection.'

'Your Nazi artefacts?'

He smiles. 'Not just Nazi memorabilia but also items from the Wehrmacht, the allied and axis forces, Japanese, and Italian objects.' He shifts uneasily. 'Inspector, you said you were here to pick my brain, but you still haven't explained what you want from me. Or am I being obtuse?'

'Sorry. I'll get to the point. How easy or hard is it to come into possession of a Luger pistol from the Second-World-War?'

He ponders the question for a moment. 'They are actually quite rare despite being produced in their millions. Many were lost or destroyed during the conflict and the surviving ones have been scooped up by collectors over the years. I do occasionally see one or two come on the market, but they are few and far between.'

'How much would a Luger typically fetch at an auction?'

'Depends on its condition and if it has provenance, but I've seen some fetch as little as one thousand and others over eight thousand pounds.'

'Have you seen any on the market recently?'

'No. It would be a few years ago since I noticed one, but I don't scour the auction houses every day looking for them.'

'No, of course not. Do you know anyone by the name of Wayne Barber?'

He shakes his head. 'No, I don't.'

'Okay, thanks for your time, Mr Dunn,' she says, rising to her feet.

Dunn is bemused. 'I hope I've been of some assistance, inspector, but I fail to see a connection between the stolen stamp and a Luger pistol. On Monday you said the jeweller who was robbed wasn't harmed,' he says escorting her to the entrance.

'He wasn't, at least not physically. The Luger is to do with a separate incident.'

'Can you elaborate?' he says, pulling open the front door.

'We believe a Luger was the weapon used in the murder of DS Jason Cartwright.' It's the first time she's used the M word, and it shocks her, but not as much as it shocks Mr Dunn.

'Mur... murder?' he stammers,

'Yes. Murder. My colleague passed away this morning.'

28

The Ford Anglia rattles and hums its way towards the small village of Ormsby. Prisha is falling for the little car. It may be noisy, the heater antiquated, and the audio system virtually non-existent apart from one radio station it picks up, but it has a charm she can't resist. By some uncanny knack, she catches the shipping forecast at least once, sometimes twice a day. She hasn't a clue what most of it means, but the strange names enthral her. Viking, Forth, Cromarty, Tyne, Dogger, German Bight, and Fisher have a poetic nuance which makes her giggle... but not today. She turns the radio off as her mobile rings. She lets it go to voicemail as she navigates the car onto a gravel driveway surrounded by a small copse. Rounding a bend, she sees the breath-taking Stonygarth Hall.

'Hell... how much money must you have to live somewhere like this? Inherited from generation to generation, father to first-born son. The upkeep alone would be astronomical.' She brings the car to a halt outside the main entrance and squints at her phone, then presses redial. It's answered immediately.

'Zac, what have you got?' she asks as she exits the vehicle.

'Nothing,' he replies, his voice sounding odd.

'What did you ring me for?' There's silence as she becomes concerned. 'Zac, are you all right? You're not in trouble, are you?'

'No,' his soft Scottish lilt echoes down the phone. 'I just wanted to talk. I'm not coping too well.'

'With Jason's death?'

'Yes.'

'It's tough, Zac, but you can't let it affect you, not yet. We have work to do.'

'Yeah, I know.'

'Can you not speak with Kelly?'

'No. She's asleep. Been on nightshift. And anyway...' he tails off.

'What about Frank?'

'No. He's old school. Bottles everything up.'

'Have a word with HR. They can organise a grief counsellor.'

'I don't want to speak to a stranger who didn't even know him.'

He sounds desperate, Prisha thinks. 'I tell you what, come around to my place about five-thirty. We'll share a beer and have a chat. How does that sound?'

'Aye, that would be good. Thanks Prisha.'

She puts her phone away, her mind distracted from the task at hand.

———

Making herself comfortable, she gazes around the room as the butler closes the door behind him, leaving her alone. Enormous windows offer a magnificent view to a courtyard, in the centre of which stands a large ostentatious fountain. Behind it, well maintained and manicured gardens. Rose bushes, in hibernation, nipped back and barren. In the distance is a large lake. The door clicks open, followed by a squeaking sound. She spins around to see an elderly gentleman in a wheelchair roll towards her, a tartan blanket wrapped around him, slippers on his feet.

'Inspector, please forgive me, but I had to answer the call of nature.' Prisha stands and shakes his hand, hoping he washed them after his visit to the loo. 'I'm afraid this room is now my prison. Living room, dining room and bedroom. Damn MS.'

'Multiple Sclerosis?'

'Yes. Had it a while now, but it's reached the point where it takes me an hour to walk from one end of the room to the other. Hence the wheelchair.'

'I'm sorry,' she says.

'Don't be! I'm fine.' He taps his head. 'As long as this is still working, I'm as happy as a sand boy. Too many damned interests and hobbies, that's my problem, always has been,' he shouts in an energetic, eccentric manner. 'Can I offer you a sherry, inspector...'

'Inspector Kumar. Thanks, but no. I'm on duty. But you feel free.' She glances at the grandfather clock in the corner.

He spins towards the drinks cabinet and pours himself a very generous glass of sherry, then reverses his wheelchair back towards a gently burning log fire. He drops his head. 'I heard the sad news. It came on the wireless. A damn rum affair. May I offer you my utmost condolences. Did you know the officer in question?'

'Yes. He was my colleague. I was with him when he was shot. You also knew him.'

He frowns. 'I did?' he questions.

'Yes. He was the officer who investigated the burglary at Stonygarth.'

'Oh, yes, I remember him now. Amiable sort of chap.' Visibly upset, he turns and gazes out into the garden. 'Because I could not stop for Death, he kindly stopped for me. The carriage held but just ourselves, and immortality,' he whispers. The only sound is the comfort of the crackling fire. 'Emily Dickinson,' he adds as an afterthought.

The words touch something deep inside Prisha as a well of emotion rises. This is exactly what she feared the most... letting emotion rule logic. She swallows hard and composes herself.

'The reason for my visit, Lord Ashton...'

His trance is broken as he takes a sip of sherry. 'As you alluded to on the phone, it's concerning the stolen artefacts from eight months ago. Have you located the missing items?'

'I'm afraid not,' she says, pulling out her notepad and flicking the pages. 'I'm investigating potential leads in the murder of DS Cartwright.'

'Oh.' Lord Ashton's clarity returns.

'DS Cartwright was shot with a Luger pistol. We don't have a lot to go on, so I'm chasing up old information to rule it in or out.'

'I see.'

'I've read the report from DS Cartwright, who visited you after you noticed the missing valuables, but I like to double check things myself. Relevant information has a tendency to get lost in translation. First of all, the date?'

Lord Ashton grimaces. 'I don't remember the exact date. But it was the Spring open day. We have three a year—Spring, Summer, and Autumn. You see, we receive some modest funding each year from the National Trust to keep the place respectable. In return, we open our house and grounds to the public. Apart from all the historical British artefacts... paintings, statues, vases, furniture, I also have a small collection of wartime mementos which has become a draw card amongst aficionados.'

'Which war?'

'The Second-World-War. My father served in the 21st Army Group as a Brigadier under Montgomery.'

'How did your father come across these so-called souvenirs?'

He pauses to choose his words carefully. 'Let's say my father was a collector.'

'Meaning?' Prisha says tersely, back on her game, not allowing his privilege to convolute her thinking.

'Meaning, he salvaged things. From the battlefield, dead soldiers, abandoned buildings. It has existed since the beginning of time. To the victor go the spoils of war.'

Prisha pulls at her earlobe, agitated. She finds the upper class tend to wrap things up in layers of unnecessary complexity. 'Lord Ashton, I don't care about a possible war crime that occurred sixty, seventy years ago. I only care about today. Let's focus on the stolen items. According to the report, the items taken were a Hitler Youth knife, an SS insignia, and a signed copy of Mein Kampf.'

'Correct. If you are unaware, Mein Kampf is the autobio...'

'Yes! I'm well aware of what Mein Kampf is, Lord Ashton! It's the autobiography of Adolf Hitler.'

He persists in that way older, over-educated people tend to do. 'It translates as...'

'My struggle or my fight! And for once in my life, I can sympathise with him!' she snaps back, sick of the condescension.

'Oh dear,' he says with an element of remorse. 'I've offended you. I apologise. It was never my intention.'

She relents, and gazes at the old man, ashamed at losing her composure. He's eighty if he's a day, and suffering from a debilitating disease, but taking it on the chin with energy and good humour, at least outwardly. He knows what awaits. A slow, crippling death. But he gets on with life and busies himself. He has an energy and a spirit, which refuses to be bullied by the disease.

She apologises. 'I'm sorry, Lord Ashton. As you can imagine, it's been a stressful week.'

'I understand, my dear,' he replies quietly as he pushes on the wheels of his chair, rolling towards her. He places a hand on top of Prisha's. 'Continue with your questions and I'll try not to be such an insufferable prig.'

'With the passing of time, has anything else come to light which could throw some light onto the burglary?'

He cogitates carefully. 'No.'

'Can you show me where the items were kept before they were stolen?'

'Certainly, follow me.' He places his sherry on the hearth and heads towards the door at pace, clattering into a small table as he does so. Yanking the door open, he hangs a left and speeds down a long corridor, Prisha in hot pursuit.

'Christ,' she mutters. 'He can certainly motor.'

'Keep up inspector, keep up!'

She breaks into a slow jog as he races away. Halfway down the corridor, he slows until he's adjacent to a long, glass display cabinet. 'This is where they were kept. As you can see, it has a small padlock at the end. Remove that and you have access to the locking mechanism. Once released, the glass panels can be lifted.'

Prisha inspects the tiny padlock. 'Not the best security,' she says, looking behind her at a camera mounted on the back wall. 'What about security footage?'

'It was installed after the theft. Once bitten, twice shy.'

'What would the stolen items be worth?' she says as her attention falls back onto the array of other objects in the cabinet.

'Hard to say.'

'A rough guess.'

'The most valuable item was Hitler's signed copy of Mein Kampf, with a friendly epigram dedicated to the purchaser of the book. Probably ten to fifteen thousand pounds, give or take. The SS insignia and Hitler Youth dagger, possibly three to four thousand pounds.'

Prisha jots down the details. 'And you're absolutely certain nothing else was taken?'

The slamming of a door and the click of heels on the wooden floor halt proceedings. Prisha looks up to see a smartly dressed older woman heading towards them.

'Ah, here's my wife. Mary, dear, let me introduce you to Inspector Kumar from CID.'

The woman smiles at Prisha as they shake hands. 'Pleased to meet you, Lady Ashton.'

'Likewise, inspector. I hope Malcolm hasn't been giving you the run-around. He can ramble on.'

'Not at all. He's been very helpful.'

'The inspector is here regarding the stolen items from the Spring open day,' Lord Ashton explains.

'And the murder of DS Cartwright,' Prisha adds.

A flash of concern shoots across Lady Ashton's face. 'I see. But where does the murder of the poor unfortunate police officer fit in?'

'We believe the murder weapon was a Luger pistol from World-War-Two. We're trying to ascertain how the gunman got his hands on such a weapon.'

Lady Ashton scowls at her husband. 'I knew this would come back to bite us, Malcolm. I think it's about time you came clean.'

The three of them are back inside Lord Ashton's so-called prison, as he pours himself another glass of sherry.

'And no more of that until tonight, Malcolm. It's not even midday,' Lady Ashton chastises, staring disapprovingly at the alcohol. 'He thinks because he has a terminal disease, he can do whatever he wants,' she explains to Prisha as though her husband isn't in the room.

'The Luger?' Prisha prompts, trying to refocus everyone's attention.

'It's like this inspector,' Lord Ashton begins, only to be cut off by his wife.

'I'll explain, Malcolm. Otherwise, we'll be here all day. Yes, there was a Luger pistol in the cabinet, inspector. It was stolen along with the other items.'

Prisha is furious but contains her anger. 'And why did you not report it stolen at the time?'

'Malcolm didn't have it registered.'

'You realise that's an offence? You must register all firearms with the Firearms Licensing Department at your local police station. Failure to do so can result in a five thousand pound fine or six months in prison.'

Malcolm stares sheepishly at his woollen blanket. 'And that's the reason I didn't report it as stolen. I thought I'd be in trouble.'

'And more importantly, you could have saved the police a lot of leg work. We could have been onto this on Monday if you'd originally reported the Luger as stolen.'

'Do you think it was the weapon used in the murder?' Lady Ashton says, gravely concerned.

'Possibly. We believe one of our suspects has a fascination with fascism.'

'Oh dear. What will happen to us?'

Her indignation subsides as she gazes upon the elderly couple. 'I'm not sure. I'll have to discuss it with my superior, but at the moment I have better things to do. I would advise you to conduct an inventory of the entire estate and register any firearms which aren't already registered.'

'Yes, of course, inspector,' Lady Ashton says. 'I'll undertake the task myself today.'

'Good. Lord Ashton, were there any distinguishing marks or features on the Luger that you can remember?'

'Yes. Engraved on the walnut grip was the name Josef Becker. On the barrel were six notches.'

'Notches?'

'Yes. I assume it was a tally of how many people Josef Becker had killed with the pistol.'

'The whole affair is ghastly,' Lady Ashton murmurs. 'The only good thing to come of the theft was that vile book was stolen. I'd have burnt the damned thing if I'd had my way.'

'It's a piece of history, Mary,' Lord Ashton replies.

'It's a piece of disgusting filth written by a maniac!'

'Ahem, Lady Ashton, your husband couldn't remember the exact date of the robbery. The police report states it was Sunday, April 6th. Is there any way for you to confirm the date?'

Lady Ashton beams broadly and leaps from her chair. 'Yes. We keep a guest book to register the number of visitors we've had during an open day,' she explains as she moves to a bookcase and pulls out a battered green book. She quickly flicks through the pages. 'Stonygarth was open to the public on Saturday and Sunday the 5th and 6th of April, respectively.'

'May I take a look?' Lady Ashton hands her the register. 'Hmm... not many visitors. I count fifteen on the Saturday and twenty-two on the Sunday.'

'It was the weather, inspector. It bucketed it down on both days. It was the Easter weekend and come Monday it was blue skies and sunshine. Typical.'

'I'll take a quick photo of the names listed,' Prisha says as she pulls her phone out and carefully fires off a couple of snaps. None of the names jump out at her. 'And how do you know the items were stolen on the Sunday? Could they have been stolen before then?'

'Highly unlikely. My cleaning lady worked all day on Good Friday before the open day and she distinctly remembers cleaning the display cabinet. She said it was definitely locked. It was Malcom who noticed the padlock was missing from the cabinet about five o'clock on Sunday not long after we'd closed our doors.'

'So, it's possible it was broken into on Saturday?'

Lord and Lady Ashton share troubled glances. 'Yes, I suppose so.'

Prisha hands the book back. 'Thank you for your time.'

29

The distinctive soulful voice of Amy Winehouse drifts from the speakers as rain taps at the windowpane.

'Grab yourself a beer from the fridge,' Prisha calls down from her bedroom.

'Are you having one?' Zac shouts back.

'No. I may go for a run later. I'm just getting changed.'

Zac saunters into the kitchen and grabs a Peroni from the fridge, cracks the top and takes a refreshing slug. 'Oh, that's better,' he mutters as his eyes take in the small but clean and tastefully decorated kitchen. He spots a postcard on the fridge door and studies it. He slides away the magnet holding the card to the door and flicks the postcard over. It's violently snatched from his hand as Prisha enters the kitchen.

'Do you mind?' she snaps angrily, flipping the postcard back over and reattaching it to the door.

'Sorry,' Zac says with a mixture of embarrassment and bemusement. 'Where's it from... Argentina?'

'Yes.'

'Family, friend, ex-lover?' he says with a grin.

'A distant aunt,' she lies.

'I see,' he says, as she ushers him from the kitchen into the cosy living room. 'You're not really going running tonight, are you? It's raining.'

'And? If I curtailed my activities because of the rain, I'd never leave the flat. I thought I might jog up to St Mary's and light a candle for Jason.'

'Aye. I suppose I better do the same. But I'll go by car,' he says, dropping onto the settee. 'So how was your day?'

'Busy. I called on Alfred Dunn again and paid a visit to Stonygarth Hall and interviewed Lord and Lady Ashton about the burglary they had last Spring.'

'Naughty, naughty. You're playing with fire,' he says with a smirk. 'Why did you visit Dunn again?'

'To find out how rare Luger pistols are,' she replies, gazing into thin air. 'He gives lectures on the war. He's even held one at Stonygarth Hall and is a buddy of Lord Ashton.'

'So?'

'A connection,' she replies with incredulity at his lack of intuition. 'I found out they omitted one tiny detail about the burglary.'

'What?'

'An unregistered Luger pistol was also stolen. They feared the consequences and kept quiet about it. There's something off about all of them,' she adds as an afterthought, distracted.

'All of whom?'

'Alfred Dunn, Garth Windsor, maybe even Lord Ashton.'

Zac frowns and leans forward, cradling his bottle. 'Prisha, I know you need to keep busy at a time like this. We all do, but...' he trails off.

'But what?'

'It's easy to chase shadows,' he begins gently, sympathetically. 'Don't become side-tracked. I'm pretty certain Alfred Dunn, Lord Ashton, or Garth Windsor didn't shoot Jason. Our main person of interest at the moment is Wayne Barber and even he's a longshot.'

'Yes, I know they didn't shoot Jason,' she snaps. 'And how's the search for Barber going?' Her question is laced with scepticism.

'Not too good. We must have questioned every bodybuilder in the area who has even a slight resemblance to Barber but they all have alibis. And none have an American accent.' He chuckles. 'It's funny, isn't it? One day we're searching for a guy with a Yorkshire accent, the next day one with a New York accent?'

'Hmm...' she muses. 'Anyway, if Barber is the killer, you won't find him with a scattergun approach. He may be a psycho, but it doesn't mean he's stupid.'

'Oh, and I suppose we'll find him by questioning retired professors and Lords of the manor?' he says with disdain. 'Your profiling is all askew, Prisha. Remember the old metaphor—birds of a feather flock together?'

'It's a proverb, not a metaphor.'

'Don't split hairs.'

'And that's an idiom. I'm telling you, Zac, I'm onto something.'

'Okay, have it your way. Have you told Frank all this?'

'Yes. He told me to sit on the info for the moment.'

'Why?'

'Duh,' she says mockingly. 'Because I've been stood down and I can't access the database to enter my report, and even if I could, Banks or Overland may see it. Then they'd know I've been working the case.'

'Oh, yeah. I could enter it under my name?'

'No. Frank said that's too risky. We're walking a tightrope already. No point embroiling anyone else.'

'Suppose. Anyway, there must have been millions of Lugers manufactured. It doesn't mean the one that belonged to Lord Ashton is the murder weapon. And even if it is, it only helps us after we've found it and link it to a suspect. It's probably at the bottom of the North Sea by now.'

'You don't get it! The fingerprint from the car matches the one from Stonygarth Hall. Whoever stole the Luger, also stole the car. Find the man who stole the Luger and we find Jason's killer.'

Zac drops his head into his hands and rubs at his face, exhausted. 'Yes, I *do* get it. We all get it. But it doesn't help. The theft at Stonygarth was eight months ago. You're starting from the wrong end. That trail is long cold. If we couldn't find the culprit eight months ago, then why would we be able to find him now? We have the supermarket footage of our man from six days ago—that's what we should all be focussing on.'

'Okay. Let's drop the subject. You have your ways, I have mine. Anyway, we're not here to talk shop. You sounded distressed when you called earlier. How are you coping?'

He takes a gulp of beer, then rolls the bottle back and forth between his big paws. 'I feel silly being here now. I was a little emotional before. It's like someone has draped a leaden overcoat around my shoulders. Everything is dreich, and not just the weather. I swear to God, Prisha, if I'm the copper to nick Jason's killer, I'm not sure I'll be able to contain myself. I'm not in control of my feelings at the moment. I could end up killing the bastard.'

She leans forward and wraps her hands around his. 'We're all going through similar feelings, Zac. Rage, anger, hatred, guilt, sorrow. Don't fight them. Roll with the punches. They'll pass soon enough.'

'How do you cope?'

She grins. 'I compartmentalise... according to my psychologist.' She points to the left side of her head. 'At this side of my brain is a box with everything to do with Jason inside it.' She moves her finger to the opposite side. 'In this box is my police work. And in this teeny-weeny box around here, at the back, there's my sex life, personal relationships, and my social life.'

He laughs. 'Thanks. I feel better already.' His smile quickly dissipates. 'I had a bet yesterday,' he says, staring at the carpet.

'Oh, Zac! Why? You were doing so well.'

'I followed Cleavage into the bookies.'

She resists a chuckle. 'Go on?'

'I've been trying to catch up with him. He was away for twenty-four hours, out on the boats. Anyway, after unloading the catch, he headed to the betting shop, and I followed him in. I see it now. It is an addiction. I have no control over it. I thought I better act the part, you know, as a punter, otherwise it may look suspicious. That was bullshit. I used it as an excuse to have a bet. I didn't have to. The punters in betting shops are concerned with one thing—the fucking horses they've backed.'

Prisha puffs out her cheeks. 'It's a minor relapse caused by extenuating circumstances. Don't beat yourself up about it. Put it behind you and move on.'

He smiles at her. 'Thanks.'

'Did you win?'

'That's the worst part about it. I put fifty quid on at eight-to-one.'

'Oh, you lost?'

'No. I fucking won. Four hundred quid.'

'Isn't that good?'

'No. It feeds the craving. Winning is like taking a snort of cocaine. I walked down the promenade afterwards and dropped half the money into the lifeboat charity box. The other half I've hidden in a sock in my drawer. I'll take the boys out and treat them. Maybe when this thing is all over. I have to hide it from Kelly. How bad is that?'

'You need to get some time with your wife to discuss your feelings. I know it must be hard with her being on nightshift, but she doesn't work seven days a week.'

'No, but I do at the moment. Anyway, things aren't good between us.'

'Oh, I'm sorry.'

'Don't be. It's my fault. She noticed a text message on my phone the other day.'

'I don't like the sound of this.'

'Last week, when I was on that undercover operation with DS Danny Beale, well, I met a girl at a nightclub in Hull. Lilly's her name.'

'Zac, you dipstick,' she whispers, shaking her head. 'Did you...'

'No. All we did was share a kiss. But I've been texting and calling her a few times a day. She makes me feel good about myself.'

'How old is she?'

'Twenty-three.'

'Bit young, isn't she?'

'Christ, you make me sound like a dirty old man. I'm thirty-three. A ten-year difference isn't that much.'

'Okay, calm down. You don't have to get so defensive. For what it's worth, you're being a dickhead. End it and forget about her. You're married. Think about your boys.'

His expression changes, but he says nothing and quickly finishes his beer, then heads towards the door. 'Thanks for the beer and chat,' he says coldly.

'Zac, stop being a prat! You don't have to get a gob on.'

Her front door slams shut. She pulls it open, but he's already disappeared from view as he skips down the first flight of stairs.

'Well done, Prisha. Subtlety never was your strong point.' She stares down at her running shoes as her stomach grumbles. 'Bugger it. I'll give the run a miss tonight. I'm starving and my mind's a mess.'

30

Prisha is in the kitchen next to the grill, urging it to hurry up. Hunger gnaws at her insides and the waft of toast and the melting Red Leicester cheese only heightens her appetite. The water in the kettle bubbles angrily, emitting a steady geyser of steam from the spout until a click ends the turmoil. She pours water into a cup and drops a tea bag into it.

Her mind is like a congested motorway intersection. The vehicles, her random thoughts. They whiz around, moving onto slip roads, crossing over bridges, disappearing into tunnels from which they never emerge. Everything is a jumbled mess, with no pattern or decipherable intent. Randomness. And yet, she knows within this cauldron of confusion there is an answer, or at least a pathway to an answer. But her blood sugar is low. She's edgy, nervous, agitated.

Pulling the grill tray out, she carefully slides a spatula under the cheese on toast and drops it onto a plate, then takes a seat. Eating calms her. She rocks back and forth, sips her tea, munches on her meal. Clarity slowly sweeps in like a cool breeze after a stinking, hot day. She has an idea.

Grabbing a marker pen and a clutch of A4 sheets from the printer, she sits down at the table in her living room.

'Okay, let's go through this logically, serenely. No flitting from one thing to another.' On each sheet of paper, she jots a name, and underneath, makes a few salient points. After five minutes, she's finished. She pushes her settee back and moves a side table out of the way, clearing a space on the floor. Carefully, she lays out all the sheets on the carpet and stands over them as her eyes slowly move from one sheet to the other.

Garth Windsor – Jeweller
Robbed – Stamp

Alfred Dunn
Collector of WWII Artefacts

Lord Ashton
Collection of WWII artefacts
Luger - Stolen

Wayne Barber – possible suspect
Interest in WWII / Nazis

Daniel Platt – possible suspect
Owner of WRX / ex-army

CLUES
Stolen Stamp
WRX
Unmatched fingerprint (car and Stonygarth)
Luger pistol

Talking to herself, she paces around the sheets, occasionally rearranging them and adding extra notes.

'Windsor and Dunn know each other. Dunn and Lord Ashton know one another. Ashton and Dunn are collectors of World-War-Two collectables. Lord Ashton had a Luger pistol stolen. When I told Dunn the Luger was the murder weapon, what was his reaction? He was shocked. Yet surely, he'd have known Lord Ashton used to have a Luger in his collection and it had been stolen? But he said nothing. Maybe he knows Lord Ashton hadn't reported it as stolen. Maybe he didn't want to drop him in it. Is that why he said nothing? Hmm...'

She makes further notes on the sheets, rearranges them again and adds arrows pointing to other sheets.

'Dunn said Lugers are quite rare, which *could* mean the murder weapon is Lord Ashton's stolen Luger. So, who stole the Luger from Stonygarth Hall, and did they sell it on the black market or keep it for themselves? Dunn's name wasn't in the guest book on the open day. Nor was Barber's. And Lord Ashton never mentioned if Dunn attended the open day. Then again, I never asked him.'

She hovers over the sheet of Daniel Platt.

'And what about you, Mr Platt? Ex-army. It wasn't your fingerprint found in the burnt-out car. Are you an innocent player in all this, or do you know more than you're letting on?'

Her eyes drift across to the next sheet.

'Wayne Barber. Who are you and where are you? You partly match the description of our primary suspect, but your eyes and accent are all wrong. Does that rule you out? Anecdotal witness statements indicate you hate the police and you're a Nazi fanatic and a loose cannon.'

She stares at the top sheet, where it all began.

'Mr Windsor. Are you another innocent victim caught up in this bloody mess or is there more to you than meets the eye? Maybe Zac was right the other night. Outwardly, I've never suspected you of anything untoward, and yet, why was I ambiguous in declaring you innocent? Something must have lodged in my brain, hidden from view, but what?'

The gin sploshes into the glass, followed by a glug of tonic water. She takes a seat and nips at her drink, her mind cogitating over the links.

'Where to now, Prisha?' she murmurs as she picks up the pen and a fresh sheet. 'Tomorrow we pull in Daniel Platt and see if he knows any of the other players in this riddle, or at least see what his reaction is when their names are read out. Then I pay a second visit to Lord Ashton and have another look at his guest book and ask him a few more questions. And Alfred Dunn, what about you? I'll leave you on the backburner for the moment, but something tells me you could be the key to this conundrum. And lastly, Mr Windsor... what is it about you? There's absolutely nothing you've said or done that should make me uneasy... and yet, something is niggling away at me, but I'll be damned if I know what it is.'

She collects all the sheets into a pile, finishes her drink, flicks the lights off and heads to bed, feeling back in control.

31

Thursday 3rd December

Frank struggles to fasten his tunic and decides to leave the top three buttons undone. His trousers are just as bad, if not worse. He gives up on the fly halfway up, afraid if he pulls it up any further, something could pop off. Apart from that, he's feeling rather pleased with his uniform. Admittedly, it's been a while since he was last dressed as an officer. Maybe four, five years ago at the funeral of a former chief constable.

'Meera, come and have a look! Do I pass roll call... and be honest now,' he shouts to Meera in the bathroom. The brushing of teeth hastily ends, followed by running water, a gargle, and a spit. She strolls into the bedroom, wiping a towel across her mouth.

'Sweet merciful Jesus,' she mutters, eyes agog.

Frank smiles. 'Still cut the mustard?' he says, puffing his chest out. 'And I know that look, Meera. You never could resist me when in full honours,' he says, glancing down at his array of medals pinned to his jacket breast. 'Well?'

Unbeknownst to Frank, he's misconstrued abject disbelief for amorous intent. 'Sweet merciful Jesus,' Meera repeats, causing a ripple of consternation in Frank.

'What?' he asks in all innocence.

'Have you actually looked at yourself in the full-length mirror?'

'Not yet,' he says, shuffling past the bed to stare at his reflection.

'Maybe you should.'

His sense of pride, optimism, and sexual ardour is diminishing at a rate of knots.

A mirror can be a cruel mistress.

He witnesses his reflection. 'Holy shit on a hot breadstick!'

'My Sweet Lord. This is going to take some creative thinking,' Meera sighs.

'What happened to my arms and legs? They're getting longer. That's not the way it's supposed to work.'

Meera mystically teleports herself behind him as they both gaze into the unforgiving mirror, both aghast at what they see.

'Sweet merciful Jesus,' she utters for the third time.

'Can you stop saying that?' Frank snaps. 'It's not helping. And why are my limbs growing longer? I'm nearly bloody sixty! They should be shrinking.' He eyes her suspiciously. 'Have you washed this on hot in the washing machine? It's only supposed to be dry cleaned.'

'It was dry cleaned. The only thing growing is your gut, backside, and the amount of fat around your body. It's pushing against the fabric which makes it ride up, shortening the trouser legs, and jacket sleeves. You look like one of those policemen from the old black and white films, you know, the ones that are supposed to be funny.'

'The Keystone Cops?'

'Yes,' she says, failing to suppress a giggle.

Frank is affronted by her snigger, but not nearly as affronted as his own cartoon image in the mirror. 'It's not that bad... is it?' he asks, dropping a huge dollop of hope into the middle of a shit sandwich.

Meera can contain herself no longer and rolls onto the bed, laughing, guffawing, clutching at her ribs.

'Oh, my! What a sight,' she cackles.

Frank is resolute. 'I think I can pull it off,' he mutters, attempting to snatch some credibility back. His words only inflame her humour. His grimace morphs into a wry smile, then a chuckle before he falls onto the bed with his wife and rolls around, crying with laughter.

———◇———

Meera sticks her hand up the inside of the trouser leg. 'Yes, there's a good three inches or more there.'

'I don't like to brag, love, but it's a damn sight longer than three inches. Add another six, possibly seven inches.'

'Dream on, old man. I'm talking about the hem.' Retrieving her hand, she studies the tunic, a harder battle.

'Well?' Frank queries.

'Hmm...' she murmurs. 'There are several pleats that could be let out. I'll call Glenis and see if she can fix it.'

'Glenis?'

'Yes, Glenis. She's retired as a seamstress, but still has her equipment at home.'

Frank flits through the memory cards of the many friends, acquaintances, and colleagues his wife has accrued over the years. 'Is Glenis the one who can talk under wet cement and has the gammy leg?' he asks nervously.

'No. You're thinking of Gladys.'

'Am I?'

'Yes. Now get out of your uniform... gently. Don't pop any buttons. I'm still not sure about the tunic, but you can always wear my girdle.'

'Girdle?' he repeats, as though the word is forbidden.

She shakes her head and stares at him, losing patience fast. 'Yes—girdle. It will pull your gut in.'

'I can't wear a bloody girdle!' he bellows, affronted at the idea.

'Why?'

He struggles to find a reason. 'Because... Well, it would make me, you know...'

'What?'

'One of those sorts of blokes who get off dressing in women's clothing. What if someone saw me in it? My reputation would be in tatters.'

'If you attend the funeral without one, I can guarantee your reputation *will* be in tatters. Now listen up, Frank—three things: one—men wear girdles, the same as women, to pull their ample gut in; two—there's nothing weird or sexual about it, believe you me; and three—who, for God's sake, apart from me, is going to see you in it?'

He shuffles nervously in unchartered territory. 'Aye, fair point, but still... I'd feel... you know...' He tapers off.

'No, I don't. You'd feel what?'

'Feminised,' he whispers, as though someone may overhear.

Meera loses patience. 'Fine. Go in your uniform as it is. But it is supposed to be a solemn occasion. Once you stand up in front of the congregation in that clown outfit to deliver your eulogy, you'll have everyone in stitches.'

He wavers. 'But from getting dressed until the end of the service is about three hours,' he groans.

'Welcome to the female world. You men don't know you're born.'

'Some days I wish I wasn't,' he grumbles as he tentatively disrobes. A rogue thought enters his head as Meera collects his discarded uniform.

It's a thought typically reserved for males.

'So, love, sweetheart,' he begins, naked apart from his baggy Y Fronts. 'Did the uniform stir something in you, wink, wink, nudge, nudge,' he says, pulling in his stomach and buttocks, as well as straightening his back and pushing his crotch out at the same time... a no mean feat for a man nearing sixty.

Meera pauses for a moment, before continuing to fold his uniform. She stands straight and eyeballs him, which doesn't fill him full of good cheer.

'Yes, it did stir something in me.'

'Really?' he replies enthusiastically, once again misreading his wife's enigmatic expression.

'Yes... really. We've both been on the same diet for the last six months. I've lost six kilos, you've gained four. Now,

I'm no super sleuth, but I suspect something is amiss. To whit...'

'To whit?'

'Yes... to whit—despite me packing you off with a nutritious, low-calorie lunch each day, I doubt you are eating it. Instead, I suspect you fill your face full of fish and chips, pork pies, bacon, and egg butties, and donuts. Am I on the money?'

Frank puffs his chest out. 'I'm wounded, Meera, wounded! How dare you say such a...'

'Thank you. I have my answer, Frank,' she replies as she marches out of the bedroom with his uniform.

'Christ! She missed her vocation. She'd have made a better copper than me,' he laments forlornly.

32

Zac bumps his backside into the door, spins around, and enters Frank's temporary office carrying two steaming mugs of tea. He places one in front of Frank and takes a seat.

'I caught up with Prisha last night,' he says.

'Oh, aye,' Frank replies, disinterested as he blows at his tea.

'She told me about the Luger stolen from Lord Ashton's place.'

'Keep that under your hat for the moment.'

'What do you reckon?'

'About the Luger?'

'Yes.'

'If it is the murder weapon, then it's good to know where it came from, but it doesn't help us until we *find* the weapon and *link* it to a suspect.'

'That's exactly what I said! Did she tell you about her suspicions?'

'Yes, she did. She sees a connection between Jason's murder and Alfred Dunn, Garth Windsor and possibly even Lord Ashton,' he replies wearily. 'Although, she didn't elaborate on what the connection was precisely.'

'And?'

'And what?' Frank asks, taking a sip of tea. 'Slap my hairy arse! How many teabags did you use—ten? I could stand a spoon up in that bugger!'

'Just the one. Anyway, what do you think of her suspicions?'

'Not much. We're chasing a muscle man. He's the one who pulled the trigger. Dunn, Windsor, and Lord Ashton are hardly likely to win Mr Universe any time soon. I'm not sure what her game is. It's been tough on everyone, and with her being stood down, I fear she's had too much thinking time.' He pushes back in his seat and attempts a half-hearted stretch, but discontinues the process as pain floods his body.

'You all right there, Frank?' Zac enquires.

'Aye. Never better,' he lies. 'Prisha is a bloody smart lass, but I think she's overcomplicating things. Police work is built on solid foundations. Sift the facts. Interview the suspects. Keep eliminating them until the facts match with your last suspect. Then it's game over red rover. It's not rocket science, but it does require patience and diligence.'

'Aye. We're singing from the same hymn book, Frank.'

'She'll be better once she's back on the team, and a little birdy tells me that won't be too far away.'

'She's been cleared of any wrongdoing by the IOPC?'

'It's not official yet. So, keep schtum.'

Their conversation is interrupted by shrill bleeps. Frank answers the phone. 'Finnegan... yes, right, good. Zac will be down in a moment.' He hangs up and stares at Zac. 'Duty solicitor has arrived. He's in the interview room with Daniel Platt. The desk sergeant is going through all the preamble. Should be done in five minutes.'

Zac sips his tea and grimaces. 'Good. How do you want me to handle Platt?'

Frank considers the question. 'Out of all the people of interest, Platt appears to be the most innocuous. I don't believe he stole the stamp or murdered Jason. But does he know who did? I want him ruled in, or preferably, ruled out. We need to start eliminating suspects. It's time we unravelled some knots. Go hard but mix it up. Don't give him time to think. Let's see how he reacts. I'll watch on the monitor. See if I can pick up any telltale tics.'

'What's Prisha's thoughts on Platt?' Zac asks, rising from his chair and picking up a folder.

'She's on the same page as us. She doesn't think he's directly involved, but maybe he's protecting somebody.'

Zac pulls at the door. 'Right, I'm away.'

'Hey, Zac,' Frank calls out.

'What?' he says, half turning.

'How are you coping with it all?'

'Oh, yeah. I've had better weeks but haven't we all?'

'How are things on the home front?'

He shrugs. 'Meh.'

'I see. Good luck, Zac... with everything.'

'Cheers, Frank.'

Zac strides into the sterile interview room. Sitting behind the table is Daniel Platt and the duty solicitor, a morose looking individual with wild eyebrows which would be a serious hazard to life and limb during a grass fire.

Zac drops his folder on the desk and takes a seat.

'Thanks for coming in to see us,' Zac says in a cheery tone accompanied with a smile, belying his inner turmoil.

Platt folds his arms defensively, clearly irritated at the imposition. 'Look, what's all this about? I came in yesterday to give my fingerprints and now you've called me back again.' He glances at the solicitor. 'And why do I need a solicitor? I told your desk sergeant I didn't want a solicitor, but he advised me I should have one. I've got nothing to hide. All I know is, my car was stolen, and was involved in some sort of robbery of which I know nothing about.'

Zac holds his hand up, trying to halt the verbosity of Platt. 'Mr Platt, Daniel, these things work best if I ask the questions and you answer them. That way, we can get through the process a lot quicker.'

Platt throws a sideways glance at his brief, who responds with a slight nod of the head. 'All right. Get on with it.'

Zac pulls a portrait photo of Wayne Barber from the folder. 'Do you know this man?' he asks.

Platt studies the photo, briefly. 'No, I don't. Should I?' he replies with an element of truculence.

'Take your time and have another look.'

Platt picks the photo up and considers it more carefully. 'No. Never set eyes on him.'

Zac removes the second photo, the one obtained from the supermarket CCTV footage.

'And what about this man?' he enquires.

Platt shakes his head. 'How the hell would I know? His face is covered, and he's wearing a hat.'

Zac runs his tongue over his front teeth and relaxes back in his seat. 'Do you know a Wayne Barber?'

Platt waggles his cheeks from side to side. 'No. Never heard the name before.'

'Are you certain?'

'Positive.'

'You said you work out in the gym when you're working on the rigs in the Middle East.'

'Aye. What of it?'

'What about when you're at home? Do you have gym membership?'

'No. I have a small gym set up in my garage. That way I can work out whenever the mood takes me.'

'So, if I were to pay a visit to your house, I'd find a gym inside the garage?'

Platt is puzzled. 'Yes, you would.'

Zac sniffs and leans forwards. 'Do you collect stamps, Daniel?'

His face scrunches. 'Stamps?' he quizzes as though he's been asked the most incomprehensible question in the world.

'Yes, postage stamps.'

'No, I don't collect bloody stamps.' He pauses. 'I mean, when I was a kid, I may have dabbled in it for a year or so, but no, I don't collect stamps.'

'Have you heard of the Two Penny Blue, Daniel?'

Another shake of the head. 'I've heard of the Penny Black,' he offers.

'What about a Mr Windsor, Garth Windsor, a jeweller from Middlesbrough?'

'What about him?'

'Do you know him?'

'No.'

'Certain?'

'Yes, certain.'

'What about Alfred Dunn, an ex-professor from Durham University?'

'Nah, not heard of him either. Are you going to tell me what all this is about? You're deliberately keeping me in the dark.'

'It's concerning an ongoing investigation. Last Thursday, a jeweller was robbed in Middlesbrough. A very rare and expensive stamp was stolen. A Two Penny Blue. The robber made off in a Subaru WRX, your Subaru WRX.'

'Oh, I see. As I proved at our first meeting, I arrived in London last Wednesday and was there for a few days.'

'You have hotel receipts, and your passport to prove you were in London, but that doesn't mean you couldn't have travelled back and forth to anywhere in the country.'

'What's going on here?' Platt barks, perturbed at proceedings. 'You don't seriously believe I made a trip to bleeding Middlesbrough to pinch a stamp I didn't know existed from a jeweller I've never heard of, do you?'

Zac doesn't answer. 'After the robber made off with the stamp, he travelled from Middlesbrough towards Whitby along the A171. The car was reported as travelling erratically. It was spotted by an unmarked police car containing two plain clothes officers. A short time later, your vehicle was seen on the forecourt of a petrol station. The officers pulled in behind the car to speak with the driver.' Zac stops and swallows hard, barely able to say the next sentence. A few seconds pass.

Platt shuffles in his seat, shoots another glance at his solicitor, worried. 'I don't like the sound of this. I'm not stupid. I watch the news.'

'One of the plain clothes officers exited the car and walked towards your vehicle. He was shot in the chest by the driver, who then took off. That officer was my colleague, DS Jason Cartwright, who sadly passed away yesterday. This has gone from a robbery investigation to a murder investigation.'

Platt raises his hands in defence, alarmed. 'Woah! Hang on a minute, you're not seriously saying I had anything to do with it, are you? I'm sorry for your loss, for his poor wife, for him... but I'm telling you, on my mother's life, I wasn't involved.'

'Do you know who was?'

'No! of course I bloody don't. If I did, I'd have told you, wouldn't I?'

'Would you?'

'Yes, of course.'

'You could be covering for a mate or a relative?'

'Don't talk daft. I'm ex-army. I know right from wrong.'

Zac stares at him, unflinching, buying time as he tries to contain his emotion and let his pulse descend a little. 'Ah, yes... ex-army. Do you know Lord Ashton from Stonygarth Hall?'

Platt is now bewildered by the line of questioning. 'I've heard of Stonygarth Hall. It's an old stately home up the road, but I've never been. And I've never heard of Lord Ashton. I'm an oil and gas operator, sergeant. I don't mix in those circles—Lords and retired professors.'

'Have you heard of the Luger pistol?'

'Yeah, of course I have.'

'Do you own one or have access to one?'

'No.'

'What about hobbies?'

'Pardon?'

'You work two on two off. That's six months of the year when you're at home. You live alone. That's a lot of time to fill. You must have hobbies, outside interests.'

Platt's arms grip around his chest even harder. 'I spend time with my lad. We sometimes go to the footy together. I work out, read a lot of fiction. There's always something good on the TV. I don't know. It's never been a problem for me, filling my time. There's always something to do.'

'What about collectables?'

'No, I don't collect anything.'

'Do you have an interest in the Second-World-War? Nazis, fascism?'

'Christ, what are you driving at?'

'Just answer the question, Daniel.'

'I like to watch a good war film as much as the next bloke, but no, I'm not obsessed or anything.'

Zac fixes him with a mean glare for a good ten seconds as Platt squirms in his seat. 'To recap. You've never met or heard of the following people: Alfred Dunn, Lord Ashton, Wayne Barber, or Garth Windsor?'

'No.'

Zac taps at the mug shot of Wayne Barber. 'And you've never seen or met this man?'

'Not to the best of my knowledge.'

'You've changed your answer.'

'What? No, I haven't.'

'When I first showed you the photo, you were emphatic you'd never seen or met him. Now, there's an element of doubt—not to my knowledge—you just said. That's what politicians say when they know they're deep in the shit.'

Platt has a bead of sweat on his brow, even though the room is cool. 'It's a phrase, a slip of the tongue. I mean, who knows? I could have been standing next to him at a footy game, or in the supermarket checkout line, or leaning against the bar in a pub. What I meant was, I don't recognise his face, have never spoken with him, and don't know who the hell he is.'

Zac studies him silently for a moment. 'That will conclude the interview with Mr Platt.' He speaks towards the video camera, recording proceedings. Collecting the photos from the table, he slips them into the manilla folder, pushes his seat back, and rises. 'Thank you for your time, Daniel. You're free to go.'

Platt has the face of a man who has just been slapped across the head with a wet fish. 'Free to go? You're not charging me with anything?'

'No. Should I be?'

Platt jumps from his seat as he senses freedom. 'No, of course not. Will you want to see me again?'

Zac shrugs. 'Hard to say. But probably not.'

'You mean I'm in the clear?'

'You're not doing yourself any favours here, Daniel. I said you were free to leave. I suggest you act upon that before I change my mind.'

Platt quickly grabs his coat as his solicitor places a hand on Platt's arm. 'I think we should have a debrief,' he whispers.

'Yes, of course.'

———◇———

Zac slumps into his chair and throws the folder onto Frank's desk.

'Pick anything up on the monitor?' he asks.

Frank jabs his fork into the pot noddle and twists. 'Only the usual. Defensive posture, irritation mixed with trepidation. Perfectly normal reactions for innocent individuals to convey when under suspicion. But you did well. Gave him a good working over. Nice touch at the end about the politicians.' Frank drops the noodles into his mouth and winces. 'Ow! That's bloody hot.'

'I take it Platt has been eliminated from our enquiries?'

'Aye. Cross him off the list. One less bugger to worry about.'

33

The wind buffets leafless trees as the ubiquitous grey clouds swirl silently overhead. A few spots of rain splatter onto the leadlight windowpanes. The fire in the hearth intermittently spits and hisses. Prisha is lost in a trance for a moment, experiencing a welcome sense of peace. Her reverie is abruptly interrupted as the door creaks open and the familiar click of Lady Ashton's heels stab across the wooden floorboards.

'My apologies for keeping you waiting, Inspector Kumar. My husband will be with you shortly. I'm afraid he had rather a fitful night's sleep.'

Prisha rises and casts an eye over the double bed in the corner of the room and the tangle of sheets and blankets.

'I'm sorry to hear that. It can't be easy with his disability.'

Lady Ashton plonks herself down on a threadbare ancient high-backed seat and rests her hands in her lap. 'It wasn't his MS,' she replies as Prisha resumes her seat. 'He's been worried sick about the pistol. We both have. Did you speak with your superior about the oversight?'

'Yes, I did.'

'And what is to be your course of action?' she asks, her face creased with anxiety.

'We can't just sweep it under the carpet. It's a serious offence.'

Lady Ashton wrings her hands together and turns a ghostly shade of pale. 'No, of course not.'

'The so-called oversight needs to be recorded, noted.'

'Indeed. Due diligence must be followed. Will either of us go to prison?'

Prisha smiles warmly. 'No. You may receive a small fine and warning letter in the post, but that's all. There will be no charges. But let it be a salutary lesson to you.'

Lady Ashton's bosom noticeably lifts as she sucks in air. 'I can't tell you what a relief that is to hear, inspector. It's a weight off my shoulders. I completed the inventory of the house yesterday and the only other firearms we have are five ancient, rusty muskets, some dating from the civil war. They were attached to various walls as decorations, but I've taken them all down and locked them in a spare room. They're all... what's the word when they can't be fired anymore?'

'Blanked?'

'Yes, blanked off. I'm not sure what to do with them.'

'I think the best course of action would be to pay a visit to your local police station. Explain the situation and they will send an officer out to advise you. That way you cover yourself.'

'Yes. Yes, indeed. That's what I'll do today. The only other guns are owned by our gamekeeper. He has two shotguns, and they are both registered to him. He showed me the firearm certificates.'

'Good. All sorted then.'

The squeak of rubber on polished floorboards announces the arrival of Lord Ashton. If he was a bubble of eccentric energy yesterday, today he's the picture of death warmed up. He wheels into the room, slowly, with much effort.

'Maxwell, some good news. The police are not going to press charges regarding the pistol. We may receive a small fine and a warning letter, but that's all.'

He clasps his hands to his mouth as Prisha suffers a heavy pang of guilt. Maybe she overdid it yesterday with the warning. She's caused them a lot of unnecessary anguish.

'Thank heavens for that. Mary, if you don't mind,' he says, nodding at the decanter of sherry on the table.

Lady Ashton purses her lips in mock disapproval but performs her wifely duties and pours him a half glass of sherry.

'Well, inspector, is that all?' Lady Ashton prompts.

'No. I had two reasons for my visit today and now we have the first one cleared up, I'll move on to the second. Lord Ashton, I believe you know Alfred Dunn, a retired professor?'

Lord Ashton pulls his head back, eyebrows raised. 'Yes, I know Alfred. Known him for many a year. Grand chap. Why do you ask?'

'On the open day, back in April, do you know if he visited Stonygarth?'

His brow furrows. 'No, not to my knowledge. Mary, fetch the guest book. If he visited, then I didn't see him, but he definitely would have signed in. He knows the National Trust check how many people we get through the doors, and he's a bit of a stickler for protocol.'

Lady Ashton retrieves the battered guest book and flicks through the pages before donning spectacles.

'No. I can't see his name for Saturday or Sunday,' she says, studying the list of names.

Prisha already knows his name is not on the list for the Spring Bank Holiday weekend.

'May I?' she says, holding her hand out.

Lady Ashton passes her the book. 'Of course.'

She quickly flicks back to the previous year. Her finger rests on a heading. 'I see last year, on the August Bank Holiday open day, you had a lot of people through the door.'

Lord Ashton appears vague, but Lady Ashton is on the money. 'Yes. It was a gloriously sunny weekend. It was our best open day for many a year.'

Prisha continues tracing the names that signed in over the weekend. 'Lord Ashton, how long have you had your war memorabilia on display? Has it been there forever and a day?'

'No, it hasn't. I used to keep it under lock and key. It was actually Alfred who suggested I should put it on display.'

'Mr Dunn?'

'Yes.'

'Can you remember when he first made the suggestion?'

'Not long before August Bank Holiday, last year. I like to think it was my collection which increased visitor numbers, but alas, I believe my wife is correct and it was down to the lovely weather we had.'

Prisha's index finger hovers over a name as another piece of the jigsaw slides into place. She pulls out her phone and taps at the camera icon, then takes a snap of the four pages of names scrawled across the pages. She hands the book back to Lady Ashton and gets to her feet.

'Thank you for your time, Lord, and Lady Ashton. I can see myself out.'

34

Friday 4th December

A funeral cortege of black cars snakes its way along Abbey Lane, both sides lined by the public, heads bowed. As it nears the access road to Whitby Abbey car park, it slows to a halt. Two mounted police gently guide their horses out onto the lane and bear left. Frank, Zac, and Prisha move forward, poised, and polished in their uniforms. Behind them, Superintendent Banks, Detective Deputy Chief Constable Martin Overland, and the top man himself, Chief Constable Critchley, follow.

The car behind the hearse, carrying the widow, starts, then abruptly stops. Amanda Cartwright throws the door open and exits. Dressed in the required black, her face devoid of colour, she addresses Prisha.

'If you don't mind, I'd like you to accompany me in the car,' she states, emotionless.

Prisha, concerned, shoots a sideways glance at Frank. He nods. Feeling extremely uncomfortable, she follows Amanda into the vehicle.

The procession continues to the sound of seagulls, wind, the sea, and the clip-clop of the two horses ahead... and the bells tolling their misery.

Prisha sits with head bowed. She tentatively reaches out to touch this stranger's hand. The gesture is not appreciated as Amanda Cartwright pulls her arm sharply away.

'I blame you,' she states coldly, staring dead ahead.

Prisha doesn't reply.

'I've seen and read everything. It was you who spotted the car at the petrol station and suggested you make an arrest. It was you who stayed in the safety of your car as my Jason went to investigate.'

Prisha's head drops further. 'True.'

She sighs. 'It won't last... the blame. I know you were only doing your job, but at this moment in time, I hate you.'

The cortege passes the old abbey, rounds the corner, and comes to a halt, greeted by six pallbearers, the members of Jason's darts team. The public turnout is huge and subdued.

As if the occasion wasn't sombre enough, the bell continues to toll, creating a Dickensian atmosphere. Prisha suppresses the urge to throw the door open and run.

'I won't cry. I can't cry,' Amanda says as the driver pulls open the door. 'It will come in a day or two. But not today.'

Prisha exits the car and stares at the column of police officers behind. She feels small, vulnerable, weak.

Frank is standing at the front of the church. His massive hands grip the lectern as he nears the end of his eulogy. Swallowing hard to quell the emotion, he continues.

'I won't lie. That's not the man I am. Was Jason the greatest police detective I've come across? No. Was he the most punctual, practical, a stickler for diligence? No.'

There's nervous shuffling in the church.

'But he was a good man who doted on his wife. He was a man who didn't carry the world on his shoulders, and always looked forward to the weekend, his darts, his football, a quiet pint or two. He relished the simple joys with a guileless innocence I envied. My officers are like my children. There are the high achievers, the dependable tryers, and... the mischievous ones. Jason was my naughty child. And what parent doesn't have a soft spot in their heart for the naughty kid? I said he was a good man, and he was. A simple platitude. But stop for a moment and think about the word, *good*. It's used with such abandon it's almost lost its meaning, but what does it really signify?'

He pauses as the packed church listens on in silence. 'No malice, no ill-will, no resentment, no artifice. Jason was a *good* man. Let's remember him, not in the way he fell, but as a bright, cheery friend who cut his own path. Our work, our profession, does not define who we are: we are born who we are with all our faults, our flaws, and our glorious individual qualities. Jason was a man who relished life. I'll miss him terribly.' He finishes with a tremor in his deep baritone. Walking down the steps, he quickly wipes the wetness from the corner of his eyes and takes his pew at the side of Meera.

A morbid hush hangs over the congregation as the pall bearers take up their position. A young choirboy makes his way to the front of the church and stands between pulpit and lectern, the rest of the choir behind him. Unaccompanied, he begins the opening verse of Tears in Heaven. The gathered mourners rise to their feet as the cherubic voice echoes around the nave. Frank staggers as Meera reaches out to steady him. She takes his hand in hers and squeezes it as tears roll down his ruddy jowls. His shoulders heave. Zac shoots him a sideways glance, then drapes an arm around Tom, pulling him in tight to his side. Prisha stares at the cold flagstone floor, unable or unwilling to bear witness. The rest of the choir joins in as the pall bearers lift the coffin and shuffle down the aisle towards the waiting hearse.

No one notices a muscle-bound man hunched in the corner wearing a puffer jacket and a woollen hat pulled low over his forehead.

35

Dunsley Hall Country House is a ten-minute drive from Whitby. Nestled in a tranquil hamlet, it's set on four majestic acres, with landscaped gardens. The early nineteenth-century mansion house is more accustomed to accommodating weddings, christenings, or shooting parties. Today, it hosts the wake for a fallen police officer.

When the mourners first arrive, the atmosphere is subdued, respectful. An hour later, and with the aid of copious amounts of free alcohol, the ambience is jovial with occasional outbursts of laughter.

Prisha is alone in a corner of the function room, overly aware of herself, anxious. She barely knows anyone, having only been in the area for a few months. Little circles and cliques have formed between long-time colleagues, friends. She nurses a gin and tonic, which she's barely touched. After the church service, Amanda Cartwright asked if she would accompany her to the crematorium. Prisha assumed it was some sort of macabre punishment for her perceived part in Jason's death. The harrowing experience has left her exhausted, and all she craves is a long walk along the coast and then to get snuggled up in her cosy flat with a good book.

'Ah, Prisha,'

She turns to acknowledge Chief Constable Critchley and Superintendent Banks as they approach.

'Sir, ma'am,' she says, nodding deferentially.

'No need to stand on ceremony. We're all off duty. Call me Gordon.' She smiles but doesn't reply. 'Apart from earlier today, I believe this is the first time we've met. Anne was telling me about the excellent work you and Jason did up in the Dales, the double murder of the elderly hikers?'

'Yes, sir... Gordon. It was a team effort. Jason was invaluable. I couldn't have done it without him.'

'And how are you coping with it all?'

She assumes he means Jason's death. 'It's painful, but I'm okay. To be honest with you, I need to be back at the coal face. I've been off work for a week now, and it's driving me insane. I feel useless, superfluous to requirements.'

Critchley and Banks exchange looks. 'I have some good news for you on that front, but keep it under your hat until tomorrow. I've heard a whisper the IOPC have completed their investigation and their report should be with us first thing tomorrow.'

'And?' she probes.

'You've been exonerated of any wrongdoing,' he adds.

Prisha expels a long breath of air. 'Does that mean I can return to work tomorrow?' she says, eyeballing Anne Banks.

Anne offers her a very rare smile. 'Yes. Back on duty first thing and you'll be re-joining the investigation.'

'Oh, thank God!'

'And I have some other good news,' she says, lowering her voice. 'Considering what's recently happened, and in concert with your recent good work, I've revisited my original decision about your promotion.'

'Yes?' she replies, desperately trying to quell her enthusiasm.

'I've consulted with Gordon and Frank, and you won't be returning to your position as sergeant.'

'You mean I'm staying on as acting inspector?'

Critchley chuckles. 'No. There's no acting about it, Prisha. You are to be promoted to inspector.'

'Give me a few days to finalise the paperwork, then I'll make the announcement,' Anne says. 'Of course, you'll be on probation for twelve months and there will be quarterly performance reviews, but that's standard for any promotion.'

'I want to scream with excitement,' Prisha says, sporting a wide beam.

'Probably not a good idea considering our present surroundings,' Critchley says, holding his hand out.

Prisha shakes it enthusiastically. 'Thank you, Gordon. Thank you, Anne. This is such a massive weight off my shoulders. You don't know what it means to me.'

He turns to Anne 'Right, well we best pay our respects to Amanda Cartwright then head back to York.'

Prisha gulps her drink down as she gazes at the pair as they make their way over to the grieving widow. Her eyes fall onto the two women behind her—Kelly, Zac's wife, and Meera, who are both slipping into their winter coats. At the bar, she orders a fresh gin and tonic and gazes around the room, feeling a mixture of exuberance and guilt for feeling exuberant. She spots Frank and Zac acting suspiciously in the garden. They appear to be keeping out of view behind a water fountain.

'What are those two up to?' she murmurs, heading towards the French doors. She creeps around the fountain and jumps out on them. 'Caught you!'

It soon becomes obvious as they both hurriedly pull cigarettes from their mouths.

'Sweet bejeezus!' Frank exclaims, 'Don't you know I have a dicky heart?'

'You bloody idiot!' Zac snaps.

Prisha cracks up laughing. 'How old are you two? Skulking here like two naughty schoolboys behind the bike sheds. I thought you'd given them up, Frank? And Zac, I didn't realise you smoked?'

'I don't. I gave them away about ten years ago.'

'Looks like it.'

'Simply de-stressing,' Frank explains, taking a hefty draw on his smoke. 'I don't want Meera catching me, otherwise she'll have my guts for garters.'

'Aye, likewise, Kelly,' Zac adds.

Prisha grins. 'I suggest you get rid of your ciggies pretty quickly because I saw Meera and Kelly preparing to leave.'

They both instantly flick their smokes into a garden bed.

'Hell fire,' Frank groans.

Prisha looks over to the function room. 'And here they come now.'

The miscreants down their shots of whisky and swill the contents around their mouths as their wives approach.

'What are you doing out here?' Kelly asks Zac. 'It's freezing.'

'Erm... just getting a bit of fresh air.'

She eyes him suspiciously. 'Hmm... I'm heading home now. Meera's giving me a lift.'

'What? Already?' Zac quizzes.

'My shift starts in two hours, and I have to make the boys their tea, and the babysitter's arriving at six. I know you need to let your hair down, Zac, but don't get hammered. Don't roll in at midnight, sozzled.'

'And the same goes for you, Frank,' Meera adds, staring at her husband disapprovingly.

'Of course not, Meera. Just a few quiet ones to farewell an old colleague, then I'll be home.'

She leans in and pecks him on the cheek. 'I believe you. Thousands wouldn't.'

Zac makes a move to give Kelly a kiss goodbye, but she deliberately dodges the move. It does not go unnoticed by all present. The trio watch on in silence until the two women disappear around a corner heading towards the car park.

'Right, Sergeant Stoker, I believe it's your shout?' Frank states.

'Same again?'

'Aye, but make it a double,' he says, pulling his cigarettes from his pocket.

'Prisha?' Zac asks, nodding at her glass.

'Go on then. One for the road. Gin and tonic, please.'

'You leaving so soon as well?' Frank asks as he sparks up his smoke.

'Yes. I want a clear head for tomorrow.'

'Oh, I see. You've been speaking with the chief constable and superintendent.'

'Yes.'

He offers her a warm smile. 'Congratulations, Prisha. I'm made up for you. I really am.'

'Thanks.'

He puffs smoke out into the chilly air and takes in his surroundings. 'Funny things... wakes.'

'What do you mean?'

'They're a relief valve and also a line in the sand. The beginning of the end of misery, and the resumption of normal play.'

'For some.' Prisha murmurs as she glances inside at Amanda Cartwright, who is making her way from the function room escorted by the chief constable and superintendent.

'Damn,' Frank says discarding another cigarette into the garden.

───────

Frank and his superiors are in muted discussion as Prisha walks with Amanda towards the car park.

'I'm sorry about earlier, in the hearse,' Amanda says wistfully. 'I have so much anger inside and I needed to take it out on someone.'

'I understand.'

'And I apologise for what happened at the crematorium. I don't know what came over me.'

'Forget it. Stress takes its toll on everyone.'

She offers Prisha a wistful smile. 'I'm relieved the funeral is out of the way. That's why it was hurriedly arranged. I can grieve now, for a while, then get on with life. Does that sound heartless?'

'No. What are we supposed to do when a loved one dies? We can live the rest of our lives in sorrow or move on. Gone but never forgotten. And you have your baby to think about.'

Amanda stops and rubs her belly. 'Yes. It's the only thing keeping me going, to be honest. It's a girl. I found out last Thursday, the day Jason...' She pauses, unable to say the words. 'It was going to be a surprise as he walked through the door. Now he'll never know.'

Prisha thinks for a moment. Sometimes a white lie can be helpful. 'I think he knew.'

'Really?'

'Yes. We were talking in the car on the way back from Settle. He was mentioning baby names. He was convinced it would be a girl.'

'You're making it up,' Amanda says, doubtfully.

'Honest to God, it's the truth. He said you liked the name Petra. He scoffed and said it was a dog's name. I told him it was Greek and meant rock. Someone who is unshakeable, resilient, strong. I said I liked it and Jason repeated Petra Cartwright, three times mulling it over.'

Amanda gazes out at the rolling countryside and the sea in the distance. 'You saw more of him in the last two weeks than I did. Maybe in a few days you could call around and have a coffee and we can talk about him?'

The very thought gives Prisha palpitations. 'Yes, of course. I'd like that.'

Frank, Prisha, and Zac watch on as the car departs, containing the chief constable, superintendent, and Amanda.

'That's a nice touch,' Zac says. 'The chief constable taking her home.'

'Aye. I dare say he's perpetually snowed under, but he's given up a full day to pay his respects. Those things don't go unnoticed by the rank and file.'

Prisha finishes her drink and hands the empty glass to Zac. 'Time for me to leave, as well.'

'How are you getting home?' Frank asks.

She smiles at him. 'As you would say, Frank—shanks' pony. I'm walking along the coastline.'

Frank stares up at the overhanging, angry clouds. 'You must be bloody mad. Rather you than me.'

'I'll see you both tomorrow. Nice and early. Don't drink too much. You need clear heads,' she calls back.

'Christ! She's as bad as the missus,' Frank mutters in mock disgust.

As she walks the coastal path towards Whitby, bittersweet emotions, and a mild sense of euphoria swirl around her mind.

———⚬———

Frank and Zac loiter with intent near the fountain, retelling funny anecdotes about Jason as they chain smoke and sip on whisky after whisky. Frank doubles over in a coughing fit. As he regains his composure, he looks up and spots a familiar figure heading his way.

'Ah, Bennett, good to see you could make it,' he says, surveying the colossal frame of Doctor Bennett Whipple, the resident pathologist.

Bennett eyes him wearily. 'Considering we are not currently occupied in our respective, official, working capacities, I acquiesce it is permissible to address one another informally... Frank.' He bears a pained expression, as if passing a very large gallstone, as he says the name, Frank. 'I found it duty bound to pay my respects and offer my condolences to the widow, not that she knows me from a stick of celery.'

'No, but all the same, I'm sure it's appreciated.'

Bennett Whipple stiffens. 'It is impossible for you to deduce whether or not my commiserations were esteemed. Only the receiver of such sympathies would be in a position to offer a conclusive perspective on the matter.'

Frank and Zac exchange a quick roll of the eyes as Whipple stares into the middle distance as if in a trance.

Frank takes up the cudgel of required banality. 'Aye, well, nevertheless,' he says, hoping the good Doctor will sod off immediately. Unfortunately, he doesn't.

'As you know, Detec... ahem, Frank, I deal with death on a daily basis. I would never consider myself a friend of DS Jason Cartwright, but I had cooperated with him in a professional capacity frequently due to the inordinate amount of deaths that regularly occur within the vicinity of your domain,' Whipple continues, eyeing Frank disapprovingly as though he were personally responsible for the deaths. 'However, performing an autopsy on a professional associate brings with it a range of emotions I have not encountered before whilst dissecting a cadaver.'

Frank is suddenly perturbed. 'Bennett, I hope you didn't discuss the autopsy with Mrs Cartwright?'

Whipple is incensed at the suggestion and momentarily forgets the informality of the situation. 'Detective Chief Inspector Finnegan, may I remind you of my exemplary due diligence! Medical ethics prevents me from any interlocution of autopsy conclusions with any person unless they are involved with the deceased in a qualified capacity. Of course, I didn't discuss the dissection with Mrs Cartwright. As far as I'm aware, she has no knowledge of who performed the post-mortem.'

Frank breathes a sigh of relief. 'That's good to hear.'

Zac finishes his whisky and grabs Frank's empty glass. 'Another?'

'Aye, go on then,' he replies.

'Bennett?' Zac asks, waggling a shot glass under his nose, already knowing the answer.

Bennett sniffs judgementally. 'I've made my position on alcohol known on many occasions before. It will lead you down the road to ruination, depravity and ultimately a miserable death. But your offer was noted, sergeant.'

'Is that a, no?' Zac asks.

Bennett's nostrils flare. 'Indeed, it was a no, sergeant! Now, I must bid you my farewell salutations. I believe Mrs Whipple has a ham shank waiting for me upon my return.'

'Lucky for some,' Frank says, shooting Zac a quick wink.

'Aye, it's been a long time since I had a ham shank from the missus,' Zac adds.

Bennett's eyes narrow as he tries to fathom if there was a hidden meaning behind the words. Despite his exceptional IQ, mental abilities, and digital dexterity with a scalpel, he has not mastered the cryptic language of crude British innuendo. Moments elapse until he's convinced there was nothing untoward in their replies.

'Indeed,' he finally says as Frank and Zac maintain deadpan expressions. 'I consider myself a master of the English language, but alas, the only word I can summon to encapsulate the tumultuous past two days is... sad. So many words to choose from and yet, none can ameliorate my emotional turmoil better than that solitary, short, three-lettered word... sad. Good evening, gentlemen.'

Lost for words themselves, Frank and Zac watch on as the hulking figure lumbers away, disconsolately.

'Fuck me blue,' Zac whispers.

'And slap my arse with a pickled kipper,' Frank adds. 'Old Raspberry Whipple has a heart, after all.'

'I need a double after that. You?' Zac asks.

'No. Make it a treble.'

'Yes, boss,' he replies as the men from Jason's dart team spill out into the courtyard, a little worse for wear, but happy and boisterous in a melancholy way.

Frank calls them over.

36

Saturday 5th December

The incident room is colder than usual because of a problem with the central heating. The occasional buzz of a fluorescent light is the only noise to interrupt the deathly silence. Prisha shivers and pulls the collar up on her winter coat. Her mind is lucid, her body relaxed. She's already completed a five-mile run around Whitby, impervious to the bleak, chilly conditions. A warm shower, a light breakfast, and a cup of strong coffee and she's raring to go. Her eyes lift from the screen as the door creaks open and PC Pembroke enters.

'Morning, Kylie,' Prisha says with a warm smile.

'Morning, Prisha.'

'You're in early.'

'Not as early as you,' Kylie says, glancing at the clock on the wall. 'What time did you get in?'

'Six. I see you were shortlisted for the weekend shift.'

Kylie takes a seat at her desk. 'I volunteered.'

Prisha laughs. 'You're keen.'

'To tell you the truth, I prefer to be at work than at home. Does that sound odd?'

'To most people, it would. But not to me.'

'Who else is in?'

'Just us two at the moment. I let the nightshift leave early. Overland has given most of the team the weekend off, which I think is a good idea. A circuit breaker. Let everyone recharge their batteries. Zac and Frank will be in about seven and the only other officer on duty this weekend is PC Clem Dinkel, who I'm not familiar with.'

'Oh,' Kylie says, indicating a negative emotion which doesn't go unnoticed.

Prisha eyeballs her. 'Oh, what?'

'Nothing.'

'Spit it out, sister. What's wrong with him?'

'There's nothing wrong with him... per se. It's just he can prattle on a bit and he's unco.'

'Uncoordinated?'

'Yes. Clumsy. Clumsy and awkward, socially awkward.'

'Maybe he's nervous. Might be his first time on a murder case working with CID. Where's he from?'

'Drafted in from York. And another thing—he's a whistler, and not a very good one. Frank's told him off a couple of times about it. Says he couldn't carry a tune in a bucket. And Dinkel tells anyone who will listen that he's recently passed his detective exam. I think he's hoping to get into CID.'

'Oh, well. You take the hand you're dealt. Has he any redeeming features?'

Kylie pouts and wiggles her head. 'I suppose he's easy on the eye. Fit body. But seriously, you wouldn't go there. You'd be up on a murder charge within the week. Hey, is it true?'

'Is what true?'

'You're officially an inspector?'

'Sort of. I'm still acting inspector until Superintendent Banks completes the paperwork.'

'Brilliant! Congratulations.'

'Thanks.'

'What's our main priority?' Kylie asks as she thinks about taking her coat off, then decides against it.

Prisha's focus returns to the computer screen. 'We need to trawl our way through all the reports in the database. There must be over a hundred of them. It's all very well collecting this intel, but unless someone analyses it, then it's not much use. We can probably discard most of it, but there may be a little nugget of gold in there that's been overlooked.' She turns to Kylie. 'Sorry. It's hardly a high-octane adventure, is it?'

'Don't apologise. Tell me where you want me to begin?'

Both women work in silence as they carefully scour the reports, occasionally stopping to jot down notes of interest to follow up on. An hour quickly passes until they can hear gruff male voices and plodding footsteps from the corridor outside. Prisha glances at the clock—7:10 am.

'That sounds like Frank and Zac,' she comments, spinning around as both men enter the room. They blink under the harsh lighting and stare at the room as if they've never seen it before.

'What...' Frank tries to formulate a sentence but fails miserably.

'My God!' Prisha exclaims. 'Look at the state of you two! What time did you leave the wake?'

Frank peers at Zac with a pained expression. 'Good question,' he replies. 'Zac?'

'Fuck knows. All I remember is we left when they closed the bar.'

'Six. It was about six,' Frank elaborates. 'Then we tagged along with the blokes from Jason's darts team and did a pub crawl around the town.'

'Was I there?' Zac asks.

'Of course you were bloody there!' Frank gripes. 'You were the life and soul of the party. Don't you remember your party trick with the cucumber?'

'Where the hell did I get a cucumber from?' Zac says, wincing in pain at a very vague memory.

'Good question, and one I fear will never be answered.'

'What time did you get to bed?' Prisha asks, trying not to smirk.

'Do you have to shout?' Zac says resting a hand on the back of a chair to steady himself.

'I'm not shouting,' Prisha replies as she exchanges a grin with Kylie.

'Not sure,' Frank says, answering the initial question.

'I hope you didn't drive to the station. You'll both be well over the limit.'

'Calm the farm, lass. Meera drove us both in.'

'I bet she was in a good mood,' Prisha says with a chuckle.

'Oh, aye. Laugh a minute. Right, enough of the interrogation. Zac, go make a brew.'

'I'm not sure I can, Frank. I've got double vision and heart palpitations.'

The debate over refreshments is halted as discordant whistling drifts through into the room.

'Oh, Christ,' Frank groans. 'Whistling bloody Willy. Is he on the weekend shift?'

'Afraid so,' Kylie says.

'It doesn't rain but pours.'

The door, which opens into the room, is pulled shut twice before it opens inward, as it should.

PC Dinkel enters, bearing an eager grin. 'Morning everyone!' he shouts, full of beans.

'Oh, fuck,' Zac groans as he grips his forehead.

'Oi, Dinkel,' Frank begins. 'Two things: quit the bloody whistling. I won't tell you again. And can you make tea?'

'Tea? Erm... well, yes... I think.'

Frank's eyes narrow to slits. 'You don't sound confident, Dinkel. It's not nano technology. Boil the kettle, drop a tea bag into a cup. Add water, milk and two... no, make it three sugars and bring it to my office.' Frank half turns, then stops and grimaces.

'What is it?' Prisha asks, slightly concerned.

'My blasted knee. I have a bit of floating cartilage giving me merry hell.'

Prisha realises it's time to take action. She focuses on Zac first. 'Zac, you're in no fit state to be of use to anyone. As your inspector, I suggest you go home. Drop a hydrolyte into a pint of water, take some pain killers and go to bed for another four hours. Then get a warm shower, have a bite to eat and get yourself back here by midday.'

'Are you pulling rank?' Zac mumbles.

'Yes,' Prisha replies sternly.

He squints at Frank. 'Can she do that?'

'Aye, she can. And I agree with her. You look like warmed up shit on a stick. You're no use to man nor beast the state you're in. And let this be a salutary lesson for you. There's nothing wrong with a couple of relaxing pints, but your problem is you don't know when to stop.'

'Hang on, it was your idea to—'

Frank holds his hand up. 'No point apologising now. The deed is done. Prisha's right. Get yourself home.'

'And I suggest you do the same, Frank,' Prisha says. 'You're both as bad as each other.'

'No. I'll be fine. I have some paperwork to attend to.' His eyes swivel onto PC Dinkel. 'Are you still here, Dinkel?'

'Erm, no sir. I mean yes, sir. Tea, three sugars. I'll get on to it right away.'

'Good lad.'

Zac staggers towards the door. 'I'll be back,' he mutters like a fucked-up, malfunctioning Terminator.

37

Prisha reads the report again, intrigued. 'Hey Kylie, I see that last Monday you interviewed three guys at that gym on Silver Street.'

'Yes. What about it?'

'In your report, you said one had a Canadian accent. His name is Scott Lincoln.'

Kylie ponders, trying to recall the name. 'Oh, yes. I remember now. Odd sort of bloke.'

'Did you get a tip off?'

'Yes. Someone rang Crimestoppers anonymously. Once we put Barber's photo on social media, the phones went off. A lot of crank calls and time wasters. I questioned over thirty blokes last week. Most didn't come anywhere near the description we circulated.'

'Tell me about this Scott Lincoln.'

Kylie wanders over to Prisha's desk. 'He was in the gym as I arrived, but was just about to leave. I asked if he could give me a couple of minutes. He matched the height and build of Barber but that was about all.'

'What about the face?'

'There may have been a very vague similarity, but that's all. He was wearing a woollen hat pulled down quite low. A few strands of ginger hair straggled down his forehead. A softly spoken man. I asked him about his accent. He said he was from Canada, Toronto. I took all his details: name, address, telephone number.'

'What colour were his eyes?'

'Brown.'

'Alibi?'

'He said he worked on the trawlers and had been at sea the previous week, during the shooting.'

'Did you ask for the name of the trawler or his skipper's name?'

'Er, no.'

'Did you check out his details?'

Kylie winces. 'No, I didn't.'

Prisha raises her eyebrows. 'First rule of CID work: never believe a word anyone tells you until you've verified it. Now, check the address and phone number.'

Kylie flushes. 'Sorry, I... there were so many people to question and check up on.'

'Don't apologise. You're just starting out and if no one's ever told you before, then how are you to know? Frank or Zac should have mentioned it at the morning briefings. Are you any good with technology?'

'Depends.'

'Photo manipulation?'

'I know my way around. Why?'

'Once you've checked this Scott Lincoln's details out, pull Wayne Barber's image into a photo editing software and plonk a woollen hat on him, then print it out.'

Kylie scuttles back to her desk with her tail between her legs, as Prisha rises and stretches. She wanders over to PC Clem Dinkel.

'How's it going Clem? Anything jump out at you?'

'No, ma'am. Not yet.'

'Don't call me ma'am unless we're in public. I'm not the bloody Queen.'

'Sorry, sir... I mean Prisha.'

'Keep at it.' She turns to head to the kitchen.

'What exactly are we looking for?' he asks, puzzled.

'Inconsistencies, nervous suspects, dodgy alibis, things which don't quite add up.'

'How will I know?'

'I hear you want to be a detective, Dinkel?'

His demeanour lifts. 'Yes, ma'am!'

Prisha eyes him wearily. 'Detectives, detect—Dinkel.'

'Detectives, detect, Dinkel,' he repeats, parrot fashion.

———◦———

Prisha returns with a fresh cup of tea and a buttered scone. She can't help but notice Kylie's worried expression.

'You okay? You look like you've seen a ghost,' she asks.

'The address he gave me...'

'68 Mount Farm Crescent?'

'Yes. It doesn't exist. There's a Mount Farm Close, but not a crescent. And Mount Farm Close is a tiny cul-de-sac with only a handful of houses on it.'

Prisha's left hand involuntarily tightens into a fist. 'Phone number?'

'Not connected. And there's this,' she says, handing Prisha the digitally altered photo of Wayne Barber, now sporting a woollen hat.

Prisha takes the image and gazes at it. 'And?'

'I think it could be him.'

'Barber?'

'Yes. The guy I spoke to wasn't as fat in the face. But with the hat on, there's definitely a resemblance. I'm sorry, Prisha.'

She grins. 'Don't be. This could be the breakthrough we're looking for. Come on, grab your coat, and bring the photo. We're going to the gym.' Both women head to the door. 'Dinkel, man the fort. We're going out. Oh, and check the emails. See if any of our overseas counterparts have come back with a hit on the fingerprint we sent them.'

'Roger Daltrey, that!' he calls out.

Prisha stops in her tracks and whispers to Kylie. 'Roger Daltrey?'

'It's another of his quirks. He thinks he's being amusing.'

'Someone needs to put him wise to that.'

They hurry down the corridor and stop outside Frank's office. Prisha raps on the door and sticks her head inside. Frank has a pen in hand and a stack of papers in front of him.

'Busy?' she asks.

He looks up, appearing marginally better than he did an hour ago. 'Bloody paperwork. Timesheets and expenses. The Super's head will fall off when she sees this little lot. Going somewhere?'

'Yes. It may be something, then again, it may be nothing. A loose end that needs sorting.'

'Aye, well, don't over-elaborate.'

'We'll be back in thirty minutes.'

'By the way, Prisha.'

'What?'

'Welcome back. You've been missed.'

She grins. 'Aw, that's sweet. And to think some people call you a grumpy old bastard.'

38

The gym owner is less than enthused to see the officers.

'This is the fourth visit your lot has made in the last six days,' he grumbles as Prisha pockets her warrant card. 'My numbers have dropped off. Everyone feels like they're under suspicion.'

Prisha bristles. 'I apologise if our search for a homicidal maniac has impinged on your business, but I think you need to put things in perspective, Mr...'

'Davies,' he says contritely, shrinking a little.

'Mr Davies. Now, a few questions. Do you know a Scott Lincoln or a Wayne Barber?' Prisha asks.

'No.'

'Can you check your membership database for them, please?' she says, in no mood to be messed around.

The owner sighs but taps at a keyboard on the reception countertop. 'Scott Lincoln, Wayne Barber,' he drawls slowly, enunciating the names. 'Nothing has come up for either. In fact, I don't have anyone with the last name, Lincoln or Barber.'

Prisha nods to Kylie, who produces the manipulated photo. 'Do you recognise this man?' Kylie says, as she places the image in front of him.

He picks it up. 'Aye, I do. Although he's lost a bit of weight since the photo was taken.'

A stab of excitement shoots through Prisha's body. 'What's his name?'

The owner shakes his head. 'Don't know. Quiet sort. Comes in and pays per session. I tried to get him to sign up for membership as it works out a lot cheaper, but he wasn't interested. More fool him.'

'When was the last time you saw him?'

'Oh, now you're asking. Beginning of the week. Monday or Tuesday, perhaps.'

'Is he a regular?'

'Fits and starts. Some weeks he comes in every day, other weeks it's a couple of times. Is this the guy you're after for the shooting?'

'We're not sure. Just chasing up a lead, that's all. Is there anyone in the gym who would know him?'

'I doubt it. Like I said. He keeps himself to himself. All I get out of him is a hello and goodbye.'

'He said he was Canadian. Do you know if that's true?'

The owner grimaces. 'Nah. I'd say he was definitely American, or at least he has an American accent. East coast, I'd say.'

'New York?'

'Aye. Possibly.'

'Have you any details about him at all: phone number, address, what car he drives?'

'Sorry, no to all the above.'

'I notice you have a security camera out front. Can you run through the footage from last Monday and Tuesday?'

He purses his lips. 'No.'

'Why not?' she asks angrily.

'Because it gets wiped after two days. They're bloody big files and it fills the hard drive and slows everything down.'

Prisha realises she'll not get anything else worthwhile and hands the owner her card.

'The next time he comes in, call me immediately, discreetly. And mention nothing to him about our enquiries.'

'Hang on, if he is your man, then he's bloody dangerous,' he says, alarmed.

'Yes, he is. That's why you need to call us.'

'Oh, I'm not happy about this, not happy at all.'

'Yes, well, we're hardly ecstatic about it ourselves, considering we've just lost one of our officers,' Prisha snaps, glaring at him.

He backs down. 'Aye, sorry about that. Yes, I'll call you if he comes in.'

They stride briskly back to the car, a spring in their step.

'Wow!' Kylie gushes.

'What?'

'You. You were so dominant. He was twice the size of us put together, and yet he was... not scared, but... I don't know, a little intimidated.'

'That's the way you have to be. Polite but forceful. You can't show any sign of weakness, otherwise they'll give you the run-around. We're not here to make friends. We have a job to do.'

'That's the problem with me; I try to be too chummy.'

'You're normally in uniform. That's different. You have to come across as a friendly and reassuring presence on the streets. But once you step into CID, then all that malarky goes out the window. We're here to catch bastards and put them away.'

Kylie giggles.

'What's funny?'

'You. You're turning into Frank.'

Prisha stops and grins at her, lifting a finger. 'Don't you dare say that! I am not a miniature version of Frank bloody Finnegan.'

'Okay. Calm down... Little Frank.'

39

Frank pops a couple of pills into his mouth and swills them down with lukewarm tea. Prisha, Kylie and Dinkel are all standing in front of him.

'Should we call the rest of the team back in?' Prisha asks.

He rubs at the back of his neck. 'No, not yet. They need a break and anyway, sometimes a small, focussed team can work better than a whole gaggle of geese running around in uncoordinated fashion. Let's play it by ear for the moment. We can always call them in as things develop.'

Prisha has already wheeled in another whiteboard and jotted down the pertinent points. Frank stares at the two photos of Wayne Barber a.k.a Scott Lincoln. 'Kylie, you stuck the hat on him?'

'Yes, boss.'

'Are you skilled enough to shave some of the excess fat off his face?'

She shakes her head. 'No, sorry, boss. I'm not that good.'

'Okay. Either pull in a random ten-year-old off the street, or, failing that, get onto HQ and find someone who can manipulate photographs. Then liaise with them until you get the photo looking like you remember him from last Monday. Make one with the hat, and one without and have a few strands of ginger hair showing.'

'Er, excuse me, sir,' Dinkel says, raising his hand in the air.

'Not now, Dinkel. Once you have the photo looking good, get it released to all the mainstream media and our own web and social media sites, asap. Oh, and put both names out there; Wayne Barber and Scott Lincoln.'

'Yes, boss,' Kylie says, excited by the responsibility.

'Ahem, sir?' Dinkel tries again.

'Not now, Dinkel!' Frank booms, making the young man quiver. Frank sticks a finger in his ear and waggles it around. 'We now have a name, two bloody names. But it doesn't mean he's our killer. Still, we need to find the bastard and pull him in. And if he was at the gym last Monday, then we can assume he's local, as we suspected, and that he's still in the area.'

'Sir, Frank, boss,' Dinkel persists with a tremor in his voice.

'For crying out loud, Dinkel! What the hell is it?'

The glass rattles in the window frames.

'It's about the fingerprint, sir. The one we couldn't get a match on. We sent it overseas.'

'Yes, I know we did. What about it?'

'We received an email from the NYPD. That's the New York Police Dep...'

'I know what NYPD bloody stands for! Get on with it!'

'They have a match for the fingerprint we sent them. It belongs to Scott Lincoln, a thirty-five-year-old New Yorker. He was doing time for murder but escaped from a high security prison. He dropped off their radar about five years ago... sir.'

'Why the hell didn't you say so earlier?' Frank bellows.

'Well, I was trying to but...'

'You can't be a shy Mary Ellen around here, lad! You need to find your voice and be heard. Speak up if you've something important to say. Right, make yourself useful and get me a number for the main precinct of the NYPD, and the name of a detective inspector or whatever they call them over there,' he grizzles, damned annoyed.

'Roger Whittaker, that, sir.'

Prisha and Kylie exchange glances as Frank grinds his teeth. 'Oh, and Dinkel, who did he murder?'

'A police officer, sir.'

40

The five officers are happily munching on fish and chips, graciously paid for by Frank, although Dinkel was the errand boy. Zac has returned, and although not one hundred per cent, there's a definite improvement in his demeanour as he wolfs his food down.

'Oh, I needed this,' he says as he sticks a handful of chips in a bread roll, smothers curry sauce over them and takes a massive bite.

'Sir, Mr Finnegan,' Dinkel begins. 'How are we going to refer to our suspect? Will it be Wayne Barber or Scott Lincoln?'

Frank eyes him wearily as he scoops mushy peas into his mouth. 'We'll stick with Wayne Barber. That's what we all know him as, and it's the alias he's been hiding behind.'

'The digital artist said the new images should be with us within the next ten minutes, boss,' Kylie says.

'Good work, Kylie.'

Prisha is oblivious to the chatter as her mind attempts to fit a square peg into a round hole.

'How are we going to flush this bugger out?' Zac murmurs to no one in particular.

'Once the enhanced photos, along with the two names, are circulated, hopefully someone will come forward with an address. The noose is tightening, Zac, my lad. The noose is tightening.'

'What are we going to do until then?'

'Sit tight.'

Prisha discards her food and rises from her seat. 'No, we're not,' she mumbles, as if speaking to herself.

Frank puffs out his cheeks and turns to Zac. 'Excuse me, Detective Sergeant Stoker, but am I *still* a DCI?'

Zac studies him. 'Aye, you are that. Unless you're an alien pod.'

'Can you two shut up for a moment? I'm thinking,' Prisha says, clearly distracted.

'Sir, Mr Finnegan, I have an idea,' Dinkel says.

'Good for you, lad. Keep it to yourself,' he replies.

'Frank, may I make a suggestion?' Kylie asks.

'Of course, Kylie. What is it?'

'What about a press conference fronted by the deputy chief constable? It would really turn the heat up on Barber if we splashed the enhanced photos of him around the country.'

'That's not a bad idea. If we arrange it now, it would be on all the news bulletins by tonight. I like your thinking, Kylie. Let's throw the bloody kitchen sink at the bugger. And if Barber sees his ugly mug on the screen, he'll be less likely to decamp. He'll not want to be in the open with the world and his wife knowing what he currently looks like. The last thing we want is for him to do a disappearing trick. What do you think, Prisha?' He waits a few seconds. 'Prisha? Prisha!' he shouts.

'What?' she says absentmindedly.

'How about we get Overland to hold a press conference with the new photos?'

'Yeah, whatever,' she murmurs as she finally slots a round peg into a round hole.

'Thanks for your input, inspector. It was much appreciated,' Frank says sarcastically as he glances at Zac, who merely shrugs and takes a huge glug of water.

Prisha walks to the whiteboard in a stupor. She picks up the marker pen and neatly writes,

CHARLES WINDSOR – STAMP – ROBBERY

Frank and Zac eyeball her cagily, shake their heads and groan.

'For God's sake, Prisha. Let it go,' Frank chastises. 'Forget about the bloody stamp. You can return to that once we have Barber behind bars.'

'She's like a dog with a bone,' Zac remarks.

'Prisha, did you hear what I said?' Frank says, raising his voice. 'Your primary focus, no, your *only* focus right now, is Barber. Do I make myself clear?'

Dinkel and Kylie glance at each other nervously, feeling the tension in the air.

Prisha turns, eyes distant, her brain working overtime. She hasn't heard a word. 'Windsor,' she murmurs, barely audible. 'Bloody Windsor. The lying toe rag.'

Frank picks up a chip, then drops it back into the paper. His barrel chest rises as he heaves a sigh. 'Go on, get it out. Let's hear it,' he says.

Prisha returns to Planet Earth with a bang. 'There was no robbery. Well, no, there was. But there wasn't,' she babbles excitedly, much to everyone's consternation.

Frank and Zac are concerned about her sanity. Maybe she's finally snapped under all the pressure?

'Easy, lass. Take your time. Deep breaths. Take a seat and have a sip of water,' Frank advises in a fatherly tone, rising to his feet.

She spins around, eyes agog. 'Frank, I need a warrant, as soon as.'

'For?' he asks.

'A search warrant for Windsor's shop. He has a safe in there.'

'And what do you expect to find in his safe - Wayne Barber?'

'He's a big lad, Frank. It would have to be one hell of a safe,' Zac chuckles.

'No. It's where the stamp will be,' Prisha says.

Frank flops back into his seat, drops his head into his hands and scratches at his balding scalp with his fingers. 'I'm not sure how to say this, Prisha, but...'

'Don't you see? Windsor faked the robbery. He either had something over Barber, or he paid Barber to carry out the robbery. Barber didn't steal the stamp. Windsor needed it to look as real as it could be to convince the police and the insurance company. That way, he keeps his precious stamp, and he claims sixty grand in insurance money. It's a double whammy. I thought it odd about the supermarket CCTV footage. Those cameras are clearly visible. Why would a robber walk straight towards them? Because he needed to be seen, to verify Windsor's account. The police believed him, the insurance believed him. And that's why he gave us the false leads about Barber. He said he had piercing blue eyes and a local accent. That threw us right off the scent. Even when Riley Miller first alerted us to the name Wayne Barber, he was only ever a person of interest and not a prime suspect. And why? Because Windsor's description of Barber differed so much from what Riley Miller told us. Windsor doesn't want us to catch Barber, otherwise his ruse could be in jeopardy. But the whole thing went tits-up when Barber shot Jason.'

The room falls silent as everyone digests the outburst. 'But how does this help us catch Barber?' Zac asks, slightly shellshocked, and still hungover.

'Windsor must have a contact number. How else could he have coordinated the robbery?'

'And if we could get hold of Barber's number, we can get a ping off a tower to locate where he is, or at least the street he lives on,' Frank says, ruminating.

'Hang on a mo. There's something else I've just thought of,' Prisha says as she pulls her phone out, taps an icon, and zooms in on the photos she took of Lord Ashton's guest book. She shakes her head, smiles, then presses the "print" button. 'Gotcha, you conniving little bleeder.'

The printer rapidly spits out an A4 sheet. Prisha collects it, strides to the whiteboard, and picks up the marker pen.

'Here we go,' Zac chunters. 'It's like watching Miss Marple on crystal meth.'

Dinkel is clearly confused. 'Who's Miss Marple?' he queries.

Frank turns to him. 'Agatha Christie? Hercule Poirot?' he explains.

Dinkel shakes his head. 'Sorry, sir. I must have missed that briefing. Are they all suspects in the investigation?'

Frank groans. 'No, Dinkel., they're not suspects. How old are you?'

'Twenty-six, sir.'

'Can you try to be a little older?'

The request bamboozles Dinkel. 'I'm not sure if... I mean... well, I suppose I could try.' He ends on an upbeat note, without a clue how he can make himself older.

'Thanks,' Frank states, praying it's the end of the matter.

Beneath the name WINDSOR Prisha writes ALFRED DOBSON – BURGLARY - STONYGARTH. She then attaches the printout of names to the board with a magnet and turns to her captivated, if befuddled, audience.

'I always knew he was dodgy,' she declares. 'Pay attention as it's a little complicated,' she advises. 'Lord Ashton's father was a major general in the Second-World-War. During his time in Europe, he collected a few little keepsakes for himself.'

'The spoils of war,' Frank states.

'That's a posh word for theft, but yes, the spoils of war. The items were obviously passed onto Lord Ashton when his father died. He kept the collection under lock and key. They were never on public display. Now, Lord Ashton became acquainted with Alfred Dunn when Dunn gave one of his talks at Stonygarth Hall about eighteen months ago. Dunn gives public lectures a few times a year on the war and the rise and fall of the Third Reich, that sort of thing. They're not big events. Maybe ten, fifteen people attend. He holds them in village halls, private residences, stately homes. After Dunn's lecture at Stonygarth, Lord Ashton showed Dunn his small collection, namely: a signed copy of Mein Kampf, a Hitler Youth dagger, an SS insignia, and a Luger pistol. Dunn convinced Lord Ashton he should put them on public display. He said they'd be a draw card for the open days held at Stonygarth three times a year.' She pauses and picks up a highlighter pen and draws a line through a name on the printout.

'Who's that?' Frank asks, squinting.

'The name is Alfred Dunn. This is a copy of the visitor book from the open day held last year during the August Bank Holiday. It was the first time Lord Ashton's war memorabilia was on display.'

'So what?' Zac begins. 'If Dunn is a friend of Lord Ashton, it wouldn't be unusual for him to pay a visit during the open day, especially as it was his idea to put the items on display.'

Prisha grins. 'That's exactly what I thought when I spotted his name a couple of days ago.' She now highlights another name below Dunn's.

Frank puts his spectacles on, to no avail. 'I can't see the name from here, but I can guess who it is. Scott Lincoln a.k.a Wayne Barber?'

'Correct! He signed in directly below Alfred Dunn. I think Dunn and Barber, or Scott Lincoln if you prefer, attended Stonygarth together to check out how secure Lord Ashton's items were.'

'What was the security like?' Kylie asks, just about keeping up with events.

'Very poor. A glass cabinet secured by a metal sliding pole fastened with a tiny padlock. Remove the padlock, slide the pole back, and it releases the locking mechanism. Then it's simply a matter of lifting the lid of the cabinet and help yourself. At that stage, there were no security cameras.'

'Hang on,' Zac says. 'How do Barber and Alfred Dunn know each other?'

'According to Riley Miller's information, he said Barber was obsessed with Hitler and the war. At some point, I believe Barber attended one of Dunn's lectures and they struck up a friendship. The items weren't stolen until the next open day, last April.'

'You think the first visit was to case the joint?'

'Yes. I believe Barber returned in April, alone, maybe with bolt cutters or something, and snipped the padlock.'

'Bit risky with all the people around.'

'Ah! Last April, the weather was atrocious. They only had twenty visitors for the whole day, and it's not a guided tour. The Ashton's lock their private rooms, but visitors can wander around the rest of the building at will. Barber would have had plenty of opportunity to break into the cabinet unseen.'

Frank removes his spectacles and rubs at his eyes. 'Let's go back to Windsor for a moment. How does Windsor know Barber? Where's the connection?'

Prisha waggles her cheeks from side to side. 'I'm not sure, yet. All I know is that Windsor used to be an acquaintance of Dunn until they had a falling out over a pair of cuff links belonging to Hermann Goring. Maybe Windsor attended one of Dunn's lectures and was introduced to Barber?'

'Okay, let's assume your theories are correct, then it means we now have two people who know Barber—Garth Windsor and Alfred Dunn.'

'That's right. But here's another thing. Last Tuesday, after I'd visited Jason in hospital, I was at a bit of a loose end, so I had a wander around town and ended up in a little café on Church Street. I spotted Dunn walking quickly down the street towards the café. He was carrying a briefcase and looked worried, harried. I exited the café and deliberately bumped into him. I asked him if he was in town for business or pleasure, you know, in a chatty way. He said he'd just paid a visit to his sister, who was ill.'

'Perfectly reasonable explanation,' Zac comments.

'Yes, except for two things. When I asked what was wrong with his sister, he said she'd sprained her ankle. A sprained ankle is an injury, not an illness.'

'Slip of the tongue, perhaps?' Frank suggests. 'What's the second thing?'

'When I first visited Dunn's house, he told me he was a bachelor. Not a single photograph of any family member was in his living room. I don't think he has a sister.'

'You think he'd visited Barber?' Frank asks.

'Possibly.'

'Why?'

'Again... not sure. Maybe Barber needed money and used the robbery on Stonygarth as leverage.'

'There's a lot of unfinished threads, Prisha.'

'Yes, I know, Frank. I don't have all the answers, but maybe Dunn and Windsor do? I think we should arrest them both and put them through the ringer. Getting a ping from Barber's mobile should be a last resort. As you indicated, it can give us a rough location, but when we're dealing with an armed, unpredictable killer, I think we need an *exact* location.'

Frank strokes the stubble on his chin, deep in thought. 'Aye, you're right. The last thing we want is to lose another officer.' His gaze drifts across to Dinkel. 'Did you get all that, Dinkel?'

'If I'm completely truthful, sir, I didn't get a bleeding thing! I don't know my Windors from my Dunns, from my Gorings, from my Barbers. Oh, hang on, Barber is our prime suspect, right?'

Frank chuckles. 'Aye. At least you're honest. I could explain it again to you, but I can't understand it for you.' He leaps to his feet, yelps, and immediately sits down again. 'Bloody knee,' he says, rubbing it vigorously. 'Well, don't just bloody sit there gawping at me! Action stations! One of you contact the magistrate. We need search and arrest warrants for Garth Windsor and Alfred Dunn. If, and when, we recover Barber's mobile number, we'll need another warrant for his telco. And one of you have a heads-up with armed response. We may need them in

the next twenty-four hours. Chop, chop, jump to it!'
he bellows. 'Prisha, you take Kylie with you and arrest
Windsor. Zac, you take Dinkel and arrest Dunn.'

'Really?' Zac says, less than enthused at the prospect of
Dinkel's company.

'Yes, really!'

41

The four officers clatter down the station steps in silence.
A quick swipe of a security pass and the door opens into
the reception area.

'Inspector Kumar!' the desk sergeant calls out.

'What is it?' Prisha yells back, determined to get out of
the front door.

'There's a gentleman to see you.'

She throws a quick glance over her shoulder at a tall,
smartly dressed man standing at the counter.

'It will have to wait!'

'He says it's important.'

'It will have to wait!' she shouts even louder as Zac and
Dinkel march outside.

The desk sergeant tries again. 'He says it's concerning a
Mr Windsor.'

Prisha halts and hands the car keys to Kylie. 'Get the
car started. I'll be there in a minute,' she orders as she

spins around. The mystery gentleman approaches, smiling warmly.

'Inspector Kumar?' he says.

'Yes. And you are?'

'My name is Clive Farmer, private investigator,' he explains whilst simultaneously showing her his ID card.

'You have something on Mr Windsor?'

'I perform a lot of investigative work for the insurance companies.'

'And?'

'Heritage Collectables contacted me a few days ago to investigate a claim by Mr Garth Windsor regarding the theft of a precious stamp.' He pulls out his notebook and flicks through the pages. 'I believe it was a rare Two Penny Blue.'

'Yes, that's correct.'

'And you're the senior investigating officer in the case?'

'Yes. Can you get to the point? I am rather busy.'

'My apologies. To cut a long story short, a rigorous search into Mr Windsor's past activities has uncovered some interesting facts.'

Prisha glances outside as the Ford Focus, driven by Kylie, pulls up near the entrance.

'Go on.'

'Five years ago, Mr Windsor was insured by Secure Investments, an insurance company specialising in antiques and rarities. He put in a claim for fifty thousand pounds for a precious broach he bought from auction. He was accosted at the back of his shop and the broach was stolen. Three years ago, Mr Windsor was with Sapphire Trust, an insurance company specialising in antiques and rarities. He bought a set of cufflinks from auction and unfortunately, he was threatened at the back of his shop and the cufflinks were stolen. This time the claim was for thirty-five thousand pounds.'

'Did these cufflinks once belong to Hermann Goring, by any chance?'

He raises his eyebrows. 'Yes, they did. And now, he has a claim for sixty-thousand pounds after being robbed of a rare stamp at the back of his shop. It appears Mr Windsor is extremely unlucky.'

'He certainly is. Three times he's been accosted at the back of his shop and robbed of precious artefacts. Poor little mite. These other two claims, were there any details about the robber?'

'Yes. A well-built gentleman. Local accent, piercing blue eyes.'

'Funny about that.'

'I can see you're in a hurry,' he says, handing her his card. 'When you get a chance, maybe we could go for a coffee and talk about Mr Windsor in more detail?'

'I look forward to that,' she says, handing over her card. 'Would it be possible for you to put together a brief bullet point list of Mr Windsor's claims and email it through to me today? My address is on the card.'

'Certainly, inspector. I'll have it to you within the hour. Thanks for your time.'

'No, thank you, Mr Farmer.'

42

Zac navigates the car down the steep incline and shoots a quick glance over the tiny fishing village of Staithes.

'Did I mention I recently passed my investigator's exam?' Dinkel says in a carefree, cheery tone usually reserved for the innocent or lunatics.

'Aye, you fucking did. About five times and counting.'

'Oh, sorry.'

Zac checks his sat-nav and slows the car. 'Right, we're here. I'll let you do the honours.'

'What do you mean?'

'The arrest.'

'The whole thing?'

Zac pulls on the handbrake and unfastens his seatbelt. 'Yes, the whole thing. The arrest, the warrant, the caution, and the handcuffs, oh, and don't forget the nice gentle bit.'

'The gentle bit?'

'Yes. When you guide him to the back seat of the car. Don't forget to place your hand on his noggin so he doesn't bump his wee head when he's climbing in. We wouldn't want that, now would we?'

Dinkel appears nervous as they both exit the car. 'You don't think he's dangerous, do you?'

Zac sighs as he performs a neck crack. 'You're dealing with a retired history professor in his late seventies, not fucking Kung Fu Panda. Don't worry, if he launches a vicious assault with his Zimmer frame, I'll Taser the fucker.'

They amble up the front steps to the door. 'Erm, what exactly is the charge?'

'Take a punt.'

'Burglary, theft? Hang on, what has he actually done?' Dinkel asks, suddenly discombobulated.

Zac rubs at his eyes, exhausted. 'Handling stolen goods.'

'Ah, okay.' Dinkel clears his throat, pushes his chest out, and pulls a stern expression. 'Alfred Dunn, I am arresting you on suspicion of handling stolen goods. You do not have to say anything. But it may harm your defence if you do not mention when questioned something which you later rely on in court. Anything you do say may be given in evidence.'

'What the fuck are you doing?' Zac asks, the last vestiges of his patience evaporating.

'I'm practising my arrest patter.'

'Your arrest patter?'

'Have you a problem?'

'Yes... you. Now get on with it.'

Dinkel raps on the door with his knuckle. They wait in silence a few seconds until Dinkel tries again. 'Maybe he's not home?' he suggests.

'Try the door.'

'I'm not sure we should. Isn't that an invasion of privacy?'

'Dinkel, you've told me a dozen times you passed your investigator's exam. You've also been a copper for three years. I'm beginning to think you've made the whole thing up and are, in fact, an imposter. What are you holding in your right hand?'

Dinkel stares at the warrants. 'An arrest warrant and a search warrant.'

'Which means?'

'We can enter the house to make an arrest and conduct a search?' he replies, although it's more of a question than a statement of fact.

'Correct. Now open the door and go inside.'

Dinkel turns the doorknob, which comes off in his hand, leaving the spindle sticking out. He grins nervously at Zac and replaces the doorknob and tries again to open the door, this time successfully.

'Some mothers do have 'em,' Zac murmurs.

Dinkel tentatively pokes his head inside. 'Hello, Mr Dunn, anyone home? It's the police. We've come to arrest you.'

'Spank my arse! You sound like the fucking cleaning lady,' Zac explodes as he snatches the warrants from Dinkel and roughly barges past him into the house.

'Alfred Dunn, I have a warrant to search your house!' Zac bellows at the top of his lungs. He strides purposefully down the hallway and pushes open the sitting-room door. 'Shit and damnation,' he murmurs as Dinkel follows behind him.

Dunn is lying crumpled on the ground, face down, immobile, with a gash to the back of his head.

Dinkel seizes his opportunity. 'Alfred Dunn, I am arresting you on suspicion of handling...'

'Shut up Dinkel, you dipstick,' Zac barks as he rushes over to the old man and carefully rolls him onto his back. He places two fingers to the side of his neck. 'He's still got a pulse, albeit a faint one. Get onto control and order an ambulance and make it quick. Then get some more uniform down here.'

'Roger Moore that!' Dinkel yells in a state of excitement. 'Oh, erm... when you said make it quick, did you mean for me to be quick or for the ambulance to be quick?'

'I swear to God,' Zac mutters under his breath.

43

Garth Windsor is playing hardball. For ten minutes he parries away Prisha's question with a two-word sentence—no comment.

Prisha glances at his solicitor, then back to Windsor. She taps her fingernail into the tabletop repeatedly, creating a small echo in the interview room.

'I can stay here all night if need be,' she says. 'Let's start again, shall we, from the beginning?'

It's a ploy. She's run a set of questions by him once and he's given his predictable reply, probably at the behest of his solicitor. But she has a few aces up her sleeve she's about to play.

'You've been rather unlucky, Mr Windsor, to be robbed of three precious artefacts in the space of five years. All of which you purchased from the same auction house. And all the robberies occurred at the back of your shop by a muscular man with piercing blue eyes and a local accent. You'd have more chance of being struck by lightning. It reminds me of that famous quote from Oscar Wilde: to lose one parent may be regarded as unfortunate. To lose both looks like carelessness. Do you want to tell me about Wayne Barber?'

'No comment.'

'Or maybe you know him as Scott Lincoln.'

He blinks. 'No comment.'

'An American. New Yorker, to be precise. Killed a police officer over there. Was serving time in a high security prison in the States, but escaped and came to England on a false passport. Do you know him?'

'No comment.'

She unzips her leather satchel and pulls out three items and carefully lines them up in front of him.

'For the record, we retrieved these items from your safe in the storeroom of your shop. It took the locksmith quite a while to get into it. But we got there in the end.'

Windsor, arms folded, stares dispassionately into the middle distance.

'Exhibit A is a rare Two Penny Blue. Exhibit B is a pair of cufflinks, once purportedly worn by Hermann Goring. And last but not least Exhibit C. A beautiful ruby encrusted broach from the late eighteenth century. It's quite exquisite. You reported all these items as stolen. And for Exhibit B and C, your insurance company fully paid you out. Is that correct?'

'No comment.'

'White collar crime,' she says with a cheeky grin. 'Doesn't really hurt anybody, does it? It's only the insurance companies who take a hit and those greedy bastards make millions in profits every year, don't they? Fuck them, eh, Garth? Instead of paying bonuses to the fat cats at the top, what's wrong with you getting your hands on some of their profits? Who cares? Everybody wants to get rich, quick, these days don't they?

And if you were caught, what would happen to you, anyway? If you repaid the money, you may get away with a fine and a slap on the wrist by a lenient judge. At worst, maybe an eighteen-month sentence in an open prison, released after nine months. Your wife could still run the business, although I'd say she's probably complicit in your deceit. We may bring charges against her; it all depends on your cooperation.'

The solicitor perks up. 'Inspector, using Mr Windsor's wife as a bargaining chip is tantamount to intimidation.'

Prisha leans back in her chair. 'Point taken. Do you want to know what I think, Garth? You probably don't, but I'll tell you, anyway.' She points at the exhibits. 'A, B, and C. I really don't give a shit about them and I'll tell you why.

Yesterday I attended the funeral of my colleague, Jason Cartwright. Afterwards, a small group of us attended the crematorium for a very brief send-off. I held his wife's hand as the casket disappeared behind the curtains, then I heard the faintest of sounds. A very soft whoosh. That was the gas burners firing up. You'd think in this day and age they'd be able to soundproof the bloody firebox, wouldn't you? Or maybe they do it on purpose to give everyone a sense of finality. There ain't no coming back from those flame throwers,' she adds in a cartoon voice with a chuckle.

Her demeanour changes to deadly serious.

'It didn't give Jason Cartwright's wife a sense of finality, Garth. Oh, no. Amanda's her name. I struggled to hold her back as she rushed towards those curtains. She'd have done it as well. If she could have opened that crematorium door, she'd have thrown herself into the flames, unborn baby and all. But you don't know yet, do you, Garth?'

For the first time, his eyes focus on Prisha. 'Know what?'

'About Wayne Barber—real name Scott Lincoln. He was your fake robber. Do you want to know what he did after your bogus play at the back of the shop?'

Windsor swallows hard.

'He got in a stolen car and drove back to Whitby. He stopped at a petrol station. I was in an unmarked car with

DS Cartwright. We pulled in behind him to question his erratic driving. DS Cartwright stepped out of the car.'

Windsor erupts. 'No! You're lying. It wasn't him who shot the officer. You're trying to trap me!'

Prisha shakes her head. 'It's true. He hates coppers. He's a neo-Nazi. You're up to your neck in this, Garth.'

'I didn't kill him! I didn't even know until just now. You can't pin anything on me. I may have committed fraud, but I had nothing to do with murder!'

'Ah, yes. Fraud by deception. Dishonestly making a false representation to gain benefit or to cause loss to another person. I think that's what the Fraud Act 2006 states. I may have underplayed it earlier, you know, about getting a slap on the wrist or nine months in an open prison. If my memory serves me correctly, I think the maximum punishment is ten years. Of course, if you willingly and honestly assisted us with our enquiries into Wayne Barber, then that could favour you in the long run. It's called mitigation. A sort of representation to the judge telling him how helpful you've been. I'm sure your solicitor could explain the nuances of it better than I can. Now, I can terminate the interview for today, or we can have a ten-minute recess and when I return, you can tell me everything you know about Wayne Barber. What's it to be, Garth? The choice is yours.'

Prisha is astounded at his confession and takes time out to compute the details. She shakes her head, then refocuses on Garth Windsor.

'Hang on, let me get this straight. You swapped the *real* Two Penny Blue for a fake?'

'Yes. Before I arrived back at the shop.'

'And how much is it worth, the fake?'

'Nothing. A few quid. You can pick them up at stamp fairs anywhere.'

'But Barber believed it was *real*, and you suggested if he wanted to make a little extra money, on top of the four grand you had already paid him for the simulated robbery, he should offer it to Alfred Dunn?'

'Yes.'

'Why?'

'Ever since our falling out, Alfred has been badmouthing me to anyone he meets. All because I outbid him for the Goring cufflinks. It was an auction, for God's sake! He swore revenge. Said he'd ruin me. I don't take kindly to idle threats, and I thought this would be a good way to pay him back.'

'Petty revenge?'

He drops his eyes, sheepish. 'I suppose so. With the benefit of hindsight.'

'But you knew Alfred Dunn was a keen stamp collector and would spot a fake a mile off?'

'Yes. I anticipated Alfred would bid for the stamp online at the auction, trying to push the price way past its reserve, making me pay more than it was worth. His so-called form of revenge. Pathetic. Well, I was willing to take the hit, as I knew I'd be getting the insurance money and the stamp.

I suggested to Barber he inform Alfred he'd stolen the stamp from me and arrange a swap late at night, in the dark. I knew it would be too much for Alfred to resist. He'd get his hands on the precious stamp and give me a bloody nose at the same time. Payback.

The fake stamp and money would be exchanged and Alfred wouldn't realise the scam until he returned home and studied the stamp with a magnifying glass. I know Barber, and there would be no way he was ever going to return the money. And what could Alfred do about it? Go to the police? Threaten Barber? No. He'd silently rage, knowing I'd pulled a fast one on him. Double the pain. It was he who vowed revenge on me, yet it was I who outsmarted him.'

'Wow! Privileged men playing a silly little game of cat and mouse with devastating results. You amaze and sicken me. Would you like to know where Alfred Dunn is right now?'

Windsor shrugs. 'I couldn't care less.'

'He's in hospital, in a coma, with a suspected fractured skull. At some point today he was attacked and robbed in his home.'

Windsor's eyes nearly pop out. 'Wayne Barber?'

It's Prisha's turn to shrug. 'What do you think?'

He hangs his head in shame 'I never anticipated the ramifications of my actions, inspector. I mean, who could?'

'Certainly not Amanda Cartwright nor Alfred Dunn. If you dance with the devil, remember to wear hobnailed boots. The time is 5:32 pm and I'm terminating this interview.'

44

Prisha enters the incident room and is greeted with a round of handclaps from her four teammates.

Frank walks towards her. 'Well done, Prisha. A full confession to all the fraud charges. You nailed the bastard.'

'Thanks, Frank.' Her words drip with disappointment.

Zac grins. 'Aye, gripping stuff. They should turn it into a movie. I couldn't tear my eyes away from the screen. Deserving of an Oscar. Although, I doubt there was much acting going on.'

'It was inspirational,' Kylie calls out from the back of the room, beaming.

Dinkel is still clapping away like a lunatic. Frank eyes him wearily. 'Okay, Dinkel. Enough with the applause. Don't overdo it. Less is more.'

'Sorry, sir.'

'Oi, and you two young ones, take note,' Frank says, pointing at Kylie and Dinkel. 'Learn from what you've just witnessed. It was textbook. You can go into the interview room with all your evidence, exhibits, witness statements, and theories and carefully lay them all out to the suspect and they'll stonewall you with—no comment or feed you a pack of lies and give you the run-around. You need to make a connection and you do that with *emotion*. People relate to emotion. When Prisha mentioned the crematorium and Jason's wife, that was the defining moment when Windsor stopped thinking about his own skin and related to someone else. That's when he cracked. Then you give them something, however innocuous or trivial. You help us and we'll help you. If you're drowning in a frothing sea, you'll cling to any lifeline.'

Prisha slumps into a chair. 'It's a hollow victory,' she laments. 'He knows Barber lives in Whitby, but doesn't know where.'

'You believed him?' Zac queries.

'Yes. Once I'd told him about the murder, he'd have bent over backwards to help us. We're no closer to finding Barber, though. Any news from digital forensics?'

'We have Barber's mobile number from Windsor's phone, and they've submitted it to the telco to see if we can get a trail from the repeater towers. But they've not got back to us yet.'

'How's Dunn?'

'In a bad way. They've given him some meds, so he'll be out of it until tomorrow morning at the earliest. That's if he comes around at all.'

'Do we know for certain if it was Barber who attacked him?'

'It was. Forensics lifted his fingerprints from Dunn's safe. Although, we don't know what was in it.'

'I could hazard a guess. A certain vainglorious book written and signed by a psychopathic dictator.'

'Show some respect. Don't speak about Superintendent Banks like that!' Frank says, much to everyone's amusement, as he glances at the clock.

'Mein Kampf,' Prisha continues unabated. 'What now, boss?' she asks, fatigued.

'You lot can go home and rest and recuperate. I'll hang on here and do the handover to the nightshift. They should be here soon. I've pulled in some extra resources.'

'Why?'

'Because in thirty minutes, Deputy Chief Constable Overland's media conference will hit the news bulletins around the country. I'm expecting heavy traffic over the phones.' He peers at Prisha's despondent countenance. 'Keep your pecker up, lass. We still have some aces up our sleeve.'

'Do we?' she mumbles.

'Yes. We have three avenues for locating Barber: the telco's cellular tower triangulation; Alfred Dunn; and Barber's ugly mug splashed across millions of TV screens. We'll find where the bastard is holed up, never fear. Right, come on, get yourself home and put your feet up. You look done in.'

'Yeah, you're right. I'll go for a run.'

Frank shakes his head. 'It's bloody snowing outside and blowing a gale. You need to relax.'

Prisha rises to her feet. 'Running is my relaxation. It clears my head and makes me feel alive. Anyway, I never got around to lighting a candle for Jason. I'll have a jog up to the church.'

Frank puffs his cheeks out. 'It beats me, but each to their own, I guess.' He turns to the others. 'Well done, gang. It's been a tough old day, but we're making progress. I'll see you all back here tomorrow morning.' He winces and gazes at the carpet. 'Right, I better call Miss Havisham and give her an update,' he mutters without enthusiasm as he heads to the door.

'Who's Miss Havisham?' Dinkel enquires. 'I don't think I've met her.'

'Superintendent Banks,' Zac says, slipping into his overcoat. 'Night Dinkel. Keep out of trouble and try not to break anything.'

45

Prisha runs up Church Street at a fierce pace and rounds the bend onto Church Lane. She launches up the 199 Steps without letting up. As she nears the top, she slows to a walk, panting hard. A yellowish light weeps from beneath the church doors, illuminating the weathered gravestones which sprout from the earth like rotting teeth. She was expecting to see a few people coming and going, but the place appears deserted, the rain and cold an adequate deterrent. A chill runs down her spine for no reason she can explain, apart from the spooky atmosphere and frigid temperature. Her hand instinctively reaches behind her lower back to rest upon the bumbag, which contains her phone.

'Damn it,' she says, sporting a grimace as the image of the bag lying on the table in her flat enters her consciousness. As she nears the entrance, she stops and glances around, biting the corner of her lip.

Something doesn't feel right.

She chastises herself. 'Stop it, Prisha. You're entering an old church on a dark night, surrounded by row upon row of headstones with a gothic abbey in the background. It's bound to feel spooky.'

The drizzle turns to rain as she scampers inside. A musty scent greets her, an amalgam of porridge and furniture polish. To her left is a rack containing tealight candles. None are alight, but there are eleven empty cups, an indication of how many people have made an effort to pay their respects. She unzips her tracksuit pocket and pulls out a tenner, and drops it in a collection box, even though a nominal fee of thirty pence is all that's required.

On the day of the funeral, the church was heaving with people, and she was in such a fog she'd not taken in her surroundings. Lighting a candle, she scans the interior of the church. She was expecting something more... romantic, authentic, but the church is a mishmash of ideas that clash with each other. Over the years, architectural structures have been added. Balconies cut across some of the original archways, negating their impact. There's a general clutter and chintzy feel about the place, with dried flowers in vases, and tacky paraphernalia adorning the walls. It's not been designed well, if at all.

She suspects a committee was involved.

With not a soul in sight, she experiences a stab of sorrow for Jason.

Is this what forty-four years on the planet amounts to... twelve candles? Twelve people who took the trouble to come here and remember you.

Fighting the urge to leave, she treads down the aisle and enters a coffin-shaped box pew. Sitting quietly, she closes her eyes and starts an internal dialogue with Jason.

I'm so, so sorry, Jason, I really am. I thought you'd pull through. What happened? Why did you let go? But you haven't gone yet, have you? I can feel you here, watching, listening. This isn't your scene at all: churches, candles, prayers, tears, and grief. You'd rather be down the pub having a pint and playing darts whilst talking about football and making crappy jokes. That's how I'll remember you, someone who was fun and enjoyed the simple things in life. I envied you some days. You were almost childlike... I said childlike, not childish. I'm missing you already. We had so little time together and, to be honest, I had little patience with you initially. Neither did anyone, if truth be told. I apologise for that. If I could turn the clock back and make everything better, I would. It was only when we spent those ten days together in the Dales that I really saw you for who you were. And... I liked you.

You grew on me. No, not like a wart... stop it, I'm being serious. I know we're like chalk and cheese, but sometimes those friendships are the best. To accept a person for who they are, not what we want them to be. That's all gone now. I know this will sound daft, but I want to be there for your unborn child, like an aunty. Of course, that means I'll have to become friends with Amanda. Sorry, that came out wrong. What I meant was, I'll have to befriend Amanda to be there for your child. Although, that's down to her. I dare say I'm not her favourite person at the moment.

A rustling noise followed by quiet footsteps interrupt her thoughts. She opens her eyes and takes a half look over her shoulder, glimpsing a shadow near the candle rack.

That's thirteen candles, now, Jason. I bet you don't care, though.

There's a creak from a few rows behind as the person takes a seat. Something flits across her line of sight, disappears, then swoops down again. A tiny bat. She shivers.

God, I hate those things. Flying rats.

Almost imperceptibly at first, the sound is unnerving. A little girl's voice, except it isn't. It's somebody in a state of despair. She breathes in the aroma of sandalwood with a fruity note.

I can smell the aftershave you wore when we were in the Dales, Jason.

Go!

What?

Go!

Jason's voice is distinct, urgent, no sign of his usual easy-going tone. It's also silent and only resonates in Prisha's head. She spins around, but all she sees two rows behind her is the top of a woollen hat and a pair of hands clasped together. A few strands of hair poke out beneath the hat. The hair is weird: limp, lank, a dark ginger. A creeping unease descends as if someone has wrapped a curse around her.

Shit! Time for me to leave, Jason. I'll speak soon.

Get out now!

His voice again.

She needs to pee.

Mouth dry.

Hard to swallow.

She rises. Legs tremble.

Sniffling from behind. Then... a squeaky high-pitched distraught voice, girlish. It drops lower, and lower, until it's a guttural growl, like the very Devil himself has materialised.

His words make no sense, spat out in rapid, angry sentences.

'The fruit of your womb will be cursed, and the crops of your land, and the calves of your herds and the lambs of your flocks. Thy Lord will send on you curses, confusion and rebuke in everything you put your hand to, until you are destroyed and come to sudden ruin because of the evil you have done in forsaking him. The Lord's curse is on the house of the wicked.'

She exits the box pew in a hurry.

'The third angel sounded his trumpet, and a great star, blazing like a torch, fell from the sky on a third of the rivers and on the springs of water—the name of the star is Wormwood.'

Her eyes dart around the church, looking for another exit. There is none.

'Don't go,' the little girl's voice, again.

Head down, gaze averted, she moves swiftly down the aisle.

A rush of movement as a hand darts out and grabs her forcefully around the neck.

'Do not be afraid of those who kill the body but cannot kill the soul. Rather, be afraid of the *one* who can destroy both *soul* and *body* in hell.'

He grins at her. His stranglehold tightening around her slender throat.

Woozy, she stares into the eyes of Wayne Barber... as her life slips away.

46

He babbles on, reciting scripture from the Old Testament.

Prisha's eyelids flutter as she desperately tries not to pass out.

Her bladder releases.

His head tilts from one side, then to the other, grinning at his prey.

Momentarily, his grip relaxes, giving her time to suck in a gasp of air.

'God is love, God is mercy,' he slavers, as the grip tightens.

Fuck you!

Eyes close as her grandmother appears before her.

She repeats the advice given when Prisha first hit puberty.

"Prisha, if a man tries to touch you, there is one thing you must do."

"What, Nanni?"

"You must knee him in the testicles as hard as you can. But remember... you'll maybe only get one chance."

Her eyes spring open.

A ghastly smile, inches away. Putrid, bad breath.

His hand tightens, again.

He speaks.

'And when you're dead, I'm going to *fuck* you on the altar. I'm going to hell. You may as well join me,' he cackles.

She leans in, as if in agreement.

Only one chance, Nanni.

That's right, Prisha.

She's a fitness fanatic.

Running is her passion.

Powerful thighs.

Swivelling her hip, her leg pivots backwards, then snaps forward as she lifts her right knee violently upwards.

Even though it's her bony patella that connects, she feels it.

Soft, squishy, yielding.

An expulsion of vile breath, entangled with incomprehensible groans as the vice from her neck is broken.

He drops to his haunches. Both hands clasp his genitals.

Gasping for air, she staggers past him and spots a vase of dried flowers in a box pew. Reaching in, she grabs the jug and smashes it down onto the back of his head.

It shatters as he collapses unconscious onto the cold flagstones.

A stream of blood trickles from his head.

Lurching, she stumbles outside into a torrential downpour and vomits.

47

The paramedic finishes the examination.

'No lasting damage. Your throat will be sore for a day or two. Take a couple of paracetamol two to three times a day.'

'Thanks,' Prisha says as she lowers herself from the back of the ambulance. She joins Frank and Zac, who are huddled under a large golfing umbrella in the car park behind the abbey. Flashing blue lights swirl around, bouncing off ancient buildings. The police radio crackles as a gruff voice declares the area secure.

The trio walk rapidly towards the church entrance.

'Are you sure he was unconscious?' Frank asks Prisha.

'Yes, definitely. It was a heavy vase. I can't believe he escaped,' she replies as the armed response unit files from the church, the lead officer, stopping to address Frank.

'We've searched it from top to bottom, Frank, and the graveyard and abbey grounds, too. Not a hide nor hair of him. There is a dribble of blood on the flagstones, but as for the man himself, he's disappeared.'

'He can't have gone far. It's only thirty minutes since Prisha raised the alarm,' Zac says, extremely disturbed by the night's proceedings.

The armed response sergeant shrugs. 'A car can get you plenty of places in twenty minutes, Zac,' he says.

Frank pats him on the back. 'Cheers, Bill. You and your gang can knock off for the night.'

Frank collapses his umbrella and leans it against a wall as they enter the church and stare at the bloodstain on the stone floor. Prisha shivers despite having Frank's long woollen overcoat draped around her shoulders.

'When are forensics arriving?' Zac asks.

'Should be here within twenty minutes,' Frank replies. 'Then we'll have a DNA sample of the bastard. Another string to our bow, along with the fingerprint.'

'Doesn't help us find him, though,' Zac says.

'True. But it helps build a case against him when we do. We'll have DNA and fingerprints. It's gold dust in court. Don't lose sight of that, Zac. It's not just about catching the bugger, but making sure he goes down for a long, long time. Prisha, can you take us through it again, step by step?'

'Really? I've already explained.'

'It may help.'

'Fine.'

———•◦•———

She spends the next five minutes reliving the ghastly scene.

'Are you certain it was Barber?' Frank says.

'Positive. Dyed ginger hair protruded from under a woollen hat. Brown eyes and he smelt bad. Horrible breath and something else...'

'What?' Frank asks.

'A faint aroma of vomit.'

'Ah.'

'What?'

'Riley Miller, the rugby lad who worked on security with Barber, he said the same thing. Apparently steroid abuse can make your sweat smell a bit like sick. Something to do with the increase in testosterone levels. The words he was reciting: did you recognise them?'

'No. But I'm guessing they're verses from the Bible. It was all about God and curses and retribution.'

'Hell, that's all we need. A killer on steroids and a God botherer to boot. Nothing worse.'

'Something else,' Prisha adds, running her fingertips across her bruised neck.

'What?'

'It wasn't a frenzied attack. It was calm, methodical. His grip was firm but gentle, if that makes sense. I could feel the power in his fingers, and he could have finished me off easily. At one point, as I felt I was going to pass out, he loosened his hold, to give me a second to take in air.'

Frank shakes his head. 'Power. He wanted to watch you die slowly. Obviously, he gets a kick out of it. We're dealing with a psychopath.'

'I'm worried, Frank,' Zac says.

'No shit,' Frank replies, kneeling down near the blood stain.

'I'm serious. How the hell did he know Prisha was visiting the church? He must be watching her, or any of us. Maybe he's on a mission to take out more police officers. I think Prisha needs to stop with one of us until he's caught. She's not safe on her own.'

Frank rises and rubs at the back of his neck. 'The imagination is a double-edged sword, Zac. It can be your greatest ally or greatest enemy. Don't turn this guy into some sort of superman because he's not.' He turns to Prisha. 'Did he say anything to imply he knows you're a copper?'

'No, he didn't.'

Frank gazes around the creepy church. 'I think he has demons in his head. Guilt over what he's done, seeking some sort of absolution from the Almighty. He's a Jekyll and Hyde type figure. Prisha just happened to be in the wrong place at the right time.'

'Story of my life,' she murmurs.

Frank smiles at her. 'It was merely a co...' He stops himself just in time.

Zac smirks. 'You were going to say coincidence, weren't you?'

'I was not! That word is not in my vocabulary. There's no such thing.'

'Go on then, finish the sentence.'

'I was going to say, ahem, what happened here tonight was merely...' He draws the words out slowly, buying time. 'It was merely a... confluence of random events.'

'A coincidence, in other words,' Zac says with a chuckle.

'But we have learnt one thing,' Frank states, quickly changing the subject.

'What's that?'

'Barber is still holed up here in Whitby. I suspect he lives on the east side of the river. And he doesn't have transport, otherwise he'd be long gone. He thinks the safest place to hide is right under our noses. Unfortunately, tonight he's fucked-up. Right, come on Prisha, I'll drive you home. Zac, you wait here until forensics arrives.'

'Christ, Frank...'

'Don't blaspheme! You're in church.' He gazes at Zac for a moment, taking in his haggard expression. 'You know what you need?'

'Hair of a dog?'

'A good night's sleep.'

'Really? I never thought of that.'

'That's what you get for burning the candle at both ends. If you hadn't gone out on a bender last night, you wouldn't be walking around like a zombie today. I'll see you tomorrow.'

'Cheers... boss,' he replies disconsolately.

'The pleasure's all yours.'

48

Sunday 6th December

The team is playing the waiting game. The telco has provided the police with data on Barber's mobile. Pings from his phone only confirmed what Frank and his team already knew—he's in Whitby. Unfortunately, his mobile has been off the network for three days, so the information is old. Even if his phone comes back onto the network, the accuracy of cellular triangulation is only accurate to within a hundred metres. The telco could detect no GPS tracking, which is typically far more specific in pinpointing exact locations. It appears Barber has GPS disabled.

The phone on Prisha's desk rings. She instantly grabs for it. 'Inspector Kumar. Yes, I see. Okay. That's good news. I'm on my way now.' She hangs up, sporting a wry smile. The other four officers stare at her.

'What is it?' Frank asks.

'That was the desk sergeant. He's just heard from the officer guarding Alfred Dunn.'

'And?'

'Alfred has woken up. He's groggy and a little sore, but he's eaten a sandwich and had a cup of tea.'

Frank emits a puff. 'Oh, that's good news. He may be a silly old bugger, but he didn't deserve any of this.'

Prisha is already slipping into her coat. 'I'll head up there now and see if he can remember what happened and, more importantly, see if he knows where Barber lives.'

'Prisha, go easy on him. He's an old man,' Frank cautions.

'Yes. Understood.' As she nears the door, she stops. 'Frank, should I arrest him?'

Frank shakes his head. 'On what grounds? Paying for a fake stamp?'

'What about the theft at Stonygarth Hall?'

'We have no evidence. When we catch Barber, and *if* he confesses all and implicates Dunn in the burglary, then we may have a case against him, but at the moment all we have is supposition. Let's keep things simple for the time being. I don't see Alfred Dunn as a flight risk, and I dare say he'll be in hospital for a few more days yet. He's still not out of the woods. No point causing him any more grief.'

'Yes, boss.'

———◆———

Prisha cringes as the acute care nurse who she saw when she visited Jason heads towards her.

'Oh, you again, inspector. What do you want this time?'

'I'm here to question Alfred Dunn.'

'Are you indeed!'

'Indeed, I am.'

'He's only recently woken up.'

'I could hardly question him while he was asleep, could I?'

The nurse narrows her eyes and looks Prisha up and down. 'Is it absolutely necessary right now?'

'Yes, it is. Mr Dunn is embroiled in a very serious investigation, and he may have information which could progress the case dramatically. And we also need a description of his attacker.'

'Very well!' she snaps. 'But five minutes is all I'll allow. He's in a very weak and feeble condition. I don't want any undue stress placed upon him. He's under my duty of care and I take that responsibility very seriously. Follow me.'

What the hell have you got stuck up your arse, you lemon sucking old shrew?

Prisha smiles sweetly. 'Of course.'

The nurse must have injected herself with performance-enhancing drugs because she flies along the corridor at a rate of knots, weaving in and out of trolleys, dodging patients clutching Zimmer frames, and sidestepping other medics like a scrum-half. Prisha does her best to keep up. The nurse stops outside a door where a uniformed officer is sitting.

'Five minutes, inspector, and not a second longer,' the nurse barks.

'Thank you,' Prisha replies, biting her tongue. She nods at the uniformed officer.

'Ma'am,' he replies.

'How long has he been awake?' she whispers.

'Oh, nearly an hour.'

She enters the room and takes a seat. Dunn is propped up in bed, eyes are closed.

'Mr Dunn?' she says in a soft, caring voice. 'Mr Dunn?'

His eyelids flicker open. For a moment, there's confusion until the fog lifts. 'Oh, inspector,' he says, dejected. 'Have you come to arrest me?'

She pats the back of his hand speckled with blood spots and broken vessels. 'No.'

'I've been foolish.'

'Who hasn't? We all make mistakes. It's part of being human.' A thin smile spreads across his cracked lips. 'Can you remember what happened yesterday?'

'Vaguely.'

'Was it Wayne Barber who did this to you?'

He nods his head. 'Yes. The man's a brute.'

'Why did he attack you?'

'He wanted more money.'

'Why were you paying him money in the first place?'

His eyes close. 'I suppose you know. There's no point in me lying. Barber was the man who robbed Garth Windsor of the Two Penny Blue. Barber rang me and offered it to me for four thousand pounds. I went around to his house and paid him the money, in exchange for the stamp. It wasn't until I got home and inspected it, I realised it was a fake.'

Prisha uses all her will power to contain her elation. 'And Barber kept coming back for more?'

'Yes.'

'But why? You must have told him it was a fake.'

'I did. He said I was lying. I'd known him for some time. He was a regular at my lectures. Had a keen interest in the Third Reich and the war. I thought he was a decent young man, but something changed. I could see it in his eyes.'

'Did you know he shot and killed DS Cartwright?'

'No, I... I mean, not until you mentioned the Luger the other day. Then I pieced the jigsaw together.' He trails off as his eyes flicker open again and gaze sorrowfully at a blank wall.

'We suspect the Luger may have been part of Lord Ashton's collection, stolen from Stonygarth Hall eight months ago.'

'It wasn't supposed to... what I'm trying to say... is...'

'Was Barber responsible for the theft at Stonygarth?'

'Yes. Well, we both were. It was my idea. I know Lord Ashton has a terminal illness. I was concerned about what would happen to the signed copy of Mein Kampf once he passed away. Lady Ashton has said on more than one occasion she intends to burn the book once he's gone. Ironic really, considering Hitler was also a book burner.'

'What about the other items that were taken? The pistol, dagger, and insignia?'

'That was Barber helping himself. I paid him to steal the book, that's all.'

'So Barber turned up at your house yesterday demanding more money?'

'Yes. I'd already paid him a total of eight thousand pounds. I knew if I agreed to his demands, he'd keep coming back for more and bleed me dry. He arrived on my doorstep and demanded money to help him escape the country. I told him no. He manhandled me inside and threatened me. He wanted the money straight away. I keep a few thousand pounds in my safe, located behind a painting.'

'A few thousand pounds? Can you be more precise?'

'Three thousand. He took that... and the book.'

'The book?'

'Mein Kampf. It's worth at least forty thousand on the black market.'

'I thought you kept all your valuable items in a safety deposit locker in York?'

'I do... all except Mein Kampf.'

'Why?'

'I occasionally take it out and hold it. Don't you realise the greatest monster of the twentieth century actually held that book in his hands and signed it?'

'And you get pleasure from that?'

'Yes!'

'You need to get out more, Mr Dunn.'

There's a loud rap on the window as the nurse with a face like smashed crab taps at her watch and scowls at Prisha. Another few minutes and she could have got the full story from him, but she has bigger fish to fry.

'Mr Dunn, where does Barber live? What's his address?'

'He lives on Church Street in a top flat.'

'What's the number?'

'The number?'

'Yes. The house number?'

'It's... oh, dear... I'm not...' His words dry up. 'Could you?' he says, pointing at a glass of water. Prisha carefully lifts the glass to his lips. He takes a nip of the liquid.

'Mr Dunn, Alfred, it's very important you tell me the number on Church Street. It's quite a long street.'

'I can't remember.'

Damn! 'Do you recall we bumped into each other last week outside a café? Is Barber's flat near there?'

'Café? Did we?'

'Is Barber's flat near the café, north of the swing bridge?'

'It could be. I'm trying to think.'

The nurse appears in the doorway. 'Your time is up, inspector.'

'Just a few more minutes, please,' she begs.

'Absolutely not. You should count your blessings you got five minutes with the patient. Now, would you kindly leave? Otherwise, I'll call security.'

'I'm a police officer!' she remonstrates.

'And I am a head nurse, and this is a hospital, not a police interview room. Now leave!'

Slowly, she lifts herself from her seat. 'Please, Alfred, I need the number of the house. Barber must be stopped.

He's a dangerous man and could kill again. You can help prevent that.'

'INSPECTOR! This is your last warning!'

'I'm sorry... it just won't come to me.' Dunn stammers, confusion etched into his features.

Prisha throws the nurse a vicious glare reserved exclusively for people she detests. She reluctantly heads towards the door. 'If you remember the number, Alfred, there's a police officer sitting outside your door.'

The nurse grabs Prisha by the arm. 'This way!' she hisses.

'Get your hands off me, you mad old hag!'

'I beg your pardon?'

'You heard!'

'Blue,' Alfred's brittle voice calls out.

Prisha breaks the nurse's grip and pops her head back inside the room. 'Blue?'

'Yes. Blue. White house, blue door, blue drainpipe. Next door to a trinket shop. Top flat.'

'Right, I'm calling security!' the nurse declares, waving at someone down the corridor.

———◆———

Frank is facing the whiteboard, marker pen in hand, planning the operation. Discordant whistling reverberates around the incident room.

He closes his eyes. 'Patience, Frank, patience,' he whispers to himself.

'I wonder if Dunn has spilled the beans yet?' Zac says, his left leg jiggling nervously up and down.

'We'll find out soon enough,' Frank says, peering over his spectacles at him before returning to the board.

The whistling continues. Frank snaps the cap back on the pen and places it purposefully down on a table. He studies Dinkel, in the corner.

'Dinkel?'

'Yes, sir?'

'What's that song you're butchering?'

'It's Fields of Gold by Sting, sir.'

'Is it indeed? Can you fly Dinkel?'

'Fly? Do you mean have I been in an aeroplane before?'

'No. I mean, can you fly? Like a bird.'

Dinkel's expression radiates confusion. 'I've never tried, sir.'

Kylie and Zac share a smirk.

'We're two storeys up, Dinkel, and if you whistle once more today, then we'll find out if you can fly, because I'll throw you out of that bloody window!' Frank explodes.

'Sorry, sir. It won't happen again, Mr Finnegan, sir.'

'Good,' he says, returning to the board as Prisha bursts into the room full of nervous energy.

'He couldn't give me a number,' she pants. 'But he gave me a description of the house. White with blue windows and blue drainpipe. Next door to a trinket shop. Barber lives in the top-floor flat. I think we have him, boss.'

'Excellent work! Zac, put your coat on and head down to Church Street and get an ID on the property and take photos of the place. Be discreet. Prisha, call armed response and get Bill and his crew in here to organise the op. Kylie, give a heads-up to the paramedics and Fire Services. We'll need a unit from each on standby. Don't give them any details. Just say we're planning a major police operation for tonight. Right, action stations everyone! This thing needs to run like clockwork. I'll call in the rest of the team and update Superintendent Banks, and Overland.'

'Sir, sir, Mr Finnegan?'

'What is it Dinkel?'

'What do you want me to do?'

'Isn't that obvious, Dinkel?'

'Erm... no, sir.'

'Put the kettle on and make us all a brew, then take food orders and get yourself into town. An army marches on its stomach.'

49

It's a stealth operation.

During the day, a team of plain-clothed officers saunters back and forth along Church Street. Some act like day trippers, others perform as locals. Covertly, they knock on doors within the vicinity of Barber's abode and request the occupants to pack silently and find alternative accommodation for the night. All pubs reluctantly close. The main thoroughfare is cordoned off. The undercover officers meander up and down the street continually. As they reach a cordon, they slip into a different coat or exchange hats, swap partners, and set off again. To a casual observer, everything appears normal. A typical seaside town wrapped in wintery conditions. In a stroke of good luck, Barber's flat is a dormer and sits back from the edge of the building, nestled into the sloping slate roof. If he is home, which hasn't been established, he would be unable to witness the amateur dramatics which plays out below.

Frank is positioned high up on the 199 Steps, night vision binoculars in hand, radio strapped to his lapel. He has a bird's eye view of the back of the house and the dormer, albeit some distance away. It's a moonless night, with a lethargic, cloying fog drifting in from the sea, making visibility less than ideal.

He checks his watch—7:55 pm. Five more minutes until Operation Silent Pursuit swings into action. He likes a good name for an operation and he's particularly pleased with this one as he thought of it himself. What he's not quite as pleased about is the company he's keeping.

'Sir, did I mention I recently passed my investigator's exam?'

Frank's left cheek involuntarily twitches. He adjusts the zoom on the binoculars. 'Aye, Dinkel, I think you may have mentioned it,' he drawls laconically.

'That means I'm illegible to apply for a detective position,' Dinkel adds hopefully.

'Eligible, Dinkel, eligible. Illegible means indecipherable, much like your personality.'

'Sir?'

'Nothing.'

Frank clicks at his radio. During the pre-operation briefing, Prisha suggested they drop all police radio protocols in the remote chance Barber has a decoder. It's one more safeguard.

'Miss K, how's it going down south these days?' he says in a jovial tone, referring to the south end of Church Street that Prisha controls.

'All good, Franky boy. Weather's fine down here.'

'Franky boy?' he murmurs to himself. He clicks the radio again. 'And how's Jock going?'

'Weather's a little chilly up north, Franky boy. But at least it's predictable, stable if you know what I mean,' Zac replies.

'And Tin Soldier, what are you up to these days?'

'I've a joint of roast beef in the oven and it's ready to take out... Franky boy,' Bill from the armed response unit says.

'Pricks,' Frank mutters, checking his watch again. He glances up the steps, past St Mary's Church, towards the abbey where a patrol car awaits. Not that he can see it from his vantage point, as it's obscured by a large stone wall.

Acrimonious whistling softly echoes out. He turns and stares at his junior colleague.

'What's the tune you're attempting to whistle, Dinkel?'

'Don't Stand So Close to Me. It's by The Police, sir.'

'How very prescient.'

'Sir?'

'Forget it and quit the hideous warbling. You ready?'

'Yes, sir.'

'Good.'

'Sir, it's extremely unlikely Barber will come this way... isn't it, sir?' he asks nervously.

'Extremely unlikely,' Frank concurs.

'Oh, good,' Dinkel replies, his nervousness dissipating.

'But possible,' Frank adds. 'The man is as unpredictable as your sense of pitch. Are you scared, Dinkel?'

'Actually, yes, I am.'

'Good. It will make you sharper.'

'What about you, sir? Are you scared?'

'Aye, I am Dinkel. Scared to death for everyone, including myself... and even you.'

Dinkel smiles, reassured by his honesty. 'It's just...'

Frank cuts him off. 'Aye, I know, lad. It can immobilise you. The thing with fear is you can't fight with it. You must let it in, accept it. Then it loses its power. Heed that, Dinkel, and it will stand you in good stead.'

'Yes, sir.'

Frank taps at his radio. 'Miss K, Jock, Tin Soldier, there's an excellent film starting on BBC1 any moment now. It's called Operation Silent Pursuit. Watch out for the lead actor. He's a rakishly handsome devil.'

Despite his flippancy, Frank isn't happy. He knows it's a risky operation. Barber could be inside the house or not. And he could be armed. If confronted, he may bolt, or shoot, or both. It's an enormous risk, and although the plan has been meticulously worked out to mitigate the dangers, there's always the rogue element. An unknown, unknown.

The house is on a slight bend, the windows old, small. Armed response are readied on the cusp of the bend, prepared. More officers from armed response are hiding in the bushes to the rear of the house. There are two ways in: back door and front door. The initial problem will be to enter the house as silently as possible, then creep up the two flights of stairs before they reach the dormer. They have a good description of the interior of the house thanks to the owners. The ground-floor and second-floor flats are holiday rentals, and are locked up, unoccupied. The dormer is one room, more like a bedsit, but the stairs are steep and narrow, only wide enough for one person at a time.

All officers are wearing bullet resistant vests in case Barber attempts to shoot his way out. Every contingency has been catered for. Back-up, paramedics, K9s at the ready... and yet something gnaws away at Frank.

He focuses his binoculars on the back windows of the house and double checks the ground-floor and second-floor, searching for movement—nothing. The house is in complete darkness.

'What's the matter, Frank?' he murmurs to himself as a flurry of snow falls. Staring up at the sky, he witnesses a million dancing flakes swirl and pirouette towards the earth. The imitation Victorian streetlamps cast a ghostly glow over the steps and weathered buildings.

The radio crackles. 'Tin Soldier here. The film is about to roll.'

'Miss K, make sure you turn your lights off,' Frank states, his signal for Prisha to give the power company the nod to cut the juice.

The streetlamps and house lights from the old part of town don't go off simultaneously but cascade down as if part of a Christmas illumination.

But there is light.

Behind, and high above him, Whitby Abbey is illuminated in glorious gothic colours of purples, reds, and blues.

The only thing to interrupt the silence is the angry waves lashing the pier accompanied by the wind as it blows up the steps towards the abbey.

The waiting is interminable and unbearable. Despite the chill, a bead of sweat slips down Frank's back. He spins around, searching for Dinkel.

'Dinkel, where are you?'

'Right behind you, sir?' he says, giving Frank a start.

'Daft bugger! Position yourself halfway down the steps.'

'It's a bit dark, sir.'

'Then turn your torch on, daft boy.'

He fumbles for the torch and reluctantly heads down the steps.

Silence is obliterated as a cacophony of angry sounds erupts through the radio. The clank and bang of a battering ram ring out, followed by splintering wood and violent shouts and commands. Alsatians, waiting in reserve, sense the excitement and howl, anticipating a fleshy forearm to bite into. The lead guy in the armed response screams his orders.

'Armed police! Drop your weapon, lay face down on the floor with your hands on your head.'

Frank has his binoculars trained on the dormer. High-powered beams dance around incoherently inside the room as more officers rush in.

'What the hell is going on?' he murmurs, mouth as dry as sandpaper. 'Come on, is he in there or not? Have you taken him down? It's one fucking room. If he's there, you should have seen him by now.'

The binoculars swing slowly to the left, then to the right, searching for any sign of movement. Something catches his eye above the dormer.

Slate tiles collapse onto one another until there's a hole. A head pops out of the roof.

'You bastard!' He presses at his radio. 'Suspect is...'

His voice is drowned out as an urgent scream transmits through the ether.

'Trip wire! Everyone out! Go! Go! Go!'

50

A thunder of boots is followed a second later by a blinding flash, then a series of sonic booms ricochets around the town. Tinkling glass can be heard clearly. Car alarms react amidst the screams and cries of anguish.

'Sweet merciful crap,' Frank mutters, a surge of adrenalin blurring his vision. He pulls the glasses away and rubs at his eyes, then refocuses on the house. He can just make out a figure slithering down the rooftop towards a drainpipe. Smoke billows out from the dormer like a gaseous tsunami. It's buffeted by the wind and slowly descends like a spectre spreading its arms, smothering everything.

He shouts into the radio. 'DS Stoker, what is going on down there? Suspect is attempting to escape via the roof!'

No reply.

'DS Stoker, come in!' he screams again. 'DI Kumar, what's the status?'

No reply.

He drops the binoculars and rushes down the steps, as his knee twinges.

The dense smoke drifts southeast, making the steps hazardous to navigate. Fearing he could fall at any moment, he clings to the handrail and takes one step at a time, as strident yelling, expletives, and cries for help rain forth from the street below.

'Fuck, fuck fuck! Dinkel, where are you?'

'I'm down here, sir.'

'Christ, I can't see a bloody thing,' Frank says, turning his torch on. The beam is useless in the thick smoke, and he switches it off and drops it into his jacket pocket. He unclips his radio and holds it to his mouth. 'DI Kumar, DS Stoker, state your positions?'

No response as the hellish nightmare continues.

'Identify yourself?' Dinkel shouts, his voice further away than it was a moment ago.

'Dinkel? Who is it?'

The sounds of a scuffle only last a few seconds before Dinkel screams out, 'Mother!'

His mournful cry sends a pain stabbing through Frank's chest as a shadow lurches up the steps.

Frank drops the radio into his pocket and pulls out his police baton.

Barber materialises, his rucksack giving him the appearance of a hunchback.

A bloody wound to his thigh makes him stagger.

Their gazes meet in the gloom.

Barber stops.

A grisly smirk curls his lips. Wild eyes. Hatred plastered over his face.

He brandishes a dagger.

Panic visits Frank.

He's alone.

Let it in, Frank, let it in.

Fear shrivels like burning plastic as every hair on his body stands to attention.

He knows this fight won't end by the sounding of a bell or a referee pulling them apart.

One man must fight for his freedom... the other for his life!

First salvo.

'Meet Long Tall Sally, Barber. You really shouldn't have resisted arrest. You're finished, you fucker,' he snarls.

Barber cackles. 'Yeah? I don't think so, fucking pig! That's another one of yours I just got back there. Crying for his momma. Boo hoo. You're next, grandpa.' Swaying forward, he lunges the dagger towards Frank's chest. He parries the blow away with the baton, then swings it in an arc above his head and whips it down with brute force into the collarbone of Barber.

Screams of agony.

He drops the knife but rushes Frank before he can raise the baton again.

They barrel into one another.

Frank is crushed against the handrail.

A dull clatter as his police radio is jettisoned from his pocket and drops over the side of the steps.

Barber tries to lift his head violently into Frank's chin, but Frank knows the move and drops his head, negating the attack.

Barber's fingers encircle Frank's neck and squeeze.

He tries to break the hold, but the grip is immovable.

Rotting seaweed, sweat, and vile breath create a pungent odour.

He knows he only has a few seconds left before his senses shut down.

Fight dirty!

He jabs two fingers hard into Barber's left eyeball. The grip is broken as Barber screams and recoils backwards, clutching his face.

Frank coughs, tastes bile, spits and throws the baton down.

It clanks and rolls down the steps.

'Okay, sunshine,' he growls. 'You're gonna cop a good old-fashioned Yorkshire belting.'

Fingers flex back and forth on both hands.

They tighten into fists, resembling raw hams.

He unleashes a fusillade of rib crushing punches into Barber's midriff, each one accompanied by an expulsion of air, and a dull thwack, as Barber staggers back with each thump.

A splintering crack, like pulling a wishbone apart, indicates a broken rib.

A slurry of sticky blood mixed with saliva splatters onto the dusting of snow covering the cobblestones.

Barber pushes at him, but Frank throws an uppercut to the jaw. The sound is like a bullwhip.

Jason's killer totters as the chaotic discord of sirens and yelling continues in the town below.

Frank smiles and licks the salt spray from his lips as he moves in to finish him off.

Searing pain shoots through his entire body.

He falters.

Staggers.

Collapses to the cobbles as his right knee gives way under him.

'Aargh! Not now!' he yells, his voice booming out.

Disorientated, Barber remains motionless before he turns and lumbers up the steps, dragging his right leg, one arm across his ribs.

Frank pants hard as the endorphins kick in and flood his body. He rolls onto his side and watches as Barber melts into the night. Gingerly, he grabs the railing and heaves himself to his feet and hobbles after Barber. He pulls his phone out and taps at Zac's image.

'Frank, I've been trying to get you on the radio. Where are you?'

'On the steps heading towards St Mary's, behind Barber. Dinkel is down. I think he's been stabbed. I've lost my radio. What's the situation down there?'

'Chaos and pandemonium. Fire Services and paramedics entering the area now. Hard to tell how many casualties.'

'Barber's injured. He can't get far. Where are those fucking dogs when you need them?'

'They were spooked by the explosion and took off. God knows where they are. Probably halfway to Newcastle by now!'

'Prisha?'

'Got some crap in her eye from the blast. Then a dog bit her on the arm. She's being treated now.'

'Those fucking K9s are a menace!'

'I'm heading your way now, boss! Don't go after him. Leave it to armed response.'

'Bugger that. I don't think he's armed, otherwise I wouldn't be speaking to you now. I'll keep you on the line.'

Frank pushes on and painfully climbs the steps as the smoke from the blast subsides. Looking up, he spots Barber as he drags himself into St Mary's churchyard, clearly incapacitated.

'Where are the bloody officers from the patrol car?' he mutters as the pain from his knee ebbs.

Gaining a second wind, he lifts his pace. As he nears the church, he rests for a moment and pulls out his torch. Barber is nowhere to be seen.

'Come on you sod, where are you? I know you went towards the church.' His powerful flashlight bobs and weaves over the gravestones smothered in drifting smog. Movement. A figure, limping, emerges from behind a tombstone fifty feet ahead. Frank gives chase albeit, slowly. With both men injured, neither has the upper hand. He passes the entrance to St Marys, hunting his prey. The shady figure disappears from view again, causing him to slow his pace.

'Christ, this guy is like the Scarlet Pimpernel.' The torchlight sweeps around in an arc until it picks out a silhouette shambling through the graveyard, putting a greater distance between Frank.

'Damn it!' He limps forward, as the gravestones thin out. The hunter and hunted near an old stone wall demarcating the end of the church boundary. The figure ahead stops at the wall and crouches, breathing hard as Frank shambles towards him, also gasping for breath. He shines the light on Barber, who slowly rises.

Barber's left eye has swollen to the size of a grotesque, bloodied golf ball. His trousers are covered in a dark stain from his wound.

'Okay, Barber, stop playing silly buggers. Enough is enough. It's over,' he says, edging closer, clutching the torch, ready to use it as a weapon if needs be.

Barber tries to smile, but it morphs into a macabre leer. 'That's what you think,' he replies as he pulls a pistol from inside his ripped jacket.

Frank freezes as his mind plays catch up. *Why's he pulled a gun now? Why didn't he use it before?*

'Put the gun down, Barber. Where do you think you're going to go? There's a small army of armed police heading this way right now. Behind you are the cliffs and the sea.' He points to the blood weeping from Barber's thigh. 'You're injured. You need to get that leg seen to. Now put the gun down.' He takes a step forward, now only ten feet away.

Barber raises the pistol and points. 'I'm warning you, copper! One more step and I'll put a bullet through you like I did to your mate!'

Frank keeps on advancing, slow, cautious. 'Go on then, pull the trigger,' he goads.

'I *will* kill you.'

'Oh, I don't doubt it for a moment, if you actually had a fucking bullet in the gun, but you don't, do you? Otherwise, you'd have used it back there on the steps.'

Barber hurls the weapon at Frank, who raises his arm to protect himself. It catches him a glancing blow on the temple, making him stagger and drop to his knees. He touches his head and feels the sticky wetness. Barber is already attempting to scale the wall. Frank rises and sways forward as Barber drops behind the wall and disappears. Zac's muffled voice speaks from Frank's pocket.

'Frank, state your position?'

He pulls the phone out. 'Back of St Mary's near the boundary wall. This bastard doesn't know when to give up. He's unarmed, by the way.'

'I'll be there in two minutes.'

Frank puts his foot onto a stone ledge jutting from the wall and heaves his large frame up. He spots Barber fifteen feet ahead, shuffling towards the cliffs. Cautiously, he lowers himself from the wall. As he lands, his knee gives way again, sending a violent shockwave of pain through his body. He gasps and grits his teeth.

'For crying out loud! Couldn't you have picked a better time?' he yells. 'Come on, body, don't let me down now,' he seethes. He gingerly gets to his feet and inches forward as a vicious wind from the sea drives snow into his face. Barber is now at the edge of the cliffs, desperately scanning the area to find an escape route. Frank stumbles up behind him.

'No more, Barber,' he pants. 'No more.'

'Fuck you!'

'On your knees and put your hands behind your back.'

'No way!' he spits, as he glares at Frank with wild eyes full of terror, still unpredictable, dangerous. He creeps further towards the cliff edge.

'There's no way down. It's a sheer fifty-foot drop.'

Barber falls to the ground, spins around, and lowers himself over the side.

'For God's sake, man! Don't you know when you're beaten?' Frank yells as Barber vanishes once more. Frank peers over the side where Barber has dropped onto a ledge some five feet below. But the ledge goes nowhere. It protrudes out from the main cliff face but is a vertical drop on all three sides. The roar of the waves thunders up the side of the bluff, angry white peaks clearly visible.

'Frank!'

He spins around to see Zac deftly drop from the boundary wall and sprint his way. A sharp pain unexpectedly stabs across his chest. Wincing, he clutches at his bicep and gasps for breath.

'Where is he?' Zac asks as he reaches him.

'On a ledge,' he says, nodding towards the cliff edge.

'Are you all right, Frank? You look fucked.'

'I'm fine. Thought I'd take Meera out dancing later.'

Zac glances down at Barber, who is pacing back and forth like a caged tiger.

'Don't go down there,' Frank yells. 'He'd more than likely take you with him if he got a chance.'

Zac smiles. 'Do I look like an imbecile?'

'The jury's still out on that one,' Frank replies, as he lowers himself down onto his backside, exhausted.

Zac lays flat on the ground and holds his arm over the side. 'Come on Barber, don't be stupid. Take my arm and I'll help you back up.'

Barber finally realises he's defeated. 'Okay. You're right. Gave you a run for your money though, didn't I?' he says with a ghoulish smile.

Zac bites his tongue as Barber grips his hand and finds a foothold, then cautiously climbs up the crag. He rolls onto his back on the snow-covered grass and breathes heavily, staring into the dark night.

Zac retrieves his handcuffs. 'Onto your front,' he snaps. 'Arms behind your back.' Barber obliges as Zac restrains his hands, violently clicking the cuffs together.

'Christ! No need for that,' Barber complains as the cuffs nip and pinch his wrists.

Zac manhandles him to his feet. 'There was no need for any of this, was there?' he growls.

Barber laughs. 'You're right. If that fat pig mate of yours hadn't waddled over to my car, then none of this would have happened. Anyway, I'll be a fucking hero in prison. A cop killer,' he sneers. 'I'll be a fucking poster boy. You know what they say, the only good cop is a dead cop. Shame that lard arse will never see his kid.'

Zac spins him. 'What did you say?'

'I said it's a shame the fat bastard will never see his kid. Probably not his anyway. His missus looks like a skanky ho. I was there in the church, you know, the day of the funeral. Got in early and sat at the back. Lovely service. It nearly brought a tear to my eye. And it was all down to me. Pity I couldn't attend the wake.' He guffaws manically. 'Fuck me! There must have been every plod from North

Yorkshire at the funeral, and there I was sitting amongst you all, as happy as a sand boy. It's true what they say about coppers—you couldn't find your arse with both hands.'

Zac punches him in the face.

'Bastard! That's police brutality. I know my rights. You can't do shit like that,' he wails as a streak of blood drips from his nose. 'I'll have you for this,' he snarls.

'Leave it, Zac. Don't let him wind you up,' Frank says, still clutching his chest as a second wave of pain hits.

'Turn around!' Zac orders

'What?' Barber says.

Zac spins him around, pulls a key from his pocket and sticks it into the lock of the cuffs.

'Zac!' Frank warns, fearing the worst.

'What are you doing?' Barber demands, confused.

'I'm letting you go,' Zac says.

Barber chuckles. 'You what? Are you fucking mental?'

'Oh, aye. I'm fucking mental,' he says removing the cuffs and dropping them into his pocket.

Barber glances at Frank. 'What the fuck is going on?'

Zac places one hand on Barber's jacket collar and one under his belt and drags him towards the cliff edge.

'Zac, no!' Frank yells. 'I'm ordering you—don't do it!'

'Oi, what the fuck are you doing?'

As the edge nears, Zac lifts his pace as Barber tries to put up resistance, his injured leg hampering his efforts.

'Zac, put him back in handcuffs, read him the caution, and escort the suspect back to the station. That's an order!' Frank bellows, trying unsuccessfully to rise to his feet.

Barber is unsure whether it's a game of bluff. Zac tightens his grip on Barber's belt and swings him around, launching him over the side of the cliff.

Barber's scream splinters the frigid night air, his arms a helicopter swirl as he hurtles towards the rocks below.

'No, no, no,' Frank whimpers. 'You fool. You stupid bloody fool.'

Zac stares down upon Barber's lifeless body as it's carried by an incoming wave and battered against the rocks before vanishing.

'That's for Jason,' he murmurs. He walks back to Frank and pulls him to his feet, then holds his hands out in front of him. 'I suppose you better arrest me,' he says, handing the cuffs over.

Frank gazes into Zac's eyes. 'Why?'

'He shouldn't have said those things. Scum like that don't deserve to live. The world's a better place without him.'

'We're police officers, Zac, not judge and executioner. We're just police officers,' he moans softly. Frank takes

Zac's cuffs and pitches them over the cliff. A silver flash is briefly picked up in the lights from the abbey. He removes his own handcuffs and passes them to Zac.

'They may take yours for DNA testing. Mine are clean. Barber lost his footing as you tried to pull him to safety. He had an injury to his leg and lost his balance on the ledge. Nothing we could do.'

Zac offers him an apologetic smile. 'Thanks.'

Frank glares at him and shakes his head. 'You'll have to carry the burden for the rest of your life, and so will I. We're finished, Zac. Put in for a transfer. I don't want you on my team anymore.'

Both men peer towards the church as a scatter of torchlights dart across the darkness, accompanied by gruff voices and yapping dogs.

'Here comes the cavalry,' Zac whispers.

'Aye. Too little too late,' Frank says as he hobbles towards them.

Zac jogs after him and takes Frank's arm and puts it around his shoulder. 'Here, let me take your weight. It will take the pressure off that dodgy knee.'

'Thanks. How's Dinkel?' he asks, dreading the answer.

'Not sure. He was unresponsive. A paramedic was with him.'

51

Tuesday 8th December – Two Days Later

Frank slurps on a cup of sugary tea, then stares disconsolately at his computer screen and his overflowing email inbox.

'I thought when the computer age was ushered in, it was going to streamline our workload? I've more mindless paperwork and useless advice now than ever,' he grumbles. 'Oh, no,' he says as he spots Superintendent Banks marching through the incident room. 'I need her like a hole in the head.'

She doesn't knock but walks straight in. 'Frank,' she says testily.

'Morning ma'am. And how are you this fine...'

'Cut the crap, Frank. What's this?' She slaps a form onto his desk.

He casually glances at it. 'That's DS Stoker's transfer request.'

'I know what it is!'

'Then why did you...'

'Why?' she hisses.

'Why what, ma'am?'

'When did he fill this in? I thought you told him to take a week's sick leave.'

'Which question do you want me to answer first?'

'Don't play smart with me, Frank. Answer the questions.'

'Yes, Zac is on a week's sick leave at my insistence. He came in earlier and handed me the transfer request. As for the why—he said it was time for him to move on.'

'Move on?'

'Yes.'

'Did you try to dissuade him?'

'I asked him if he'd considered it carefully and he replied in the affirmative.'

'I don't get it. His children are settled in school here. His wife has a good job. Why would he want a transfer? You've worked with Zac for nigh on ten years. He's almost like a son to you. I'd have thought you'd have been rather more robust in deterring him.'

'He's a grown man and can make his own decisions.'

She puffs out her cheeks and sighs. 'I don't know what's happened lately,' she reflects.

'I don't follow.'

'This station, Whitby: it used to be a parochial backwater. I remember a time when you went about your business quietly and efficiently. Got the job done. No fuss. Now I have officers from all over the county clamouring for a transfer to Whitby—*to get a piece of the action*—as they put it. We can hardly regard Operation Silent Pursuit as a resounding success. Nor did the name live up to its intent. Thousands of pounds of windows smashed. A blackout. Explosions. Car sirens. It was a complete fiasco. You should have named it Operation Four Horsemen of the Apocalypse.'

'Ha-ha, very droll, ma'am.'

'I'm not being funny, Frank. I'm deadly serious! The explosions could have been lethal.'

'You're exaggerating, Anne. It was a series of low-yield smoke bombs. Granted, they were loud and created a dense smokescreen, but there was never any threat to life, unless someone was standing directly on top of them.'

'No one knew that at the time. What about the injuries to DI Kumar?'

'It was a piece of grit, ma'am. Nothing more.'

'And a bite to the forearm.'

'I have voiced my concerns, many times in the past, about those bloody K9s. I think they're trained to attack law enforcement officers.'

'We had a junior officer who was almost fatally stabbed.'

'It was a minor knife wound to the buttock, ma'am. Nothing fatal about it. Dinkel is out there now, chewing Prisha's ear off,' he says, nodding towards the window.

She doesn't bother to look. 'It could have been a lot worse if not for his evasive action. And how is Prisha, mentally?'

'You know Prisha. She's as hard as nails.'

Shaking her head, she pulls a vicious pout. 'And our prime suspect fell to his death.'

Frank reflects. 'True. A tragic and unfortunate ending, but I'm not alone in thinking good riddance to bad baggage. He murdered one of our own, plus an officer in the States. He put Alfred Dunn in hospital, and stabbed Dinkel not to mention his attack on Prisha in the church. I, for one, won't lose any sleep over the bugger. He was a bad egg, Anne, a bad egg.'

She gazes at him, annoyed at his flippancy. 'Frank, the police aren't simply here to catch criminals and prevent crime.'

'Aren't we?'

'NO! We have a higher duty, obligation.'

'Which is?'

'To engender, foster, and promote the social contract between the police and the public.'

'Strike a light! I suspect you've been on one of those aspirational team-building weekends again.'

'This isn't a laughing matter, Frank. And I find your blasé manner unprofessional. In two days' time, the internal investigation panel will begin, and things could unravel.'

'Calm the farm, Anne. I received a call from Chief Constable Critchley twenty minutes ago, and he says the internal review is merely a formality. We've nothing to worry about.'

'Chief Constable Critchley?'

'Yes. The guy with the pointy hat, white cloak and burning cross.'

'Don't test me, Frank. I'm not in the mood.'

'Look, Anne, the media have lapped the story up. A cop killer reaped his *just* deserts. It even made the news in America. Okay, I admit, it didn't go as planned. A few slight hiccups but...'

'A few slight hiccups! It was a fucking disaster!'

Frank reels back in his chair. It's probably the second time in thirty years he's heard Anne use the F word. 'Anne, why do you always search for the negatives? A killer is off the streets.'

'A killer is off the planet!'

Frank continues unperturbed. 'Looking on the positive side, we've charged Garth Windsor with three counts of fraud. The stolen items from Lord Ashton's estate have been recovered and will be returned to him once the internal investigation and the coroner's report are finalised. Admittedly, the signed copy of Mein Kampf is slightly water damaged due to it being in the backpack of Barber when he entered the water.'

'And what about Alfred Dunn? Why are we not pressing charges against him? He masterminded the theft of the artefacts.'

'Because we're on a hiding to nothing. When he confessed to Prisha, he wasn't under caution and wasn't offered a solicitor. It would be inadmissible in court.'

'What's wrong with arresting him and seeing if he admits his wrongdoing again?'

'And if he does, then what? We send a respected, retired, octogenarian history professor to prison? He'll be humiliated. It will only shorten his life. What he did was foolish, but he didn't organise the theft for his own benefit. He was worried that once Lord Ashton passed away, Lady Ashton would destroy Mein Kampf. He wanted to save the book for posterity. I don't see any mileage in pursuing Alfred Dunn. It could turn into a public relations disaster that even DCC Overland would struggle with.'

She emits a heavy sigh, her anger dissipating as she offers him the thinnest of smiles.

'Yes, I suppose you're right. We're short-staffed and under-funded. We need to prioritise. How's your angina?' she adds in a softer tone.

'Under control. I missed a couple of days' medication, that's all.'

'And your knee?'

'Aye, a little sore, but give it a few days and it will be as good as new.'

'And your head?'

Frank touches the band-aid with a finger. 'All good. Where there's no sense, there's no feeling.'

Her smile morphs into disappointment. 'You're falling apart, Frank,' she adds as she picks up Zac's transfer paper and rips it in two. 'You can tell Zac I'm refusing his request for a transfer. We can't afford to lose officers of his calibre. And while I'm on the subject, I've come to my decision on a replacement for Cartwright.'

'Oh, good,' Frank says, eager to change the subject.

'I believe PC Dinkel would be a suitable addition to our small team. I'm not sure if you're aware, but he recently passed his investigator's exam.'

Frank's head nearly rolls off his shoulders. 'Dink... Dinkel?' he stammers.

'Yes. Why? Do you have any reservations about him? Because if you do, then now is the time to air them.'

'Reservations, ma'am?'

'Yes.'

Frank mentally counts them but gives up when reaches ten. 'Dinkel, you say?' he replies, scratching at his chin.

———◦———

Prisha opens the top drawer of her desk, pulls out a packet of paracetamol, pops out two pills and places them on her tongue.

Dinkel is animated. 'So, there I was, Prisha, almost blind. Darkness encircled me as the smoke swirled around like a ghostly apparition. I detected a menacing figure heading my way. I said *halt, who goes there?* He rushed at me, wielding a Hitler Youth dagger. I intuitively fell into my Karate pose, fearless. He thrust the dagger towards my heart and I Karate chopped his arm. The blade clattered to the harsh, unforgiving earth. I pirouetted on one leg to deliver a roundhouse kick to the head, which would have immobilised him, but due to the snow beneath my feet I momentarily lost my balance. As quick as a beetle, he grabbed the knife and delivered the near-fatal blow. I pulled the blade from my weeping flesh and gave chase. Unfortunately, my blood loss was so great I lost consciousness.'

Prisha picks up her glass of water, tilts her head back, takes a gulp and swallows the painkillers.

'That is bullshit on a breadboard, Dinkel. I've read the official report. You were stabbed in the arse cheek, whilst running away, then fainted.'

Dinkel is offended. 'I wasn't running away. I was taking evasive action.'

'Whatevs.'

Frank and Anne stride into the room

'PC Dinkel, I have some good news for you,' the Super declares.

'Yes, sir?' he replies expectantly.

She frowns but continues. 'I have approved your application for the position of detective constable. Once the internal review of Operation Silent Pursuit is complete, you will return to York for two weeks, after which you will join Whitby CID.'

'Roger Federer that, ma'am!' he yells, punching the air.

Prisha pulls open her drawer again, pops another two pills from the packet, puts them in her mouth and takes a drink of water.

'So help me, God,' she mutters.

A Word From The Author

A Word From The Author

Thank you for reading **Whitby Toll**, book 4 in the DCI Finnegan series. A few things before you go. Book 5 in the series, **House Arrest,** is available now. Here's the link for e-readers. QR code below for paperback readers.

Book 5 – **House Arrest** – Escape Can Be A Deadly Road – **Out Now** / eBook / Paperback / Kindle Unlimited

Why not sign up to my entertaining newsletter where I write about all things crime—fact and fiction. It's packed

with news, reviews, and my top ten Unsolved Mysteries, as well as new releases, and any discounts or promotions I'm running. I'll also send you a free copy of the prequel novella , **Aquaphobia – The Body In The River.** Here's the link.

Sign up to Ely North Newsletter

Alternatively, you can follow me below on Facebook, Amazon or Bookbub to keep up to date with new releases. Links below.

 facebook.com/elynorthcrimefictionUK

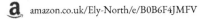 amazon.co.uk/Ely-North/e/B0B6F4JMFV

bookbub.com/profile/ely-north?list=about

And lastly, if you enjoyed **Whitby Toll**, then a review (or rating) on Amazon, Goodreads, or a share on Facebook would be appreciated. Or even better, why not tell someone you know about the book? Word of mouth is still the best recommendation.

I thank you for giving me your time, a very precious and finite commodity.

All the best,

Ely North

Also By Ely North – DCI Finnegan Series

Book 1: **Black Nab**

Book 2: **Jawbone Walk**

Book 3: **Vertigo Alley**

Book 4: **Whitby Toll**

Book 5: **House Arrest**

Book 6: **Gothic Fog**

Book 7: **Happy Camp**

Book 8: **Harbour Secrets**

Book 9: **Murder Mystery** – Pre-order (Dec 2024)

DCI Finnegan Series Boxset #1: **Books 1 – 3**

DCI Finnegan Series Boxset #2: **Books 4 – 6**

Prequel: **Aquaphobia** (Free ebook for newsletter subscribers)

*Note: All books are available from Amazon in ebook, paperback, and in **Kindle Unlimited** (excluding Aquaphobia). Paperbacks can be ordered from all good bookshops. **Boxset print editions are one book compiled from three books. They do not come in a box. *** ** Pre-orders only apply to ebooks.

Contact

Contact: ely@elynorthcrimefiction.com

Website: https://elynorthcrimefiction.com

Follow me on Facebook for the latest
https://facebook.com/elynorthcrimefictionUK

Sign up to my newsletter for all the latest news, releases, and discounts.

Newsletter
Sign Up

Printed in Great Britain
by Amazon

49621767R00239